"Just because you're riding in my truck doesn't mean we're back together."

"No, of course not. That's not what I meant." Did Rory think she hoped for reconciliation? After ten years? Ridiculous. "That's one nice thing about living in Boise. I can walk down the street and nobody knows me."

"Or your past."

"Or my past. Yes." Lacey didn't even try to keep the bitterness out of her voice.

"You're not the only one," he said grimly.

"I'd ask you in, but you—"

"Need to go," they said in unison.

To say she'd forgotten the effect he had on her would be a lie. He still had the power to warm her with his presence, to make her yearn for his kiss.

Why hadn't Rory married and started a family of his own?

Why hadn't she?

Dear Reader,

When I visited central Idaho and the beautiful Salmon River country, I knew I had to set a story there. And so the town of Silver River came into being, along with its namesake river and the surrounding mountains.

As the story goes, ten years ago a horrible murder was committed in Silver River, a crime the town never forgot and that profoundly affected the lives of Lacey Morgan and Rory Dalton. They were high school seniors and planned to spend the rest of their lives together. The crime shattered those plans. Rory and Lacey became virtual strangers.

Now new evidence regarding the murder comes to light. But is it too late for Rory and Lacey? And what if revealing the truth adversely affects others? Might there be circumstances in which the truth should be kept secret?

These were just a few of the questions I encountered while writing *Silver River Secrets*. Good thing Rory and Lacey took over, and I didn't have to answer them! I hope you will agree they made the right choices.

Visit my website at lindahopelee.com or email me at linda@lindahopelee.com. I'm also on Facebook and Twitter (@lindahopelee).

Linda

HEARTWARMING

Silver River Secrets

——

Linda Hope Lee

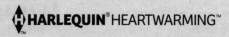

Recycling programs
for this product may
not exist in your area.

ISBN-13: 978-0-373-36818-1

Silver River Secrets

Copyright © 2016 by Linda Hope Lee

All rights reserved. Except for use in any review, the reproduction or utilization of this work in whole or in part in any form by any electronic, mechanical or other means, now known or hereinafter invented, including xerography, photocopying and recording, or in any information storage or retrieval system, is forbidden without the written permission of the publisher, Harlequin Enterprises Limited, 225 Duncan Mill Road, Don Mills, Ontario M3B 3K9, Canada.

This is a work of fiction. Names, characters, places and incidents are either the product of the author's imagination or are used fictitiously, and any resemblance to actual persons, living or dead, business establishments, events or locales is entirely coincidental.

This edition published by arrangement with Harlequin Books S.A.

For questions and comments about the quality of this book, please contact us at CustomerService@Harlequin.com.

® and TM are trademarks of Harlequin Enterprises Limited or its corporate affiliates. Trademarks indicated with ® are registered in the United States Patent and Trademark Office, the Canadian Intellectual Property Office and in other countries.

Printed in U.S.A.

www.Harlequin.com

Linda Hope Lee lives in the Pacific Northwest. She likes traveling to new places, especially to small towns that might serve as settings for her novels. In addition to contemporary romance, she writes in the romantic suspense and mystery genres. When she is not writing, she is busy creating watercolor paintings or drawing in colored pencil or pen and ink. Another pastime is photography, which she uses as inspiration for her art and for her stories. She also collects children's books and anything to do with wire fox terriers.

Books by Linda Hope Lee

Harlequin Heartwarming

Return to Willow Beach

Eva's Deadline
Her Summer Crush

Visit the Author Profile page
at Harlequin.com for more titles.

CHAPTER ONE

"SHE'S B-A-ACK," Sam Porter announced.

"That so?" Rory Dalton didn't bother to look up from under the hood of Sam's '66 Ford Mustang. Instead, he focused on installing the car's new water pump.

"Yep. She's just about to head over the bridge. Aren't you gonna come look?"

Rory gave the wrench another twist. "I'm busy fixing your car, in case you didn't notice. Besides, how do you know it's her?"

"She's driving a convertible with the top down. A white Camaro. Could be a classic."

"No kidding." Rory straightened and regarded his friend, who stood at the open end of Dalton's Auto Repair. He and Sam had been buddies since they played football for Silver River High ten years ago, and both shared an interest in classic cars.

Sam laughed. "Thought that'd get your attention. Hurry up or you'll miss her. She travels."

Rory tossed the wrench on the workbench and trotted over to stand beside Sam. From the shop's hilltop vantage point, he had a sweeping view of the highway leading into Idaho's Silver River. Her car was the only one on the road. As Sam said, it was a Camaro. A '75, to be exact, not quite old enough to be considered a classic. Still, a fine set of wheels.

The car held his interest for only a moment, and then he zeroed in on the driver: Lacey Morgan. Her long, dark brown hair swirled around her face. Sunglasses shaded her eyes, and a sleeveless top exposed her tanned arms.

Rory's throat went dry.

Just then, she looked up to the hilltop. Rory jumped back, hoping she hadn't spotted him. He didn't want her to think he had the slightest interest in her return to Silver River.

Sam shoved his hands into his pockets and rocked back on his heels. "Wonder how long she'll be here this time."

"She never stays more than a week. Just long enough to check on her grandmother."

"Might be longer. Remy broke her hip. She went straight from rehab to Riverview. Lacey's here to help her get settled and to clean out her old apartment."

"I heard about Remy's accident. I'm sorry she's had trouble. But how do you know so much? Or would that be violating lawyer-client confidentiality?"

Sam laughed. "Not at all. That bit of info comes from Ida Capshaw. She's our para-legal, you know, and she plays bridge with Remy."

"Ah." Rory stepped forward again in time to see Lacey's car sweep over the bridge and join the traffic on Main Street. Then a delivery truck pulled in behind her, and she was lost from his view.

He gave his head a quick shake and frowned at Sam. "Why are we standing here wasting time when there's work to be done?"

Sam's eyebrows peaked. "Because she's back?"

"So? No business of mine."

"So you keep telling me. But I have a feeling you're in for trouble, this time. Big trouble."

LACEY MORGAN HEADED down Main Street with the image of Rory Dalton imprinted on her mind. She hadn't intended to look up at his auto shop when she rounded that last curve in the highway, but she had, and there he had been, gazing down at her as though he'd been waiting for her to drive by. Which was crazy. Why should he care that she'd come to town again? He knew she made the trip from Boise to Silver River periodically to visit her grandmother. When their paths crossed, they said little more than a brief "hello."

The events of that fateful day ten years ago, just a week before they both were to graduate from Silver River High, with their whole future ahead of them—a future they planned to spend together—had ripped them apart and turned them into strangers.

An overhead banner advertising the town's annual Silver River Days caught her eye. This year's dates were August 10–15. She'd be long gone by then. Cleaning out Gram's apartment and settling her into Riverview would take no more than a week, tops.

Lacey's boss at the Boise Historical Society was generous about her visits to Silver River, and especially about the extra time she needed for this trip. Even if she'd wanted to

stay for the celebration—which she didn't—
she wouldn't ask for more time off.

Leaving the downtown behind, Lacey was
soon in the country again. Rambling mountain ranges surrounded her, and here and
there the river popped into view, sparkling
in the sunlight.

Another mile brought the turnoff to Sophie's
Bed and Breakfast, where globe lights along
the driveway guided Lacey to the Victorian-
style house painted bright lavender with white
trim.

She parked in the guest lot and pulled her
suitcase on wheels up the flagstone walk to
the porch. Several middle-aged guests sat in
wicker chairs chatting and drinking iced tea.
They exchanged "hellos" with Lacey as she
passed by.

Inside the house, Sophie Bennett came from
around the counter with arms outstretched.
"Lacey! I've been watching for you."

"Hello, Sophie." Lacey returned Sophie's
hug, catching a whiff of her lilac-scented per-
fume.

Sophie stood back and held Lacey at arm's
length. "Good to see you."

"You, too."

Sophie's bright blue T-shirt and orange

slacks fit smoothly over her trim figure. An orange scarf holding back shoulder-length blond hair revealed a hint of gray at the temples.

Sophie returned to her post behind the counter to check Lacey in. That completed, she took a key from a drawer and motioned to Lacey. "Come on. I'll take you up to your room."

They went down a carpeted hallway to the stairs. The rooms they passed offered Lacey glimpses of wood paneling and wallpaper, brocaded fabrics and patterned carpets, hurricane lamps and heavy draperies. The B and B had long been a dream of Sophie's, and when she finally convinced her husband, Hugh, to buy the place, she fixed it up in style.

"Sorry to hear about your grandmother's accident," Sophie said over her shoulder as they climbed the stairs. "How's she doing?"

"Determined to walk again, but agrees it's time to be in a place where someone can look after her."

"There's no better place around here than Riverview."

"I know. We're so lucky the owners decided to build their retirement home here rather than in Milton."

On the second floor, Sophie stopped at one of the rooms and slipped her key into the lock. "Here we are."

Lacey followed her inside, her gaze taking in a queen-size bed with a colorful patchwork quilt, an armoire, an overstuffed chair and a round rosewood table. A Tiffany lamp decorated with yellow roses hung over the table.

"I love it!" Lacey exclaimed.

"Fabulous view, too. Take a look."

Lacey parked her suitcase next to the luggage rack and followed Sophie to the window. In the courtyard below, water gushed from a stone fountain, and walkways wound through gardens full of flowers. Beyond lay the river and neighboring farms.

Then her gaze landed on an all-too-familiar copse of willow trees and a two-story house with peeling white paint. Her stomach dropped. "Oh…"

"What's the matter?" Sophie's voice rose in alarm.

"Our old house. Gram's house."

"You can see it from here?" Sophie peered out the window. "Oh, my. Lacey, I'm sorry. I never realized…" Sophie pressed her fingers to her lips and looked at Lacey. "You don't have to stay in this room. You can move across the hall."

Lacey shook her head. "No, I want this one."

"But to be reminded whenever you look out the window..."

"Sophie, not a day goes by that I don't think about what happened in that house."

"I'm sorry, honey, so sorry. But I do wish you could put the past behind you."

Lacey shook her head and bit her lower lip. "Not possible."

Sophie let a moment of silence pass and then said, "Okay, if you're sure you don't want to change rooms, I'll let you get settled. You probably want to go see your grandmother right away."

"Yes, I'm having dinner with her, but that still gives me time to unpack."

"If you need help bringing in more stuff, Hugh is around somewhere."

"I'll be fine. Thanks." Lacey lifted her suitcase onto the luggage rack and unzipped it.

Sophie walked toward the door but then stopped and turned. "Don't forget the party tonight."

Lacey looked up. "Party?"

"Yes, I mentioned it when you made your

reservation. We're having a kickoff party for Silver River Days, here in our courtyard."

"Oh, right. I saw the banner in town. But I don't think—"

"Please come, Lacey."

Lacey pressed her lips together. "But I won't be here for the celebration itself. And, well, you know I feel uncomfortable at town gatherings."

Sophie slowly shook her head. "Lacey, it's been ten years. Do you really think people are looking at you and thinking only that your father was a...was..."

Lacey closed her eyes. "Go ahead and say it, Sophie. A murderer. You, along with everybody else in this town, believe that my father shot and killed Rory Dalton's father in cold blood. But he didn't. I know he didn't."

"The jury convicted him."

"They were wrong."

Sophie stepped close and put her arm around Lacey's shoulders. "You know Hugh and I were friends with your parents, hon. We used to go out together. And, okay, your dad was a hothead sometimes, but we put up with him. No question we loved your mom. Nobody mourned her death more than we did. I miss her to this day. But don't you think it's time for you to move on?"

"If only I could prove his innocence…"

"Let it go, Lacey."

Lacey squeezed her eyes shut. "I can't. I just can't."

CARRYING A VASE of pink roses, Lacey knocked on the door to her grandmother's apartment at the Riverview Retirement Community.

"Come in," came the cheery reply.

She opened the door and stepped into the apartment's compact kitchenette and from there into the living room.

Remylon Whitfield, looking crisp and cool in a pink cotton blouse and white slacks, sat in her wheelchair near the patio door. She held out her arms. "Lacey, love! I've been waiting for you."

"Good to be here, Gram." Lacey set her purse and the flowers on a table and then hurried to Remy's side and gave her a warm hug.

"I've missed you," Gram said when they ended their embrace. She glanced over Lacey's shoulder and clapped her hands. "You brought me some roses. Thank you."

"You're welcome. The best housewarming present I could think of."

"They're perfect. Did you get your room at Sophie's? You're staying for dinner here, though, right? We can play Scrabble afterward."

Gram's eyes behind her glasses were hopeful.

"I should have time for a game or two, although Sophie wants me to come to their Silver River Days party tonight. I told her I'd think about it."

"You should go, dear."

Lacey sighed. "I just don't feel comfortable in this town."

"I know, honey. Sometimes, when I get to thinking about the past, I don't, either." Gram looked down at her hands.

"But it's different for you. Having your son-in-law accused of murder is not the same as having your father, your flesh and blood, accused."

"Not accused, dear. Convicted," Gram said in a reproving tone.

Lacey opened her mouth to argue but then clamped her jaw shut. No sense in firing up their old disagreement, especially when she'd just arrived. Her gaze landed on two cardboard boxes sitting beside the patio doors.

"Looks like you've already done some moving."

Gram nodded. "Cousin Bessie helped me gather some things together before she left. Vernon brought the boxes over when he came to pick her up."

"That was nice of him. I could start unpacking them now. We have some time before dinner."

"Might as well."

While Lacey tackled the boxes, which contained mostly linens that she stowed away either in the bathroom or in the hall closet, her grandmother filled her in on her new life at Riverview. The food was good, the aides were nice and she'd met the woman next door, who was also a bridge player.

"Sounds like you're settling in," Lacey said.

Gram sighed. "Maybe so, but I'm sure gonna miss Cousin Bessie."

"I know. I'm glad you two were apartment neighbors these past years. But I can understand her wanting to go with her son and his family when he was transferred. You have a lot of close friends in town, especially your bridge club."

"Not like family. Not much left of our family now… Just you and me." Gram gave her a sidelong glance.

Lacey knew what was coming next. Sure enough, Gram let a few seconds go by and then said, "Would be nice to live closer to each other."

Lacey tucked the last pair of sheets and pillowcases into a drawer in the hall closet. "Anytime you want to move to Boise, I'll find a place for you."

Gram folded her arms. "Only way I'd ever leave Silver River is in a pine box, and then I'll go only as far as Restlawn. I'll not run away like you did."

Lacey's stomach churned. "I didn't run away. I went away to college, which I had planned to do before…before…" She shut the drawer and spread her hands. "Gram, please, let's not spoil my visit."

Gram wrinkled her brow. "You're right. I'm sorry, honey. I just wish you would come back home where you belong."

Where you belong. Gram's words brought an ache to Lacey's heart. No, as much as she might wish it were so, she did not belong in Silver River. Not anymore.

If she could somehow prove her father's innocence, then she could hold her head high and live here again. But, after ten years, what hope did she have of that?

CHAPTER TWO

BY THE TIME Lacey returned to Sophie's, dusk
had spread a rosy glow over the landscape.
The globe lights lining the driveway shone
like miniature moons. Inside the B and B,
the sounds of lively music, talking and laughter drifted in from the courtyard. Instead of
joining the party, Lacey went toward the
stairway. Despite Sophie's encouragement,
she'd decided to skip the party. She wouldn't
be here to celebrate Silver River Days, anyway. If not for her grandmother, she wouldn't
come to town at all. Ever.

"Lacey?"

Uh-oh, caught.

She turned to see Kristal Wilson enter the
front door. Lacey warmed at the sight of her
old high school friend, one of the few who
stood by her after the tragedy.

"I heard you were staying here," Kris said
as they exchanged a hug.

Lacey shook her head. "The grapevine in

this town never ceases to amaze me. I just arrived this afternoon. I planned to give you a call."

Kris tucked a lock of silver-blond hair behind her ear, revealing a dangling silver heart earring. "I know, but here we are, and we can go to the party together." She gestured toward the door to the courtyard.

Lacey shook her head. "Uh-uh. I decided to skip it. It's been a long day, and besides, I'm not dressed for it." She pointed to her sleeveless blue tunic top and black tights.

"Who dresses up in Silver River?"

"You do. You always look like a million."

Kris grinned as she smoothed the collar of her bright yellow blouse, which she wore with a brown pencil skirt and high-heeled shoes. "That's because I'm a walking advertisement for the shop."

"No, you love clothes. You always have."

Kris waved dismissively. "Okay, okay. But, Lacey, come to the party, just for a little while, so we can catch up. Otherwise, we'll have to wait till we go to lunch, and who knows when that will be?"

"Well…okay, for a little while."

Still, Lacey felt her muscles tense as she stepped into the crowded courtyard. There were so many people. Had the whole town come out? On the way to the bar, she nodded and smiled at familiar faces. Then, glasses of Chardonnay in hand, she and Kris strolled the walkway circling the burbling fountain. Music from the four-piece combo filled the air, and balloons and streamers added a festive touch. They chatted about Remy's move and Kris's job at her aunt's clothing store and the problems of being a single parent to eight-year-old Lucas.

"Thank goodness for day camp," Kris said. "It's been a lifesaver this summer."

At the buffet table, they sampled the appetizers.

"Has anything changed between you and Sam?" Lacey asked, plucking a potato chip from a napkin-lined basket.

Kris munched a cracker topped with cream cheese. "Not really. He'll never forgive me for breaking up with him and marrying Nolan."

They chatted for a while longer, and then Lacey said, "I really should go. But we'll get together for lunch soon."

"I look forward to that… Oh, oh…" Kristal placed her fingers to her lips.

"What?"

"If you leave now, you'll run smack into him."

"Him, who?"

"Rory. He and Sam just arrived."

RORY DRAGGED HIS steps as he followed Sam into the courtyard at Sophie's B and B. He wasn't really in a party mood. After a busy day at the shop, all he wanted was to go home, snap open a beer, kick back and relax. But he'd told Sophie and Hugh he would come and help celebrate the upcoming festival. On the way in, he'd met Sam, and so here they were. He wouldn't stay long, just say a few "hellos," and then leave.

Sam pulled two bottles of beer from an ice-filled tub. "Here you go." He handed one to Rory.

"Thanks." Rory opened the beer and took a sip. The cold liquid made his taste buds tingle.

"Hits the spot, doesn't it?" Sam held up his bottle.

"Yeah, but I could drink beer at home."

"Not with all the food you'll find here." Sam gazed around. "Let's head over to the buffet table… Uh-oh."

"What's the matter?"

"Kristal's here."

"That's okay, isn't it? You two are on speaking terms."

"Yeah, but are you and Lacey? 'Cause she's here, too."

Rory followed the direction of Sam's nod, and sure enough, Kristal and Lacey stood at the buffet table. Feeling his chest tighten, he took a deep breath. "I never expected Lacey to be here. She keeps to herself when she comes to town."

"Not this time. But Kris spotted us, so we might as well say hello."

Rory frowned. "But I…"

"What? You two do speak to each other, don't you?"

"When we have to." He took another sip of beer while he debated. Finally, he said, "Okay, let's get it over with."

Still, as he and Sam approached the two women, who were now turned to face them, he found breathing difficult.

"Hello, Kris, Lacey," Sam said. "Saw you this afternoon coming into town, Lacey. Nice set of wheels."

"Thanks, Sam." Lacey's gaze shifted to Rory. "Hello, Rory."

"Lacey." Rory nodded without smiling.

Lacey's long brown hair curled about her heart-shaped face, and her eyes were as big and brown as he remembered. His chest tightened even more.

"Good crowd," Sam said, looking around.

"It is." Kris nodded.

An awkward silence fell. Then, just as Rory was about to say, "Nice seeing you," or some other phrase to signal his exit, Sam said, "Kris, you need a refill."

Kris looked at her half-full glass of wine and then at Sam. "I do?"

Sam tilted his head.

"Oh, I guess I do," Kris said.

Sam lifted the glass from Kris's hand. "You two excuse us?"

Before either Rory or Lacey had time to respond, Sam steered Kristal toward the bar.

Rory stared after them. *Thanks a lot, Sam.* He turned back to Lacey, intending to say, "See you around," but what came out was, "Sorry to hear about your grandmother's accident. Being laid up must be tough on her."

"It is, but she's recovering." Lacey shifted her feet and looked toward the door.

Okay, she's as anxious to get away as you are. Let her go.

"She's at Riverview now, right?" he said.

"Yes. That's why I'm here again, helping her to move."

"I figured that."

Why else would she be in Silver River? Certainly not to see him. And why were they standing here making conversation, anyway?

"Your business doing well?" she asked.

"If you mean the shop, yeah, business is great."

"Still working for your grandfather, too?"

He nodded. "Part-time." Working for his grandfather's real estate investment business was more an obligation—and a necessity— than a pleasure. "What about you? Still with, what? Some historical society, right?"

A smile lit up her face, the first he'd seen all evening. "Yes. The Boise Historical Society. I'm doing what I love—writing about history."

They'd both made lives for themselves without each other. And yet, after what had happened, he should be glad they'd managed to move on.

They fell silent while the music and conversation swirled around them. *Okay, now go!* Then his gaze fell on her empty glass. "Looks like you're ready for another drink."

She frowned but said, "Why, I suppose I—"

"There you are, Rory!"

Rory looked around to see Helen Lewis hurrying along the walkway.

Helen skidded to a stop. "I've been looking for you. I just had to tell you how well our car runs since you gave it a tune-up. Jasper and I were about to trade it in, but not now."

"Glad it's working for you," Rory said.

Helen turned to Lacey. "This man is a wonder." She peered through her black-framed glasses. "Oh. I don't think I know you."

"This is Lacey Morgan," Rory said. "Lacey, Helen Lewis. She and her husband are new in town. He works for Thompson's Building Supply, and Helen works at the Visitor's Center. Lacey, ah, used to live here," he added to Helen.

Helen's eyes widened. "I've heard about you. You're the one who—"

Catching Lacey's stricken look, he finished quickly, "Went to high school same time as I did."

Helen frowned as she cut her gaze to Rory and then back to Lacey. "Oh. Right. You were high school buddies."

"Buddies" didn't exactly describe his and Lacey's relationship back then, but he wasn't about to correct Helen. "We were on our way to get Lacey another glass of wine." He nodded toward the bar.

Lacey shook her head. "No, I really need to leave now. Busy day tomorrow. Nice meeting you, Helen. Good to see you again, Rory."

The words tumbled from her mouth, and before Rory could reply, he was staring at her back as she hurried along the walk to the B and B's door.

Helen pressed her fingers to her lips. "Oh, dear, I hope I didn't run her off."

Rory raised a hand. "Don't worry about it. Lacey and I were only saying hello."

INSIDE THE B AND B, as Lacey set her empty wineglass on a table, she realized her hands were shaking. She felt queasy, too. Bad enough to have spent time talking to Rory, but then to meet a stranger who apparently knew all about her past… Too much.

Taking a deep breath, she hurried through the dining room to the stairs. She put her foot on the bottom step, but then on impulse swiveled around and marched toward the front door.

Five minutes later, she sat in her car at the entrance to the highway, waiting for traffic to clear. She rolled down the window and, along with sounds of the music from the party, the fresh air rushed in, tinged with the smell of grass and hay and the river.

Once on the highway, she pressed her foot to the accelerator, watching the speedometer inch up past the speed limit. Except for a pale glow of light lingering behind the mountains and the lights of the houses she passed, darkness covered the land.

She sped along for a few miles and then came to her senses and eased her foot off the accelerator. No point in risking a ticket. Calmer now, she loosened her grip on the steering wheel and leaned back against the seat. Putting distance between herself and the party—and Rory—was just what she needed.

And yet her thoughts lingered on their meeting. They'd exchanged more words tonight than during any other time their paths had crossed when she'd come to town. So what? Trapped by circumstances, they were only being civil to each other, exchanging small talk that didn't mean anything. In a few days, she'd be gone again.

Meanwhile, she'd be sure to keep her distance.

LACEY SURVEYED THE array of food displayed on the B and B's dining room sideboard, from scrambled eggs and hash browns to waffles and oatmeal and fresh fruit. She breathed in all the enticing aromas, and her stomach rumbled. After her unsettling encounter with Rory, she'd spent a restless night, but that hadn't dulled her hunger this morning. The conversation of other guests drifted through the room. The door to the courtyard stood open, admitting a fresh morning breeze.

Sophie bustled in carrying a tray of coffee cups. "Good morning, Lacey." She set the tray next to the coffee urn.

"Hi, Sophie." Lacey slowly shook her head. "I don't know how you do it."

Sophie quirked an eyebrow. "Do what?"

"The party last night, and now this fantastic breakfast." She made a sweeping gesture to include the sideboard.

Sophie laughed and fingered the turquoise scarf holding back her hair. "The committee prepared last night's food, and this spread is our cook's doing. She's a marvel. Still, compliments are always welcome… I was glad to see you at the party," she added, as she unloaded the cups.

"Kris caught me as I came home from Gram's."

"Ah, so I had a little help, did I? Well, you came, anyway. I saw you talking to Rory—" She cast Lacey a cautious glance.

Lacey picked up a plate and helped herself to the scrambled eggs. "All these years, we've never said much more than 'Hi,' and then last night we actually had a conversation. Sort of."

"Maybe that's a good thing."

Lacey shrugged and added hash browns to her eggs. "I can't imagine why. We won't get together again."

"You never know." Sophie finished unloading the cups and picked up the tray. "Oh, by the way, are you going up to Restlawn to visit the graves sometime this trip?"

"Yes, I'd planned to go this morning, before I start cleaning out Gram's old apartment."

"Feel free to take some of the flowers in the courtyard." Sophie gestured toward the open doors.

"Why, thanks, Sophie. That's thoughtful of you."

"That way, Hugh and I can pay our respects, too. He's outside now. You can get a bucket and some clippers from him and choose the flowers you want."

Half an hour later, Lacey found Hugh outside folding up the tables from last night's party. Dressed in blue overalls and a white T-shirt, he looked more like the farmer he used to be than the proprietor of an elegant bed-and-breakfast.

"Looks like you're getting your courtyard back in shape," Lacey said.

"That was some party." Hugh lifted his baseball cap, smoothed his gray crew cut and then settled the cap back on his head.

They chatted a bit, and then Lacey said, "I'm going up to Restlawn this morning, and Sophie said I could take some of your flowers, and that you'd have something I could put them in."

"Sure. Wait here a minute."

Hugh disappeared inside a toolshed, emerging a couple minutes later carrying a plastic bucket and a pair of clippers. He handed them to Lacey. "These should do the job."

"Thanks, Hugh."

"Take some of the pansies." Hugh indicated the flowers clustered in one of the beds. "Your mother's favorite."

"They were, and I will take some."

"Don't suppose Rick would care what flowers you put on his grave," Hugh said in a dry tone. "Not that he deserves any."

Lacey dropped her jaw and stared at Hugh, his unexpected slam at her father taking her off guard. Then she lifted her chin and said crisply, "Well, I care."

Hugh shook his head. "You're probably the only one who does."

CHAPTER THREE

ON THE DRIVE to Restlawn Cemetery, Hugh's unkind remark about her father rang in Lacey's ears. But, like many of the townspeople, he believed that Rick Morgan had, in fact, shot Rory's father, Al Dalton, Jr., in cold blood. Standing by her father hadn't been easy for Lacey, since the murder had resulted in her mother's death, too. Sometimes, she had her doubts, but, oh, she didn't want to believe he could commit such a terrible crime.

If only she could find some proof of his innocence. But little chance of that, especially now that ten years had passed.

She reached the turnoff to Restlawn and followed a narrow, winding road to the iron gates marking the entrance. Spotting the tall oak tree that shaded her grandfather's and her mother's graves, she pulled to the side of the road and parked. Bucket of flowers in hand, she trudged over the freshly mowed grass, breathing in the pine-scented air and listening to the twittering birds. Cemeteries always seemed so peaceful, and Restlawn was no exception.

She stopped in front of the headstones, her grandfather's on the left, her mother's to the right. On her grandfather's other side, an empty plot waited for Remy.

When Lacey knelt to place the flowers in the embedded vase on her mother's grave, she saw that the holder already contained pansies. A glance at her grandfather's vase revealed his, too, held the delicate blossoms. They were wilted, as though they'd been there for several days.

Who had brought the flowers? Gram used to visit, but not since she'd broken her hip and been confined to her wheelchair.

A sudden unease gripped Lacey, and she glanced over her shoulder. No one was nearby, and no other cars were on the road. Still, she had a creepy feeling someone was watching her.

Lacey turned back to the graves. She thought about removing the wilted flowers but then decided to leave them. Pouring fresh water from the bucket into the vases, she added a few of the flowers she'd brought to each of the embedded vases.

She ran her fingers over her grandfather's engraved name on the marker, Jason Carl Whitfield, remembering him as a happy man who took pride in his work as a carpenter and who doted on his wife and daughter. Lacey's mom was spoiled and self-centered, as might be expected of one who'd been the center of her parents' universe.

On the whole, she'd been a good mother to Lacey, though. Lacey especially remembered the bedtime stories and poetry they shared.

Lacey touched her mother's carved name, too, and then whispered a prayer for both of them. Grasping the bucket, she stood and, still uneasy, looked around again. Seeing no one, she turned her steps toward her father's grave, which was some distance away.

I won't have that murderer near my family! Gram had declared.

He wouldn't be here at all but for Lacey's insistence. When he died in prison, she arranged to have his remains returned to Silver River and had with her own money purchased the plot and the marker. She chose an especially pleasant spot, with a nearby fountain shaded by several maple trees. But unlike her grandfather and her mother, who'd both been mourned in public services, only

Lacey—and the grave digger—were present to witness Richard Mark Morgan's burial.

As she knelt to place flowers in the vase, she saw purple-and-white pansies, the same flowers that were in her grandfather's and her mother's vases. Apparently, the same person had visited all three graves. Who? Someone who believed in Rick's innocence, as she did?

Lacey added her flowers to the vase, whispering, "I still believe in you, Dad. And maybe someone else does, too."

Before leaving the cemetery, Lacey pulled into a viewpoint overlooking the town. From here she could see Main Street, busy as usual, with vehicles and pedestrians. Beyond the business district were blocks of homes, and then the river, sparkling in the sunlight.

Sadness filled her. Silver River was a pleasant and peaceful town. She'd been happy living here until that fateful day ten years ago. Now she lived in exile. Not that she didn't like Boise. She did. And she liked her job with the historical society. But Boise could never replace Silver River and the happiness she had known here.

RORY DROVE ALONG the highway connecting Silver River with Milton. Not that he was going all the way there. He'd turn around soon and head for Dalton Properties, where he worked most afternoons. He'd taken this long drive today to check out the overhaul he'd given the '58 Dodge, one of his classic car acquisitions bought from a man in Fork City, who'd kept it hidden away in an old shed like buried treasure.

Rory tuned his ear to the engine, but his mind wandered to last night's party and Lacey Morgan. They'd actually talked to each other. Their conversation had been awkward, but what did he expect?

Their encounter didn't mean anything, though. Probably wouldn't happen again.

Thinking of her reminded him that the turnoff to the old Whitfield farm was up ahead. The house still sat there, empty and in disrepair, a constant reminder of the tragedy. Usually, as he passed by, he gritted his teeth and stepped on the gas, eager to put the place behind him.

But today, as the turnoff approached, he found himself slowing down, and in the next moment swung the Dodge off the highway and onto the dirt road leading to the farm. He bumped along, jerking the wheel to avoid potholes and overgrowth pushing through the barbed wire bordering the road. Reaching the house, he put on the brake and gazed out the window at the two-story structure. Paint had peeled off the siding and holes dotted the roof. Ragged curtains hung in a few of the windows.

Memories flooded his mind: bringing Lacey home from school. Doing homework at the kitchen table while sampling her grandmother's cookies. Hiking down to the river where they lazed in the sunshine or splashed around in inner tubes.

He stepped from the car and walked around to the back of the house. Beyond a stretch of overgrown grass and weeds sat a garage with the door off its hinges, a barn missing part of the roof, a couple of weathered sheds and a chicken coop. And farther yet, past a row of willow trees, a trail led to the river.

He looked up at the house's second story, focusing on one of the windows. The window where Lacey's father had stood when he pointed his shotgun at Rory's father and pulled the trigger. Rory swung his gaze back around to the ground, picking out the spot where his father had died. He shuddered and felt sick to his stomach. He stood there, clenching and unclenching his fists, until he got a grip on himself. Then he marched back to his car, climbed in, slammed the door and drove off.

That house should not still be standing there, he thought, while rumbling back down the dirt road toward the highway. It should have been torn down long ago so that he didn't have to look at it and be reminded of what had happened there. Ten years ago. Ten long years. High time he did something about that house.

BACK IN TOWN twenty minutes later, Rory parked in his reserved slot behind the Scott Building on Main Street. He sat there a moment, his mind spinning with his new plan.

A knock on the window interrupted his musings. He looked up to see Stuart MacKenzie, one of his grandfather's employees.

Rory rolled down the window. "Hey, Stuart. Where are you off to?"

Stuart smoothed the lapels of his lightweight sports jacket. "The Cooper ranch. Old man Cooper is ready to talk business."

Rory opened the door and stepped from the car. "Good for you. Hope you land the deal."

Stuart grinned. "Thanks, buddy. But I'm not doing anything you can't do—if you'd forget about your cars and tend to business here." He nodded at the Dodge. "That is a great-looking car, though."

Rory pocketed the keys and ran his hand along the car's engine-warm hood. "Yeah, well, I guess restoring old cars does for me what owning land does for my grandfather. To each his own."

"Ri-i-ght. Try telling that to A.J. When you gonna take your rightful place around here as the 'heir apparent'?"

Rory shook his head. "Don't hold your breath."

Stuart laughed. "If I were a betting man, I'd bet on A.J. But I don't want to get involved in your family feud. I'm not taking sides, either."

Stuart headed for his car, and Rory entered the building. The smell of wax and varnish from the first floor's furniture store drifted along the hallway. He took the back stairs to the second floor where the offices of Dalton Properties were located. His grandfather's middle-aged administrative assistant, Sheila Cobb, sat at her desk.

"Morning, Sheila."

"Glad you're here, Rory. He's been wondering." She tipped her head toward the door to A.J.'s office just as it opened and his grandfather stepped out.

At seventy, Alfred James Dalton was as fit and trim as he'd been in his younger years, thanks in part to heredity, but also to regular rounds of golf and visits to the local gym.

A.J. spread his feet apart and propped his hands on his hips. "About time you got here."

Rory glanced at his wristwatch. "I know, I'm a little late, but with good reason—"

"Never mind. Sheila put some new proposals on your desk. Look 'em over, and then we'll talk."

"I'd just as soon talk now—about something else."

A.J. raised his eyebrows. "Hmm, all right. I've got half an hour until my two o'clock arrives. Come on in."

Once in his office, A.J. pointed to a straight chair. "Have a seat."

Rory sat, while A.J. rounded his desk and sank into a black leather chair that always made Rory think of a throne. Unable to find a chair locally that suited him, A.J. had ordered this one over the internet. When it had arrived, the delivery guys had one heckuva time getting it up the narrow stairs. But they succeeded, and there it was, and A.J. fit into it as though it were made especially for him.

A.J. opened a file folder on his desk and idly rifled the papers inside. "So, what's on your mind?" he said without looking up.

"I want to buy the Whitfield property."

A.J. jerked to attention. "Yeah? You know I've tried for years to get Remy to sell, and she's flatly refused. What makes you think you can change her mind?"

"I'm betting she needs the money, now that she's living at Riverview. That place doesn't come cheap."

"Maybe Lacey is helping out."

"Maybe. Still—"

A.J. rubbed his jaw. "Okay, let's say you get her to sell. What do you see happening to the property?"

"First thing is tear down the house. It's an eyesore, and I'm sick of it. Always reminding me—"

"You think tearing it down will erase your memory of what happened there?"

"It'll go a long way to helping."

A.J. closed the file folder and leaned forward. "And then what? A subdivision is what I see. Ought to be enough land for fifty or sixty houses."

Rory shrugged. "Getting rid of the house is first and foremost. You hate the sight of that place as much as I do."

"I'll agree with that."

His voice cracked, and his gaze strayed to the framed photo on his desk, a picture of him with his son, Alfred James Dalton Jr., better known as "Al Jr." Their arms slung over each other's shoulders, big grins on their faces, they stood in front of the Ross Building, one of their many projects.

"So, what do you think?" Rory asked.

"I need to know more. You plan to use Lacey to get to Remy? Heard you two were cozying up at Sophie and Hugh's party."

Rory clenched his jaw. "We weren't 'cozying up.' We happened to find ourselves face-to-face and exchanged a few words, that's all. As for using Lacey, ten years ago, you told me I couldn't have anything more to do with her."

"That was then. This is now. That property has sat there in a time warp, and I agree with you that enough is enough. You get it and you'll have a big bonus."

"All right—"

"Wait a minute. I'm not letting you completely off the hook."

Rory narrowed his eyes. "What?"

A.J. pointed a forefinger. "I need you to take more responsibility around here. This business will be yours someday, and you need to know how to run it. Stuart knows more about our operation than you do."

Rory shook his head. They'd had this discussion before, many times. "I'm giving as much here as I can. I have my own business to run—"

A.J.'s mouth turned down. "Oh, yes. Cars again. Collecting 'em isn't enough. You have to tinker with them, too."

Rory pushed to the edge of his chair. "If we're done here—"

A.J. put out a staying hand. "Not quite. Don't forget that I own that prime piece of property Dalton's Auto Repair sits on."

"So?"

"So Silver River could use another motel."

"Go ahead and sell the property." Rory made a dismissive wave. "I can always re-locate."

"You could if you had the money. But you don't. It's all tied up in cars."

Rory pressed his lips together. "Okay, we are done here." He stood and strode to the door.

"Keep in mind what I said."

"I'm sure you'll be reminding me again," Rory said as he went out the door. *And again, and again.*

"Get back to me ASAP about those proposals," A.J. called after him.

IN HIS OFFICE, Rory hung his jacket on the coatrack and paused to look out the adjacent window. Instead of facing the street, like his grandfather's office, Rory's office looked out on the back parking lot. He didn't care. Not even the best view in the world could make him want to be there.

His gaze landed on his Dodge, and a smile touched his lips. That was one fine car. Then he saw A.J.'s shiny new BMW, and his mouth thinned. No, his grandfather would never understand or share his love of the classics.

He turned away and crossed the room to his desk. His office had no personal touches. No photos, no certificates on the wall, nothing to identify him as the occupant. He hadn't put down roots here, and he never would.

A.J. knew how to play the guilt game, though, making him think he should be grateful for the opportunity to take his father's place in the company. If his father were still alive, Rory had no doubt the situation would be different. His father had understood Rory's need to work with his hands, to create something. He was proud of Rory's talent and never passed up an opportunity to brag about him.

But Al Jr. wasn't alive. He was dead. Shot in the back on that fateful day when he went to see Norella Morgan.

Guilt gave way to anger. Anger at Rick Morgan, the hothead who pulled the trigger. And yet at the time, he'd wanted to stand by Lacey. He'd loved her, and planned to marry her.

But that was all over now.

Now, what he wanted most of all was to get rid of that house. Somehow, he'd find a way. Pushing aside his troubled thoughts, he sank into his desk chair. For a moment he only stared at the file folder lying there. Then he took a deep breath, opened the file and began reading.

"I VISITED THE graves at Restlawn this morning," Lacey told Gram while they enjoyed a cup of tea on her patio. The afternoon sun had cleared the mountains and shone brightly from a cloudless sky. A brisk breeze swayed the cottonwood trees lining the riverbank. Still, the air was hot, even in the patio's shade.

Gram smiled. "That was nice of you, dear. I've missed going myself."

"I took some of Sophie and Hugh's pansies to put in the vases, but there were already pansies in them."

"Really?"

Gram's tone sounded more matter-of-fact than surprised.

"Yes. Do you know who could be responsible?"

Gram kept her gaze on her teacup. "Does it matter?"

"Yes, it does. You know something. Come on, tell me." Lacey leaned forward.

"Well…maybe the person was Claire Roche. Hank and Lena Nellon's daughter."

"Of Nellon's Hardware?"

Gram nodded.

"Why would she leave flowers?"

Gram bit her lower lip and looked off toward the mountains.

"Gram—"

Placing her teacup on the wrought-iron table, Gram folded her arms. "Oh, all right," she said in a grudging tone. "She liked Rick. He was a frequent customer at the store when she worked there. She was separated from her husband, Clint, at the time."

"But Dad wouldn't—"

Gram set her jaw. "You don't know what your father would do. He was a murderer, wasn't he?"

Lacy flinched. Her first impulse was to fling back, "No, he wasn't!" Instead, she took a deep breath and said calmly, "Why didn't this come out at the trial?"

"Why should it have? Claire's crush had nothing to do with Rick shooting Al Jr."

"Is Claire still in town?"

"Oh, yes. She and Clint got back together." Gram shook a finger at Lacey. "But don't you go asking her about the flowers. What does it matter who put them on the graves? That doesn't change the fact that your father was a murderer, and if it hadn't been for his crime, your mother would be alive today."

"No, Gram, he wasn't a murderer."

"Oh, you always say that. You have no proof."

Yes, she needed proof. But how to obtain that was still a mystery.

And yet, as she washed and dried their teacups in the apartment's kitchenette, she thought about what Gram had said about

Claire having a crush on her father. Had he returned her affection? She'd always thought her father was devoted to her mother, but maybe that hadn't been the case. Even so, did that make him a murderer?

CHAPTER FOUR

LACEY UNLOCKED THE door to Gram's old apartment and stepped inside. Having been vacant several weeks, the apartment's air was hot and stale. She strolled through the rooms, bare of furniture except for a sofa, a couple of overstuffed chairs and a few end tables. Those items could be sold to the town's used furniture store or donated to the thrift store. She would deal with them another day. Today, her task was to clean out the basement storage unit.

She took the elevator to the basement and located Remy's locker. Cardboard boxes were stacked from the floor nearly to the ceiling. Lacey sighed. Chances were, very little of the boxes' contents could be kept. Gram's Riverview apartment was nearly full now, and although the building had basement storage as well, that space was much smaller than this one.

A peek in one box revealed a set of dishes

with a pink rose pattern. Gram's "company dishes," brought out when they had guests for dinner and sat at the farmhouse's dining room table under the crystal chandelier.

She'd bet they hadn't been used since Remy moved out of the farmhouse, and that would have been right after the murder. Unable to bear living in the house where the crime had occurred, she and Lacey moved into this apartment. Lacey had soon graduated high school and had gone off to college in Boise, where she'd stayed. She hated leaving Gram alone, but Cousin Bessie and her family were nearby, and so she knew Gram would have someone to look after her. Plus, she made periodic trips to Silver River to visit.

Even though Gram hadn't used the dishes for years and probably had no plans to use them now, she wouldn't want to give them up. Gram hung on to her possessions. The empty farmhouse was a prime example.

Retrieving a hand truck from the hallway, Lacey loaded it with several boxes. She wheeled them out the basement's back door to the parking lot, where she'd parked her car.

The Camaro's top was down. She opened the trunk and stacked the boxes inside, and then returned for another load. These she put in the backseat. The last box was heavier than she expected, and it slipped from her hands and fell to the ground. The top burst open, and the contents tumbled out. A trinket dish made of pink glass broke into several pieces. Oh, oh, Gram wouldn't like any of her treasures damaged.

Lacey retrieved a plastic bag from her car's glove box. As she gathered up the pieces, she realized the dish belonged not to Gram but to Mom. She'd seen it on the dresser in her parents' bedroom. Examination of the rest of the box's contents revealed they were her mother's, as well. Included were several more trinket dishes, a blue silk scarf, a pair of black high-heeled shoes, a long black skirt and a frilly white blouse, and a scattering of books.

One book, which had a picture of pansies on the cover, caught Lacey's eye. She had often seen her mother writing in it.

What are you writing? she once asked. *Poetry?*

Her mother smiled. *Some. Mostly, I just… write.*

Lacey picked up the book and ran her fingers over the pansies on the cover. Now, she could find out for herself what her mother had written. She opened the cover and idly flipped the pages. Yes, there was some poetry, but other pages with dated entries appeared to be a journal.

Excitement rippled down Lacey's spine. Perhaps her mother had written on the days leading up to the murder and her own death. Maybe she'd recorded something on that very day.

Lacey turned more of the pages but then stopped and closed the book. She'd wait until later, when she had time and privacy. Now, she must finish the task at hand.

Should she replace the journal in the box or put it aside? She and Gram planned to go through everything, and she would surely notice if the book were missing.

Lacey didn't want to go behind her grandmother's back, but what if Gram forbade her to read the journal? She stood there clutching the book and debating what to do.

RORY DROVE ALONG Park Street on his way to work at his auto repair shop. Ordinarily, he'd take Main Street, but today he drove down Park Street so that he could stop by Alice Helmer's. He'd put a new battery in her Chevy last week and wanted to make sure it was running well. When he arrived at Alice's, he found no one at home. Her car was gone, too, which answered his question.

As he rounded a corner, he saw the Towne Apartments and recalled that was where Remy Whitfield had lived before moving to Riverview. A familiar white Camaro convertible sat in the parking lot. Lacey's car. And there was Lacey, too, standing by a broken cardboard box and a scattering of the contents.

He pulled into the lot and lowered the window. "Need some help?"

She looked up from the book she'd been studying. "Rory!"

"On my way to the shop. Saw you and thought you might need some help." He nodded at the broken box and the scattered items.

She closed the book and laid it on her car's front seat. "I'm cleaning out Gram's storage unit."

"I figured." He cut the engine and stepped from the car. Approaching the box, he knelt to examine it. The flaps and one side were torn. "I have some tape in my car. I'll fix this for you."

She put out a hand. "Thanks, but you don't have to. I can—"

"I know I don't. But I'm betting you don't have any tape."

"No, but I can find another box."

"No need." He went to his car, opened the trunk and rummaged through his toolbox. "Okay, we're in business." He held up a roll of tape and a pair of shears.

She held the pieces of cardboard together while he taped them. Their fingers tangled in the process, sending him an unexpected rush of heat. He shot her a glance. She was looking down, but he could swear her cheeks were pink.

When the box was mended, he helped her replace the contents. "Remy has quite a collection of fancy little dishes," he commented.

"These are my…my mother's."

The catch in her voice made him wince, and he fell silent. When they finished packing, he taped the lid shut and added the container to the others in her car's backseat.

"Is this all?" he asked.

She rolled her eyes. "I wish. No, there's more in the storage locker. I'm looking at another load, at least."

"Maybe not, if I help you."

"Oh, no, no, no." She vigorously shook her

head and then frowned. "Don't you have to go to your shop?"

"John's there. Best assistant I ever had."

"Still, no. I can manage." She folded her arms and stood with feet planted apart.

"Is that the door to the basement?" He pointed.

"Yes, but—"

"We'll have you and the boxes back to Riverview in no time." He headed toward the door.

She ran to catch up. "Why are you doing this?"

"Lacey, don't make a big deal out of it, okay? Let's just get the job done."

"You always were kinda bossy."

"Huh! So were you, as I recall."

They managed to load all the boxes into their vehicles and were soon on the road to Riverview. As he followed Lacey's white Camaro along the highway, he experienced a wave of guilt. His offer to help was an honest one, but at the same time, he also hoped to see Remy Whitfield. Not just see her; talk to her. He went over in his mind what he would say. Since working for his grandfather, he'd had plenty of experience sealing the deal. He might not especially like working in the investment property field, but he was good at it.

LACEY PULLED UP to the service entrance at Riverview with Rory's truck right behind her. She jumped from the car and went back to him. "Some of the boxes need to go to Gram's apartment and the rest to her basement storage unit."

"Just tell me which is which."

She found a hand truck, and they sorted the boxes, transferring those to the basement first. "I can take the ones to her apartment," she told him.

"I got 'em." He kept a firm grip on the hand truck. "You lead the way."

"But—"

He waved her on ahead of him.

Okay, she'd stop him at the door to the apartment.

But when they reached the door and she opened it, he swept by her, pushing the truck inside.

"That you, Lacey?" her grandmother called from the apartment's interior.

"Yes, it's me." She followed on Rory's heels, unable to squeeze ahead of him in the kitchenette's close quarters.

"Rory Dalton? Is that you?" she heard her grandmother exclaim.

"Yes, it is, Mrs. Whitfield."

Lacey finally reached the living room. Her grandmother sat in her wheelchair staring at Rory. "What are *you* doing here?"

Surprisingly, Gram's voice held more curiosity than the anger Lacey expected.

Rory propped his foot on one of the truck's wheels. "I just happened to be passing by your old apartment and saw Lacey loading up in the parking lot and stopped to help."

Gram slowly shook her head. "You always were the helper. Why, just last week, I was on the shopping bus, and I saw you take Agnes Crawley's arm and walk her across Main Street."

Rory grinned. "Aggie'd just given up her crutches after a broken ankle, and she wasn't too steady yet. But where do you want these?"

Gram looked around. "Ah, over in that corner." She pointed to a space near the bedroom door.

Lacey helped Rory unload the boxes. The sooner they completed the task, the sooner he could leave.

"So, how're you doing, Mrs. Whitfield?"

he asked when the last container had been stowed away.

"Pretty good. But I'll be a lot better when I can walk again."

"I hear you on that."

"Well, thanks for your help today, Rory," Lacey said stiffly. "You can put the hand truck back by the door on your way out."

"Now, wait, Lacey." Gram held up a hand. "Least we can do is offer Rory a cup of tea."

Rory shook his head. "No tea, thanks, but I'd go for a glass of cold water. That sun's blazing today."

Gram turned to Lacey. "There's a pitcher of water in the fridge."

Lacey tried to catch Rory's eye to glare at him, but he was gazing around the apartment. She went into the kitchen and opened the refrigerator.

"Sit," Gram told Rory, pointing to an overstuffed chair across from her.

Rory sat, leaning back, settling in. He gazed around. "Nice place you got here."

"I like it," Gram said. "What're you up to these days?"

"My car shop. Working for A.J."

Lacey returned to the living room with the glass of water and handed it to Rory.

When he looked up, she got in her glare. He seemed not to notice, smiling as he accepted the water. "Thanks so much." He took a long swallow. "Ah, that hits the spot."

"Would you like something, Gram?" Lacey asked.

Gram shook her head. "No, I'm fine. Had tea a while ago with my next-door neighbor."

No one said anything. Lacey shifted from one foot to the other. Gram smoothed her skirt. Rory drank his water.

Then he cleared his throat and sat forward. "I drove by your old farm the other day…"

"Rory—" Lacey began.

Gram interrupted. "The other day? I 'spect you drive by it quite often, being it's on the highway to Milton."

"True enough," Rory said. "Anyway, it occurred to me what a fine piece of property you have there."

"If you're about to make me an offer, save your breath. I've told your grandfather time and again I won't sell. There's plenty of land around here for him to play with. He doesn't need mine."

"Would you consider selling to me?"

"You? Why would you want the place?

Never mind, it don't matter. It's not for sale. Never will be."

"I just thought that now you're living here, you might find a use for the money." He named a sum.

Lacey sucked in a breath.

Gram dropped her jaw. "That much?"

Rory smiled. "That much."

Gram frowned and turned away to gaze out the patio door. Long moments passed. Lacey's stomach clenched. Should she tell Rory to leave? She'd been itching to since he'd pushed his way in. She was about to speak up when Gram turned back to them. Her eyes were misty.

"No amount of money will make me change my mind, Rory. I don't expect you to understand, but—" She dug into her blouse pocket and pulled out a tissue.

Lacey ran to Gram's side and placed a hand on her shoulder. "It's okay, Gram." She looked up at Rory. "We need you to leave. Now."

Rory stood. "Of course. I didn't mean to upset you, Mrs. Whitfield… I thought my offer would interest you."

"Enough." Lacey grabbed the glass from

his hand. "Leave the hand truck. I'll take it back myself."

Rory strode to the truck, grasped the handle and wheeled it into the kitchen. "Goodbye, Mrs. Whitfield."

Lacey plunked the glass on the counter and all but pushed him out the door. Instead of letting him go, she followed him down the hall, seething inside.

When they reached the entrance, he set the hand truck back in its cubbyhole. "I didn't mean to upset her."

"Did you honestly think she's changed her mind about selling the property?"

"How should I know? I haven't spoken to her for quite a while." Rory went through the door and into the alley.

His defensive tone fueled her anger. She followed him, not about to let him leave yet. Thankfully, no one else was around. "And you didn't stop earlier to help me. You were using me to get to Gram."

Rory fished in his jeans pocket and pulled out his truck keys. "No, Lacey. I really did stop to help you."

"Okay, but while you were helping you got the idea that if you followed me here you could make your offer to Gram."

"Yeah, that's probably the way it happened."

"Probably. Huh. And why do you want the property? You'll just resell it to someone who wants to build mini-ranches or condos or a motel."

"I want to get rid of that house."

"The house is the main reason Gram hangs on to the farm."

Rory propped his hands on his hips. "Lacey, you can't tell me you like having that house still standing."

Lacey winced and then steadied herself and lifted her chin. "It's not for me to decide. Or you, either. The house—and the farm— have nothing to do with you."

Rory's eyes blazed. "Nothing to do with me? My father was murdered there. Shot in the back by your father, while he was running to his car. And then, your father turned on your mother, and as she crawled from the bed trying to escape him, he pushed her, and she cracked her head on the fireplace hearth. Fell into a coma and died a week later. Isn't that what the prosecutors proved in the trial that sent your father to prison?"

Tears burned Lacey's eyes. She slapped her hands over her ears. "Stop. Stop. You have no right to come here and talk to me like that."

"You want my sympathy?"

"No, of course not!"

She spoke the truth. Whatever she and Rory had together all those years ago—the fresh, bright new beginnings of love—was long gone now. As dead and buried as their parents.

The rumble of a delivery truck in the driveway brought them both to attention.

"Gotta go," Rory mumbled and, without looking at her, flung open the door to his truck and climbed in.

"My father was not a murderer, Rory Dalton. And I'm going to prove he wasn't."

But between the delivery truck's approach and the start of Rory's truck engine, her words were lost.

When Lacey returned to Gram's apartment, she found Gram where she'd left her, sitting in her wheelchair by the open patio door, gazing outside. She went over, knelt in front of her and took her hands.

"I'm so sorry. I tried to keep Rory out of the apartment, but he barged his way in. I had no idea what he was up to."

"That's all right, honey. I'm fine. Just had a little lapse for a few minutes. Don't blame Rory. He was doing his job."

"He wants to tear down the house. He told me so just now. I told him you'd never let that happen."

"No, I won't."

"Let's not talk about it anymore." Lacey checked her wristwatch. "It's time for lunch. Then we'll play Scrabble or do something else fun this afternoon. The boxes can wait till tomorrow."

RORY SPED AWAY from Riverview, twisting the wheel so hard on one curve he nearly careened off the road. He hadn't intended to lose his cool with Lacey, but she'd been so angry with him, at what she considered a betrayal, that he couldn't contain himself and had lashed back.

Still, he wasn't sorry he'd stopped to help her or that he'd gone to Riverview and seen Remy Whitfield. The one other regret was Remy's discomfort. He hadn't meant to upset her. But they all were upset, and had been all these years. That was why the situation needed to be dealt with. He firmly believed that once the house was no longer standing, they all could heal and move on. Somehow, he needed to convince Remy.

Lacey would be leaving town soon. Once

she was gone, he would contact Remy again. He hadn't sensed she disliked or rejected him; in fact, she'd been downright friendly until he started talking about the Whitfield farm.

Rory drove through town and across the bridge, catching the road leading up the hill to his shop. He parked in his spot in the back, under a maple tree.

Inside the garage, he approached John, who was changing the oil in a Honda. "What's happening?"

John straightened and stepped away from the car. "Lots. Harry Selznick dropped off his Chevy." He pointed to the car sitting in the adjacent bay. "Tire keeps going flat. I took a look. Needs a new rim. Subaru's waiting." He gestured to the SUV on the other side of the Chevy.

Rory stroked his chin. "We'll need to check the junkyards to see if they have a tire rim that'll fit the Chevy. If not, we'll go to the internet."

John nodded. "I'll finish up with the Honda, and then I'm on it. Oh, there were a couple of calls, too. Messages on your desk."

"Thanks. I'll check those and then get started on the Subaru's transmission."

Rory went into the office, feeling much better now that he was back at the shop. Being on the job he loved allowed him to put aside all his other problems and frustrations—at least for a while.

LACEY CLOSED THE flaps on the box she'd finished unpacking and added it to the other empty boxes ready for the recycle bin. As she'd promised Gram, they'd waited until Sunday afternoon to tackle the boxes from her old apartment. This morning they'd attended the church service in the Riverview chapel and then enjoyed lunch in the dining room with the other residents.

"We probably should quit now," she told Gram. "But we did manage to weed out a few things to donate." She pointed to several decorative plates, a few old cookbooks and some costume jewelry piled on the sofa.

Gram reached out and ran her fingers over the embossed roses decorating one of the plates. "Giving away these things is like giving away pieces of my life."

"I know. But we've kept a lot, too."

Gram pointed to the one container that remained. "What happened to that one? I don't remember all that blue tape."

"The box split apart in the parking lot when I was loading it into my car. That was when Rory came by, and he taped it. It's full of Mother's things."

Gram's shoulders stiffened. "If you think I'm giving away any of her belongings, think again."

"No, I wouldn't ask you to do that. But one of her trinket dishes broke." She pulled off enough tape to remove the plastic bag enclosing the pieces. She laid the bag in Gram's lap and opened it.

Gram reached into the bag, pulled out a couple pieces and held them up. "Ah, the dish your granddad and I got her for Christmas. She admired it at Trinkets and Treasures. Can you put it back together? There's some superstrong glue in my kitchen drawer that ought to work. Did you get all the pieces?"

"I'm sure I did, and, yes, of course I'll mend it."

Lacey retrieved the cement, and while she carefully glued together the broken dish, she listened to Gram's stories about Norella and her collection of decorative boxes and dishes. Some were gifts and others were souvenirs of places she'd visited.

By the time Lacey set the mended bowl on the side table to dry, her mother's presence was so alive in the room she almost expected her to step from the shadows.

"I don't want to see any more from that box," Gram said. "Take it down to storage."

"Just one other thing we need to discuss." She picked up her purse and pulled out the book with the pansies on the cover. She held out the book to Remy. "I found this in the box, too, and put it aside."

Gram nodded but made no move to take the book. "Norella's journal."

"Yes. Have you read it?"

"Of course not. A journal is private."

"But Mom's gone now. I'd like to read it, but I wanted to ask you first."

"And I'm saying no." Gram held out her hand. "Give me the journal, Lacey," she said in a tight voice.

Lacey pressed the journal to her chest and took a step back. "It's as much mine as it is yours. I'll give it a look and then put it back with the rest of her things." She tensed, waiting for further argument.

Several moments passed before Remy leaned back and gave a resigned sigh. "All right. But I'm betting you'll be sorry."

Lacey tucked the journal back into her purse. "Maybe so, but that's a risk I'm willing to take."

"WHICH BLOUSE DO you like, the white one or the pink?" Lacey pulled the blouses from Gram's closet and held them up. Five o'clock had rolled around, dinnertime, which called for a change of clothes. For Gram, anyway. For Lacey, her jeans and navy T-shirt would have to do.

Gram tilted her head. "Hmm, the white has a pretty lace collar, but pink is my favorite color."

"Pink it is." Lacey handed her the pink blouse and returned the white one to the closet. Her cell phone rang. "Who could be calling?" she wondered aloud. *Maybe Kris wants to set up a lunch date.*

Lacey pulled her phone from her pocket. The number was local but unfamiliar. Could it be Rory? Why would he call? Hadn't they parted yesterday with a finality that discouraged further contact? Just in case it was him, though, she wandered into the living room, where she'd be out of Gram's earshot. Strolling to the patio door, she idly gazed out. The lowering afternoon sun sent long shadows through the willow trees bordering the river.

The caller turned out to be Elton Watts, publisher of the *Silver River Sentinel*.

"Remy gave me your number," Elton said. "I hope you don't mind."

"No, not at all. What can I do for you?" As a high school senior, Lacey had written a few articles for the paper to fulfill assignments in her journalism class. Since then, she'd had no contact with Elton, other than to exchange greetings during chance encounters around town.

So, why was he calling her now?

"I'd like to discuss something with you, but not over the phone. Can you drop by the *Sentinel* tomorrow morning? You'll still be in town, won't you?"

"Yes, I'm here for a few more days. But can't you tell me what this is all about?"

"I'd rather talk to you in person."

"Well…all right."

They settled on nine thirty. Lacey ended the call and rejoined Gram. "That was Elton Watts. He wants me to come to his office tomorrow."

Gram looked up from fastening the last button on the pink blouse. "I forgot to tell you he called this morning, and I gave him your cell number. Was that okay?"

"Of course. But did he tell you what he wants to talk to me about?"

"Not a word." Gram shook her head. "Are you going to meet with him?"

"Yes, of course." Elton was one of the few people who had not taken sides when Rick Morgan was accused of killing Al Jr. He might have had an opinion, but if he did, like a good journalist, he kept it to himself.

"Good." Gram smiled. "Now, how do I look?" She straightened her shoulders and lifted her chin.

Lacey smoothed the blouse's collar. "You look gorgeous. Come on, let's go wow 'em."

CHAPTER FIVE

IN HER ROOM at Sophie's, Lacey sat by the window. Outside, the sun had disappeared behind the mountains, leaving a golden haze in the sky. The valley lay in semidarkness, and here and there a farmhouse light flickered on. Ordinarily, such a view would hold her attention. But not tonight. Tonight the book lying in her lap was all she could think about.

The book with the pansies on the cover.

Her mother's journal.

Should she read it? Or honor Gram's request and let her mother's thoughts remain hers alone?

Finally, she picked up the book. She ran her fingers over the picture of pansies and then opened the cover.

"My Story" was written on the first page in her mother's flowing handwriting. Under that, Lacey read:

In this book perhaps will be
Some glimpses of the real me.
We'll see…

Lacey smiled at her mother's attempt at writing poetry. She rifled through the pages, catching a phrase and a word here and there. Finally, she decided that rather than skip around, she would read the journal from beginning to end. She turned back to the first page and began. But after reading several entries, disappointment set in. Instead of deep, insightful thoughts, her mother's writings were rather mundane:

Helped Mom bake pies today. Rick and Dad building cabinets at Fred's Feed Store.

The entries had large gaps in time, often a week or more. Abandoning her thought to read straight through the journal, Lacey thumbed through the pages, checking the dates. She found one entry dated a year before the tragedy and stopped there:

I suddenly find myself alone much of the time. Rick works out of town a lot.

Mother has her friends and her bridge club. Lacey is busy with school and with her boyfriend, Rory Dalton. I need something to do. Bonnie says she can help me get a job at The Owl Restaurant. The money's good, especially the tips. Rick won't like me working, but when he sees the money he'll change his mind. He won't see all the money, though. I know work isn't the only thing he does when he's out of town.

The next entry was a month later:

Rick was angry about my new job at The Owl, but I'd already been there a week before he came home from Forksville and found out. I showed him the money but he acted like he didn't care. That's okay. I was hoping to save at least some of it for Lacey's college. I want her to go. I wish that's what I had done instead of marrying so young.

Working was scary at first. So many people. So busy. But I'm doing okay. Jorgen, my boss and The Owl's owner, is very patient. And Bonnie is my coach.

Two months later:

I'm learning. Bonnie showed me how to get tips, mostly from the men. But she says to be careful not to give the wrong impression. Last night I brought home $30, just from a few smiles and a little extra attention. Sometimes, I see Jorgen giving me a look, but he hasn't said anything. No one has complained about me— that I know of.

Farther on:

I'm making a lot of new friends. Okay, they're mostly men, but they're customers. Rick definitely doesn't like my working there. He says he doesn't care about the money, but he didn't turn down the $50 I stuck in his shirt pocket.

I like working! I'm important. Jorgen said so. He's protective, though. Like Dad used to be. I told him I can take care of myself.

One of my customers asked me if I wanted to have a bite to eat with him after I got off my shift. I said no, but I really wanted to. He's nice. I'm not going to write his name here, in case someone reads this. But he's very handsome. I feel he's interested in knowing the real me. Whoever that is. Ha, ha.

Was her mother referring to Rory's father, Al Dalton Jr.? Was this the beginning of their affair? Did they have an affair? No one had ever proven that, one way or the other.

Lacey read on, but found nothing more about the mysterious man. Then:

Oh, my, have I gotten myself into trouble? Jorgen says I'm too friendly with the men customers and someone complained. He won't say who, just that I'm "too friendly" and should back off.

Someone followed me home last night. When I turned in the drive, the car went on by. I'm not sure who it was, but I think I know.

The next entry:

Today I said to _____, "Did you follow me home last night?" and he said yes.

The entry after that:

Something awful happened today. I lost my necklace. The one Dad gave me with the amethyst stones that I wear almost every day. I don't think Rick took it, although he's asked me more than once how much it's worth. "It's priceless," I always say, "and will never be sold to pay your gambling debts."

The clasp was loose, but I wore the necklace to work yesterday, anyway. I noticed the necklace was missing just before closing. After closing, I looked everywhere. Bonnie helped, and Jorgen gave me a flashlight so I could search the parking lot. I didn't find it. I am sick! Daddy gave me the necklace on my sixteenth birthday. It belonged to his mother, my grandmother Ella, and was designed especially for her. I promised to pass it on to my daughter, if I ever had one. Which I did. And it will be Lacey's someday.

I must find the necklace!

Two days later:

Someone found my necklace! I've been home from work with a bad cold. Things are not good at work. Two nights ago, someone followed me home again.

Anyway, the one who found my necklace wants to bring it to me here at home. What to do? I'm better now. I don't want to go back to work, though—but I want my necklace.

Was that the last entry? Holding her breath, Lacey turned the page. Ah, good, there was more. Not much, though. Lacey stared at the date, and her heart skipped a beat. The day of the tragedy. The last day of Al Jr.'s life and the last day of her mother's conscious life. Under the date was written:

I'm waiting, scared but excited, too.
This visit promises something new.
Will I be happy? Will I be blue?
I don't know, but I'm waiting.

The remaining pages were blank. Those words were the last her mother wrote before she slipped into a coma from which she never awakened.

A lump rose in Lacey's throat, and tears burned her eyes. Reading the journal revealed a mother she had never known. She felt sorrow for her mother, for a life not fully lived. Norella yearned for more, not only from others but also from herself. Those yearnings were never fulfilled.

Lacey closed the book. She gazed idly out the window into the dark night, her thoughts focused on the last entry. Where had the book been when her mother's visitor had arrived? The visitor must have been Al Dalton Jr. He must have been the person who'd found her necklace and was returning it.

Nothing was said about a necklace at her father's trial. The prosecutor's contention was that Al Jr. had come to the house because he and Norella were having an affair. Rick came home unexpectedly and caught them. He shot Al in the back from the upstairs bedroom as he ran from the house to his car. Then he ran, too, only to be apprehended later.

Gram came home from a bridge game and discovered Al's dead body in the yard and Norella lying unconscious on the floor of her bedroom. She'd hit her head on the fireplace's raised hearth. The prosecutor theorized that in trying to escape Rick's wrath, she either had tripped and fallen, or he had pushed her. Neither theory could be proven, but that didn't keep the jury from declaring Rick guilty of Al's murder.

But what had happened to the necklace Al was supposed to have been returning? Had Gram known about that? The next time she had the opportunity, she would ask her some questions. It was time for the truth to be known.

LACEY PARKED HER car in front of the *Silver River Sentinel's* Main Street office at exactly nine thirty the following morning. Curiosity had kept her nerves humming since she'd arisen and prepared for this meeting. Why did Elton Watts want to talk to her?

As Lacey entered the office, she spotted Clio Bertram at the desk behind the counter. In her forties, Clio was Elton's only child and main employee.

Clio looked up, and a smile lit her round face. "Hello, Lacey." Then she turned to the hallway leading to the office's back rooms and called, "Dad! Lacey's here!"

"Coming!"

Elton Watts appeared. Hand outstretched, he approached Lacey. "Lacey, by golly, good to see you."

"You, too, Mr. Watts." His friendliness eased her tension, and she relaxed as she shook his hand.

He grinned. "Cut the mister stuff and call me Elton."

"All right… Elton."

Elton Watts hadn't changed much in the past ten years. A little more stoop-shouldered, maybe, and hair more gray than brown. He still favored jeans, a plaid shirt and a bolo tie. The tie ornament was a cowboy hat, and the braided strings had leather tips.

Clio left her desk and joined them at the counter.

"You remember Clio, don't you?" Elton gestured to his daughter.

Clio was shorter and heavier than her father but shared his intelligent eyes and wide smile. In contrast to his Western look, her dress, made of a gauzy green fabric, seemed more appropriate for the dance floor than a newspaper office.

"I do remember you," Lacey said.

"I was busy raising kids when you lived here before." Clio absently straightened a stack of newspapers on the counter. "Now they're old enough to be on their own while I help Dad."

Elton turned back to Lacey. "Well, Lacey, I'll cut to the chase. I've got a job for you."

Lacey widened her eyes. "A job? But I already have a job—in Boise."

"I know, but I'm hoping your boss will loan you to us for a while. We really need you."

Lacey shook her head. "That's not possible."

"Come on back to my office, and I'll explain." He gestured toward the hallway.

"I'll bring you some coffee," Clio said and headed for the cart holding the coffeemaker.

"Mister, ah, Elton," Lacey said, "I really don't want to waste your time…"

"You're not. Quit worrying."

Lacey bit her lip. "Well…all right. I admit I am curious."

He grinned. "I figured you would be."

Elton led her to a windowless room with florescent ceiling lights, where a desk and computer shared space with file cabinets and shelves overflowing with books and papers. Sitting behind his desk, he motioned Lacey into a side chair.

"Here's the deal," he began. "For this year's Silver River Days celebration, we're publishing a special edition of the *Sentinel*, with articles about the history of the town and—"

"Here we are." Clio bustled in carrying

a tray holding the coffee, and the next few moments were spent with Lacey saying no, thank you to creamer and sugar, and Elton doctoring his with both.

After Clio left, Elton continued, "Sara Hoskins started the project. She's one of our freelancers. Then her husband had major heart surgery, and she had to quit and take care of him."

"That's too bad, but—"

Elton held up a hand. "There's more. The job also includes writing some articles for our regular issue about the Silver River Days activities."

"The assignment sounds interesting, but I can't do it. I won't be in town that long."

"Can't you get time off from your job? You'd be doing us a huge favor. Plus, I know your grandmother would like to have you here longer."

Lacey shook her head. "My boss has already granted me some extra time for this trip."

"Think about it. Maybe you'll find a way."

"I don't want to keep you from asking someone else."

"There is no one else. Not with your experience. At least say you'll give my proposal some thought." He plucked a business card from a holder on the desk and handed it to her.

Lacey tucked the card into her purse. "All right. I'll think about it overnight and give you a final answer tomorrow."

RORY DROVE DOWN Main Street on his way to Dalton Properties. He usually worked afternoons, but this morning A.J. wanted him to attend a meeting with potential buyers for several houses they'd acquired at auction. He'd rather be at the shop, of course, but for now, he juggled both jobs. One of these days, though…

While waiting at a red light, he idly looked around. Lots of people out and about already. His gaze landed on a familiar car parked in front of the *Silver River Sentinel's* office. A white Camaro convertible. Lacey's car. Had to be. There wouldn't be two cars like that in town.

Just then, she stepped out the office door. Behind her was Elton Watts. They stood talking for a moment, and then Lacey turned away and approached her car. At the same time, the light changed, and Rory drove through the intersection.

He wondered what business she had with Elton. Probably placing an ad to sell some of her grandmother's stuff. Or maybe she'd just stopped in to say hello. Naw, that wasn't like her. As far as he knew, when she came to town she confined her visiting to her grandmother.

A COUPLE HOURS LATER, after the meeting was over and the last buyer had left the conference room, A.J. turned to Rory. "That went well. Those old houses will soon be replaced by a new subdivision." He scooped up some papers from the table. "Speaking of old houses, anything new on the Whitfield place?"

Rory followed A.J. from the room and into the hallway. "As a matter of fact, I saw Remy yesterday…"

"Hey, fast work."

"And I made her the offer. Which she turned down."

A.J. stopped at the door to his office and turned. "I told you you'd be wasting your time."

Rory held up a hand. "I'm not giving up. Lacey was there, too, of course, and she was being very protective of her grandmother. Once she's gone, I'll try again."

"Huh. I'm not going to hold my breath waiting for that deal to go through."

AFTER LUNCH IN the Riverview dining room, Lacey and Gram took a walk. They followed the paved path that meandered through the grounds, past flower gardens and picnic tables and benches.

Lacey wanted to enjoy the outing, but she was preoccupied. And she couldn't discuss Elton's job offer or the matter of her mother's journal with her grandmother. Gram would encourage her to take Elton's offer, and she wouldn't approve of Lacey's having read the journal.

Rory's image popped into Lacey's mind. If only she could confide in him. When they were in high school, they shared everything, from their day-to-day problems to their hopes and dreams. But of course she could never confide in him now.

They reached the river and followed the path along the bank. The water flowed steadily along, sparkling in the sunlight. On the opposite side, farmland stretched to the foothills, and beyond stood the mountains.

"Let's stop awhile." Lacey pointed to a

wrought-iron bench under a stand of cotton-wood trees.

"All right."

After positioning Gram's wheelchair beside the bench, Lacey sat. She leaned back and rested her hands in her lap, relishing the soft breeze cooling her cheeks. Still, her problems kept her tense.

"As long as I can visit the river now and then," Gram said, "I feel at home. Your mother loved the water, too."

Lacey let a few moments elapse and then said, "I, ah, read some of Mother's journal last night…"

She expected an angry outburst from Gram, but none came. She cast her a cautious glance. "Don't you want to know what she wrote about?"

"No, I don't." Gram clamped her jaw shut and folded her arms. "Like I told you, a journal is private."

"I'm going to tell you anyway, because I have some questions."

Gram shifted in her chair so that she faced Lacey. Her eyes were angry. "Is that why you brought me here? To make me a captive audience?"

Lacey spread her hands. "Please, bear with me, just a little."

"All right, say what's on your mind and get it over with."

Lacey took a deep breath. "She wrote about the amethyst necklace Grandfather gave her, the one that belonged to his mother. And how upset she was when she lost it at the restaurant."

Silence, except for the shushing sound of the flowing water and the twittering birds perched in a nearby tree.

"And that someone found it—she didn't write his name—and planned to return it to her on…on that day."

"So?"

"So was Al Jr. the one who found it? Was that why he came that day? The necklace wasn't mentioned at the trial. The prosecutor wanted everyone to believe Al came to see Mother when no one else was home." Lacey looked down at her hands. Talking about her mother's adultery—supposed adultery—always made her uncomfortable.

"I knew she lost the necklace at work, but she never said anything to me about anyone finding it."

"Did the police ever see the journal?"

"No. Although I would see her writing in it, she never left it around for anyone to read. Months after she passed away, I found it behind some books on the shelves in the living room, by the fireplace. Like I told you, I didn't read it. I put it with the rest of her things that I'd been gathering up."

"Did you ever see the necklace again after that day?"

"No."

"It wasn't found on Al. That surely would have come up in the trial. So what happened to it?"

Gram pressed her lips together and shook her head. "I don't know, but let's say Al did return the necklace. Then I'm guessing that after your father shot Al, he took it."

"But it wasn't found on Dad, either, when he was arrested. We would have heard about it in the trial."

"He probably pawned the necklace before the police caught up with him."

"Pawned it? Why would he do that?"

"Oh, come on, Lacey, you know your father always needed money to pay his gambling debts."

Lacey bit her lip. Gram was right. She'd heard her mother and father arguing about his gambling often enough, and her mother had mentioned the problem in her journal.

"But what if he didn't pawn it?" she insisted. "What if someone else took the necklace?"

"Someone else was there that day and they shot Al? That's what you want to believe, isn't it?"

Lacey straightened her shoulders. "Not want to believe. That's what I do believe."

BACK AT GRAM'S APARTMENT, Lacey opened the box of her mother's belongings.

"I told you I'm not going to give away any of her things," Gram said in a cross tone.

"I know. But the necklace might be here. You might have overlooked it in a pocket or a purse. If I could find it, the mystery would be solved."

"And then would you stop fussing?"

"Maybe. I don't know." Lacey dug into the box and brought out a navy blue cotton jacket. She stuck her hand in one pocket and then the other. Nothing.

"I can't stand this." Gram wheeled around so that her back was turned and she faced the patio door.

Lacey kept digging, but she did not find the

lost necklace. When she finished, she taped the box shut again and set it in the kitchen for later transfer to the basement storage closet.

They went to dinner and then joined some of the other residents in the activity room for a sing-along, which restored Remy's good humor. When Lacey took her leave, her grandmother gave her a warm hug.

"Thank you, dear one, for all that you do for me," Gram said.

"You're welcome, Gram. You know I love you."

"I know, honey. And I love you, too."

IN HER ROOM at Sophie's, Lacey took out her mother's journal and reread some of the entries. Then she went to the window and gazed out. Darkness hid the farmhouse, but she knew instinctively where it was and focused on the spot.

The missing necklace nagged her. She was sure it was the key to the identity of Al Jr.'s true murderer. If only she knew what happened to it. Then she might be able to identify the killer and clear her father's name. And then, once and for all, she could live in peace.

She left the window and as she walked

by the table, her gaze fell on the business card Elton Watts had given her. The card reminded her that tomorrow she must call him with her final refusal of his job offer.

She picked up the card and tapped it against her palm, an idea forming. If she took the job, staying in town would give her an opportunity to look for the necklace. Maybe it was in one of Gram's other boxes. Maybe it was still in the farmhouse, hidden in a drawer or a closet.

Also, the job would involve talking to people. Maybe someone knew something that would help in her search. Of course, she couldn't blatantly ask about it. She'd have to be circumspect.

Excitement quickened her pulse. Then she sobered. Did she really want to stir up the past? Did she really want to talk to the townspeople? Did she want to endure the censures from those who believed her father to be a murderer?

Then she thought of her father and the last time she visited him in prison. They'd sat with dozens of others in the crowded visitors' room, sharing soft drinks and snacks from the vending machine and trying to carry on a conversation despite the lack of privacy.

I didn't kill Al Jr., he'd said. *You believe me, don't you, Lacey?*

Yes, Dad, I believe you.

A week later, after a fight in the prison yard with an inmate who had a knife, Rick Morgan was dead.

This might be her last chance to prove his innocence. If she didn't grab it, she might regret it for the rest of her life.

CHAPTER SIX

THE FOLLOWING MORNING, Lacey phoned Ed Norton, her boss at the Boise Historical Society.

"I know more time off is a big favor to ask," she said when he came on the line, "but my grandmother's move is more complicated than we'd at first thought."

True enough. She still had to arrange for the disposal of Gram's leftover apartment furniture and finish sorting through the boxes.

"I'm sorry, Lacey," Ed said. "I've already granted you more time off than your contract allows. Maybe you can get someone there to help your grandmother?"

"No, it's personal stuff—you understand."

"I understand, but I can't grant you more time."

"Then I—" Lacey gripped the phone, indecision waging a war inside her. She closed her eyes, and when she opened them again she saw the copse of trees where the farm-house stood. "I won't be back at all."

Silence. And then Ed said, "I see. Well. We'll be sorry to lose you, Lacey."

"Me, too, Ed."

Lacey's hands shook as she ended the call. Had she really just quit the job she loved so much and worked so hard to obtain? Thrown her promising future away for a few more weeks here in Silver River chasing a dream that might turn into a nightmare?

"HERE'S YOUR OFFICE." Elton Watts led Lacey into a room at the *Sentinel* and then stopped and studied her. "What? I know it's probably not as big and fancy as your office in Boise, but won't it do?"

Lacey surveyed the dimly lighted room with a scarred desk and dented filing cabinets and thought of her office at the historical society, where the furniture was new and modern and large windows overlooked the city park. But, then, that wasn't her office anymore.

"This is fine, Elton," she assured him in a strained voice. "I'll be out and about most of the time, anyway."

"True enough. Okay, then." He pointed to a microfiche reader. "We have every back issue of the *Sentinel*. Sara Hoskins's work is on the computer, and there's also a printout. And here's a list of the articles to publicize the celebration's featured events." He picked up a sheet of paper lying next to the computer. "Sit and we'll go over this."

Lacey sat and opened her tablet, ready to take notes.

Elton pulled up a chair next to her. "There's a pie contest. Hester Hartley's in charge. And there's a special exhibit at the museum. See Del Ford about that. He's the curator."

Elton put down the list and sat back. "Speaking of the museum, we'll need an article about the new wing Cora Trenton's providing in memory of her husband, George, and her son, Cal. George was mayor a while back. You probably remember him. And Cal passed away a few years ago from a brain tumor."

"Uh-huh." Lacey's fingers flew over the keyboard as she attempted to keep up with Elton's chatter.

"The flower show is Claire Roche's baby. You might remember her, too. Her folks own Nellon's Hardware."

Yes, the person Gram thought might have put the pansies on the graves at the cemetery. Lacey definitely wanted to talk to Claire.

"She and Clint live on Lewis Avenue. Be sure to take a look at her garden. It's something."

"I'll do that." Especially to look for pansies.

Elton picked up the list again and adjusted his glasses. "The downtown business association is sponsoring a raffle aimed to get people into the stores during the celebration. Millie Nixon, at Millie's Boutique, is in charge of that."

"I can talk to Kris, too, since she works for her aunt."

"And of course we can't forget the classic car show. That's Rory Dalton's project." He frowned. "That won't be a problem, will it?"

Lacey's stomach tensed. The last thing she wanted was more interaction with Rory. She forced a smile. "Not as far as I'm concerned. If interviewing Rory is part of the job, then of course I'll talk to him."

Elton's frown faded. "See, you're a professional. That's one reason I wanted you for the job." He sat back and studied her. "I'm curious, though, about why you accepted my offer when you were so against it at first."

"I, ah, well, it will give me more time with Gram." True enough.

"Your boss was okay with giving you more time off?"

Lacey looked down at her tablet. "We worked out an arrangement." That was true, too, even if the "arrangement" meant quitting her job.

"Good, good. I was afraid you wouldn't want to be involved with the project because interviewing people who knew your folks might be a problem."

"I won't let that bother me," she said in a decisive tone.

Elton beamed. "See? Like I said, you're a professional."

"YOU'RE STAYING IN town to do a special job for Elton Watts?" Gram gave Lacey a puzzled look as she set her teacup in its saucer.

They were having tea in the activity room, elegantly furnished with picture windows and double doors opening onto a sun-filled courtyard. Several residents worked on a jigsaw puzzle, while across the room, a woman played classical music on a baby grand piano.

Lacey plucked off the teapot's crocheted

cozy, releasing the aroma of Earl Grey, and then refilled Gram's cup. "Yes, I'll be here for a few extra weeks."

"So that's why Elton called you. But what about your job in Boise? Did your boss give you more time off?"

Keeping her gaze focused on her task, Lacey added tea to her own cup. "We, ah, came to an agreement."

"Did you quit your job? Or get fired?"

"A little of both." Lacey replaced the cozy back on the pot. "But aren't you glad I'm going to stay longer?"

"Of course. But I didn't expect you to lose your job. This doesn't have anything to do with Norella's missing necklace, does it?" Gram narrowed her eyes.

"It might."

Gram shook her head. "You've ruined your career to chase after the silly notion that the necklace had something to do with Al Jr.'s murder and that finding it will somehow prove Rick's innocence."

Lacey tapped her fingers on the arm of her chair. "I guess that's it in a nutshell, as they say."

"I should have burned that journal," Gram said.

THE MINUTE LACEY rounded the corner of High Street and Lewis Avenue, she spotted Claire Roche's garden. Enclosed by a white picket fence, it filled the entire backyard of the modest two-story home.

Lacey parked at the curb, but instead of getting out, she remained behind the wheel. On her job in Boise, she'd conducted countless interviews. She loved talking to people, gathering information to use in a report or one of the society's publications.

But today, Lacey also had a personal motive for visiting Claire Roche, and that put her on edge.

Finally, she gathered up her purse, took a deep breath and stepped from the car.

Peering over the fence, she glimpsed a woman on her knees digging in one of the flower beds. "Mrs. Roche?" Lacey called.

The woman stopped digging and looked up from under the brim of her yellow straw hat.

"I'm Lacey Morgan. We spoke on the phone this morning."

"Yes, I've been waiting for you." Claire Roche put down her trowel, stood and approached the gate.

In her fifties and not more than five feet tall, Claire's slight body was all but lost in baggy jeans and a short-sleeved, cotton print blouse. She wore little makeup, which brought into prominence her large and soulful brown eyes.

"Come in." Claire unlatched the gate and held it open.

Lacey followed her into the yard, breathing in the variety of fragrances in the air. "I appreciate your seeing me on such short notice."

"No problem. I need a break about now, anyway."

Claire led them along a stone path through beds of roses, impatiens, dahlias and geraniums. Figurines of fairies and dwarves tucked among the blossoms gave the garden a fanciful air.

She watched for pansies but didn't see any. Perhaps Gram was wrong about Claire being the person who had put pansies on the graves.

Claire motioned to several lawn chairs under a maple tree. "This is a good place to talk."

Lacey sat and took out her tablet and tape recorder. Claire removed her gloves and hat and laid them in her lap. She ran her fingers through her short gray curls.

They chatted about Sara Hoskins's husband's heart surgery and Remy's broken hip and her move to Riverview. Claire's friendly manner put Lacey at ease.

After a while, Lacey directed the conversation to the upcoming flower show. "The show's at the town hall, correct?"

Claire nodded and then said in a wistful tone, "I wish we had the convention center that A. J. Dalton wants to build. That would give us ever so much more space."

At the mention of Rory's grandfather, Lacey stiffened. "I hadn't heard about that. Where does he plan to build it?" Was that why he and Rory wanted Gram's property?

Claire shrugged. "I'm not sure. But he's done so much for this town. Where would Silver River be without him?"

Lacey gritted her teeth to keep from answering that question. Instead, she said, "Why can't you have your show at the county fairgrounds?"

Claire shook her head. "Too far away. We want everything connected with the celebration to be here in town. That's what Silver River Days are all about. Our town."

At last, Lacey sat back and turned off her tape recorder. "You've answered all my questions for the article, so I'll let you get back to your gardening."

"It does keep me busy." Claire put on her hat and picked up her gloves.

On the way back to the gate, Claire again leading the way, Lacey took a last look around for pansies. She was about to give up when she spied their purple, blue and red blossoms tucked away in a bed near the house.

"What lovely pansies," she said.

Claire paused to look at the flowers. "Yes, they are. Such delicate little blossoms."

"I saw some just the other day," Lacey said as they continued walking.

Claire shrugged. "Not surprising. Lots of people grow pansies."

Lacey took a deep breath. "The ones I saw were at Restlawn. I took some flowers to my family's graves. Someone had put pansies on all three, my grandfather's, my mother's… and my father's."

"Is that so?"

"Yes, and I'd like to know who that person is."

"Why?"

"Why? Because…because I'd like to thank them."

They reached the gate. Claire put her hand on the latch. She turned to Lacey, her mouth set in a tight line. "Maybe they don't want to be thanked. Maybe they want to remain anonymous. Maybe the person puts flowers on lots of graves, even the grave of a murderer."

"My father was innocent." The words tumbled from Lacey's mouth. "I know he was."

Claire scowled. "Doesn't matter what you think. He had a trial, and according to the jury, he was guilty. Justice was served."

LACEY DROVE AWAY from Claire Roche's house wondering about the woman's sudden change from friendly and open to angry and defensive. While she hadn't actually admitted to being the one who'd left the pansies, Lacey would bet she knew who did. But perhaps, as Claire insisted, the gesture meant nothing special.

Still, Lacey wanted to know the person's identity.

Now, though, she needed to turn her attention back to the task at hand. Her next interview was with Helen Jacobs, owner of Jacobs Gallery, who was coordinating the festival's art walk.

At the gallery, Lacey spent a pleasant half hour with Helen discussing her event. She had moved to town only a few years ago, and if she knew Lacey's history, she didn't mention it.

Afterward, Lacey stood on the sidewalk debating what to do next. She had time for one more appointment today. Maybe she should get Rory's interview over with. Should she call first and see if he had time to talk to her? Or drop in unannounced? She decided on the latter. If he were too busy to talk, then she'd set up an appointment.

As Lacey drove up the hill to Dalton's Auto Repair, she wondered how Rory had managed to hang on to his business location. As Claire Roche had said, A. J. Dalton never let a prime piece of property go undeveloped. Some of the townspeople agreed with him, while others thought Silver River should remain a quiet rural community.

Lacey wasn't sure what she thought. Since she didn't live here anymore, her opinion didn't matter, anyway.

She pulled up in front of the garage. All three bays were occupied. In one, a late-model Chevrolet sat on the hoist; in the second, a red sports car; and in the third, an older-model Honda.

Rory was bent over the Honda's open hood.

Lacey suddenly had another attack of nerves, although quite different from what she'd experienced at Claire Roche's. She couldn't do this, after all. She'd go back to the newspaper and tell Elton he'd have to find someone else for the job.

No, she *had* to do this. *Pretend he's just another person to interview.*

Yeah, right.

She cut the engine, took a deep breath and climbed from the car.

Rory stepped out of the garage. He wore jeans and a tight-fitting blue T-shirt, which showed off his muscular arms.

"Can I help—" He stopped and stared. "Lacey? What are you doing here? Car trouble?" His gaze traveled over her shoulder to her car.

"No, my car's running fine. I'm here about Silver River Days."

He propped his hands on his hips. "What do you have to do with that?"

"Elton Watts hired me to finish the newspaper's special edition and write articles for the regular edition. You're on my list for the Classic Car Show."

"Ah, so that's why you were at his office yesterday."

"You saw me?"

"I was waiting for the light to change when you and he came out."

"If you'd rather talk to someone else—"

He waved a hand. "No, no. Your coming here is just so…unexpected."

"I should've called. I'll come back some other time." She turned to go.

"Now's fine. John's on an errand, but I have time to talk. Come on in my office." He nodded toward an open doorway inside the garage.

She followed him into a room with a counter and a cash register, a couple vending machines, a cart with a coffeepot and cups, and a row of chairs. From there, another door led to his office, which was little more than a cubbyhole. He waved her into the one extra chair and then sat behind a scarred wooden desk. He pulled a file folder from a desk drawer, shuffled through it and took out a sheet of paper.

"Here's the map I made." He cleared a spot on the desk and laid the paper between them.

"Elton can publish this along with your article. We assemble at Fifth and Main."

She leaned over the desk at the same time he did, and their heads were inches apart. Her heart started to pound. "Ah, how many cars do you expect to participate?"

"At least fifty."

He sat back, putting some distance between them, but still dangerously near.

She licked her dry lips and swallowed. "I'd better make some notes." She pulled her tablet from her purse. "Okay, go on."

"Where was I?" He laughed.

"Ah, people. Participants."

"Oh, right. We have entrants from all over the state, as well as Washington and Montana. There aren't that many shows around, and there's nothing a classic car owner likes more than to show off his car."

Lacey tapped her tablet's keys. "So, it's free?"

"No, there's an admission fee. Proceeds go to the summer sports camp for kids. Prizes, too, for People's Choice, Best Antique, Best Custom and Best in Show."

A bell tinkled and a door slammed. Rory looked over Lacey's shoulder to the outer room. "Carl Schroeder, picking up his car.

Back in a sec. Here, you can look through this stuff." He slid the file in her direction.

Lacey flipped through the file, making notes on her tablet as she went along. Once, she glanced into the outer office to see Rory punching his computer's keys while Carl stood nearby.

Carl had been a carpenter friend of her father's. But when Rick was arrested for Al Dalton's murder, Carl joined the other townsfolk who believed him guilty.

Carl's wandering gaze landed on Lacey. He widened his eyes and stared. Oh, great. Soon it would be all over town that Lacey Morgan was in Rory Dalton's cozy garage office. Lacey sighed. She'd been crazy to take this job.

Rory and Carl left the office and went into the garage. Lacey returned to reading through the file, recording more of the information. The men's voices, along with the sound of a car's revving engine, drifted in from the garage.

Lacey closed the file folder. Restless, she stood and stretched. She could leave. She had all the pertinent information. Her gaze idly scanned the office, landing on a file cabinet with papers sticking out of the drawers and a cactus plant in an orange pot sitting on the top. A worktable held a paper cutter and a pile of wrenches.

Her attention moved to the wall. A calendar featured a Ford from the '70s, and several framed photos showed Rory—and sometimes other people, too—posing with various cars. A '50s Hudson, a '40s Ford, and a '57 Chevy that looked familiar.

"Sorry to keep you waiting," Rory said from behind her. "Carl likes to talk."

Lacey turned. "And I'm sure he will—all over town."

He raised an eyebrow. "Will that upset you?"

She shrugged. "I'd think it would upset *you*."

"I'm used to small-town gossip. I don't let it bother me—anymore," he added, looking away. Then his attention moved to the photos. "What do you think of my gallery?"

"Very impressive. You've restored all these?"

"Yep. Starting with the '57 Ford." He pointed to the photo. "You should remember that one. You were with me when I bought it." He added in a low voice, "A couple weeks before the prom."

That was why the car looked familiar.

Memories washed over her. The excitement of their upcoming graduation, and of the prom, and of their future together. All wiped out with a shot fired from her father's rifle.

Feeling suddenly sick to her stomach, she turned away from the photos.

"Lacey—"

She met his gaze, and something seemed to pass between them. Her heart beat faster. "I— I'd better be on my way. I have more stops to make."

"Yeah. Sure. Did you get what you need from the file?" He gestured to the desk.

She nodded. "I would like a copy of the flyer, though."

Rory picked up the flyer and stuck it in the copy machine. While the machine hummed and the copy printed, neither spoke. When he held out the paper, she plucked it from his hand with her thumb and forefinger.

Rory led her from the office and out to her car, where he opened the door and held it while she slid onto the seat. Once the door was shut between them, she took a relieved breath. Soon, there would be even more distance between them, and then maybe she could start breathing normally again.

She looked up at him. "Thanks for the information."

"No problem. But I gotta say one more thing. I never meant to upset your grandmother the other day…"

"I don't want any more discussion about that—even if I had the time. Which I don't." She stuck the key in the ignition.

He backed away. "All right. I hear you."

She turned the key, expecting to hear the sound of the engine firing.

Instead, she heard only a dull click.

CHAPTER SEVEN

LACEY TURNED THE key again—and heard the same dull click. She tried a third time. Nothing happened. "Come on!"

Rory stepped forward again. "You're not going anywhere. Not right now, anyway. Pop the hood, and I'll take a look."

Lacey froze. She needed to get away from there, away from him.

And now this.

"Lacey?"

Heaving a sigh, she reached under the dashboard and pulled the latch. She leaned her forehead against the steering wheel and wanted to cry. Or maybe scream.

Rory entered the garage and returned with a toolbox. "Could your problem be the battery?"

Get a grip. You have to deal with this. Lacey sat up and took a deep breath. "Not likely. I had a new one put in a couple of months ago."

"I'll check it anyway, and then the fuel line."

"And I'll look at the connection," she heard herself say.

He raised his eyebrows. "You'll do what?"

"I still remember a few things from Mr. Callahan's class. Give me a wrench." She stepped from the car and held out her hand.

He stared at her open hand, and a slow grin spread across his lips. He pulled a wrench from his toolbox and handed it to her. "Okay, go for it."

Lacey ducked under the hood and went to work. For the next few minutes, neither spoke. Then Rory said, "The battery's good and the fuel line is clean."

"I don't see any problem with the connection. What about the ignition cylinder? I know it can go bad with no warning."

"You're right about that." Rory spent the next few minutes removing the cylinder, and then they both examined it.

"Sure is dirty," she observed.

"To be expected in an old car like this. But see how it's all worn along here?" He indicated the spot with his screwdriver. "Pretty much shot."

"So, I was right," Lacey said with a note of triumph.

"Mr. Callahan taught you well." Rory tossed the screwdriver into his toolbox.

"Taught *us* well," she corrected.

"That was a good class. I learned what was to become my livelihood and—"

She waited for him to finish.

"And I met you." He picked up his toolbox and headed for the garage. "C'mon, let's wash up."

Yes, Rory, best we not say any more about those days.

"I'll need to order the part," he said while they washed their hands.

His statement confirmed what she already feared. An ignition cylinder for a car as old as hers was not something he'd keep in stock. "How long will it take, do you think?"

He tore a paper towel from the dispenser and handed it to her. "Shouldn't be more than a few days."

She wiped her hands and tossed the towel into the trash can. "Guess I'll have to rent a car."

"No need for that. I have a loaner you can use. It's at home, though. As soon as John gets back, we'll go get it."

"And when will that be?" The high from solving the car problem was wearing off and, once again, Lacey was eager to leave.

Rory made the call on his phone. "He's on his way," he said when he'd talked to John. "You can wait in the office. Or out back. There's shade there, and a breeze, most days."

"Sounds good." That would put distance between them, anyway.

Behind the building, she sank into a lawn chair next to a picnic table. She called Gram to tell her of the delay. While she explained the situation, Rory appeared, carrying a bottle of water.

"Thought you might be thirsty."

"Thanks." She accepted the bottle with her free hand.

"You're *where*?" Gram shouted in Lacey's ear.

"I'll explain everything later," she said, sorry she'd started to say anything.

Rory disappeared into the garage.

Lacey drank the refreshing water. She fiddled with her tablet and recorder and returned to the office. Rory was on the phone when John Lawton arrived. In his early twenties, John of course had not been one of their high school friends, but she remembered him especially because their grandmothers were friends.

"Hey, Lacey." John tipped his baseball hat to reveal a shock of blond hair. "That sweet car of yours giving you trouble?"

Lacey nodded. "It appears so."

"If it had to happen, this is the best place to be."

Lacey could think of a lot of places she'd rather be, car trouble or not, but instead of sharing that thought, she said, "Sorry if my problem rushed you to return."

He shook his head. "I was on my way, anyway. Heard you're going to be in town for a while this time."

"Right. I'm doing some writing for Elton Watts. That's why I came here today—to talk to Rory about the Classic Car Show."

John shoved his hands in his jeans pockets. "I'm looking forward to that. Should be a good time."

"Are you into restoring old cars, too?"

"Oh, yeah. Not as much as Rory, though. I've been working on an old Hudson—used to be my uncle's. Hope to have it ready for the show."

Rory hung up the phone and turned to them.

"The part's ordered. Should be here in a couple days."

"That's good news. Can you take me to your loaner now?"

"Yep. All set." He pulled car keys from his jeans pocket. "Back soon," he told John.

"No hurry. I'll hold down the fort."

On the drive down the hill in Rory's truck, instead of appreciating the view of the river and the mountains, all Lacey could think about was the man sitting beside her. It felt almost like they were driving home from high school or on one of the rides they often took through the town and countryside.

But if that had been the case, they'd be talking and laughing instead of sitting in stony silence.

Her gaze landed on his bare arms. How many times had she felt the strength of those arms around her?

How would being in his arms feel now?

"—is where we'll start."

Rory's voice broke into her thoughts. "What?"

"This is where the car show will start. We're assembling at Johnson's."

She looked around and saw they'd reached

Main Street and Johnson's Food Mart. "Their parking lot will be a good place to meet."

"That's what I thought. If you're still in town, you should join us."

"I won't be. My work for Elton will be finished before then."

When Rory stopped for a traffic light, someone parked at the curb honked a horn. Lacey recognized the driver as Lon Trainer, who owned the local bowling alley. His wife, Trillie, peeked around him from the passenger's seat.

Rory waved.

Mouths gaping, the Trainers waved back.

The light changed, and Rory stepped on the gas.

"Oh, great," Lacey said. "Thanks to Carl Schroeder and now the Trainers, you and I being together will be all over town by tomorrow."

He frowned. "Just because you're riding in my truck doesn't mean we're back together."

"No, of course not. That's not what I meant." Did he think she hoped for a reconciliation? After ten years? Ridiculous.

"So what did you mean?"

"Just that people in this town gossip. That's

one nice thing about living in Boise. I can walk down the street and nobody knows me."

"Or your past."

"Or my past. Yes, that's something I live with every day of my life." She didn't even try to keep the bitterness out of her voice.

"You're not the only one," he said in a grim tone.

Lacey clamped her jaw shut.

Rory turned off Main, entering a residential area where modest frame homes lined the street. A couple blocks later, he swung into the driveway of a house painted cocoa-brown with white trim. "We're here," he announced.

This wasn't the first time she'd seen Rory's home. A few years ago, she'd overheard where he lived and, curious, had dared to drive by when she figured he'd be at work.

Rory parked in the driveway and turned off the truck's engine. "The loaner is in the garage, but the keys are in the house. I'd ask you in, but you—"

"—need to go," they said in unison.

Rory walked down the driveway to the house's back door. She took in the swing of his broad shoulders, the stride of his long legs. To say she'd forgotten the effect he had on her would be a lie. He still had the power to warm her with his presence, to make her yearn for his kiss.

The sound of children's laughter caught her attention. She glanced in the rearview mirror in time to see several kids on bicycles ride by. Like most residential areas in town, families filled this one.

Why hadn't Rory married and started a family of his own? Why hadn't she?

Rory reappeared and then disappeared again into the garage. The garage door swung open. The hum of a car's engine drifted along the air, and then a late-model sedan, painted a metallic blue, emerged from the garage.

Lacey stepped from Rory's truck. "Pretty fancy car for a loaner," she said when he pulled up beside her.

He leaned his head out the window. "Only the best for my customers." Leaving the engine idling, Rory got out of the car and held open the door.

She slipped into the driver's seat, passing dangerously close to him in the process.

"I don't think you'll have any problems, but the owner's manual is in the glove box, and you can always call me." Rory closed the door. He pulled out his wallet and took out a business card, handing it to her through the open window. "This has my number."

She dropped the card into her purse, and then took out one of hers and gave it to him.

Rory pocketed the card. "I'll let you know when the part arrives."

"Okay. And thanks, Rory."

"Sure. It's my job."

IF LACEY THOUGHT leaving Rory standing in his driveway would banish him from her thoughts, she was sadly mistaken. The car he'd loaned her had "Rory Dalton" written all over it. Hanging from the rearview mirror was a tiny, silver-plated four-leaf clover, his favorite good-luck charm. He'd given her a similar one long ago. It didn't hang in her car anymore, but instead was tucked away in a jewelry box.

She switched on the radio to find another reminder—Rory's favorite country station. They always listened to it while driving home from school, singing along.

Now she was stuck driving this car for the next several days. Well, then, drive it she would. Lacey straightened her shoulders and gripped the wheel.

She'd made good progress with her interviews today, and even though she hadn't discovered anything new about Al Jr.'s murder, she was confident she eventually would.

The truth was out there. She had only to find it.

AFTER LACEY LEFT, Rory climbed into his truck and drove back to the shop. As he pulled into his parking spot behind the building, he saw Lacey's Camaro, which John had moved from the driveway. He had to admit he and Lacey had worked well together figuring out the problem, just like back in the high school auto repair class. He especially remembered an old Dodge with a broken steering wheel. When they'd fixed that, they'd grinned at each other, high-fived and then, in front of Mr. Callahan and all their classmates, he'd kissed her. Their first kiss. Everyone had cheered.

That was the beginning.

A rifle shot from a farmhouse window was the end.

Footsteps sounded on the gravel. Someone tapped his window. "Earth to Rory."

He looked around to find Sam peering at him.

Pulling the key from the ignition, Rory opened the door and stepped out.

"You okay?" Sam asked.

"Sure. Why wouldn't I be?"

"I don't know, maybe because Lacey's car is here. What's going on?"

Rory explained the situation as he pocketed his keys and headed around to the garage's front entrance. Sam fell into step beside him.

"So, what was it like?"

Rory skidded to a halt and faced Sam. "What was *what* like?"

Sam waved a hand. "Talking to her again. You two haven't spoken much in ten years. Well, except for the party the other night."

"We talked business. About the car show. And then about her car's problem." He resumed walking, turned the corner and stepped from the sunlight into the cooler interior of the garage. In the office, John stood at the computer. He looked up and nodded a greeting.

"Something's going on," Sam persisted. "For ten years she pops in and out of town for no more than a few days, and now she's taken a job here. Why?"

Rory shrugged. "If she has some ulterior motive, it has nothing to do with her and me.

What brings you here, by the way? Run out of crooks to defend?"

Sam snorted. "I'll ignore that because I know you really hold my profession in high regard. No, I was on my way back from a meeting in Milton. Stopped to see when I can bring in the Mustang again. Want to make sure it's ready for the show."

"How 'bout tomorrow night? I got nothing going."

"Me, neither. See you at about six?"

"You're on."

Sam left, and Rory headed into the office to talk to John.

Later, he thought about Sam's suspicion that Lacey had an ulterior motive for taking the job with the newspaper. If she did, what could it be? Did it have something to do with him? With them? No, there was no "them." What, then? Okay, if Sam was on target, he figured he'd find out sooner or later. Nothing stayed a secret for long in this town.

CHAPTER EIGHT

LACEY TAPPED ON the door to Gram's apartment, turned the knob and stepped inside. "It's me, Gram."

Gram sat by the patio door talking on the phone. She looked up and met Lacey's gaze, fluttering the fingers of her free hand.

"Here's Lacey now," Gram said into the phone. "I'll find out and call you back." She punched off the call and laid the phone in her lap. Grasping the wheels of her chair, she turned to face Lacey. A puzzled frown creased her brow.

Lacey set her purse on the table. "Find out what?"

"Why you were riding through town with Rory Dalton."

Lacey shook her head. "This town's grapevine rivals the internet."

"Maybe. But you didn't answer my question."

Lacey held up the keys to the loaner car.

"This is the reason. After I make tea, I'll tell you all about it."

A few minutes later, Lacey brought their cups of tea into the living room and pulled up a chair by Gram. As she related the afternoon's events, her grandmother's expression ran the gamut from raised eyebrows to the hint of a smile and then back to a puzzled frown.

"I thought you knew how to fix cars," Gram said, "from that class you took in high school. When my car battery died in the parking lot at the grocery store and you hooked up your battery to mine, I thought you were pretty smart. Do you remember that time?"

Lacey smiled. "I do. I thought I was smart, too. But the problem my car has now is a lot different than a dead battery. I don't have the tools or the part to fix it."

"Does this mean you and Rory are getting back together?"

Lacey choked on a swallow of tea. "Of course not. Why would you think that?"

Gram turned toward the patio, where sunlight streamed in through the glass. "I'm just asking. I always liked Rory. So polite and helpful."

Lacey laughed. "The kind of guy who helps old ladies across the street."

Gram nodded. "I never had a quarrel with him after the tragedy. I felt sorry for him. He'd lost his mother when he was, what? Ten years old. And then he lost his dad, and they were so close…"

"I never had a quarrel with him, either," Lacey said softly.

"Is that why you want to go digging into the past? You think if you can prove Rick didn't kill Al Jr., then you and Rory—"

Lacey caught her breath. Was that why she was on her quest? So that she and Rory might be a couple again?

"Of course not," she said. "I want to know for myself. And for my dad."

"Who's dead and gone."

"But his spirit lives on. His memory lives on—in me."

Gram fingered the handle of her teacup. "Did you ever consider that, if your father was innocent—and I'm not agreeing that he was, mind you—that there's a murderer out there somewhere? And you might be putting yourself in danger?"

Lacey nodded solemnly. "Even with that possibility, it's a risk I'm willing to take."

ROSY TWILIGHT HAD settled over the mountains when Lacey left Riverview and drove to Sophie's. She parked in her assigned space and walked up the path to the porch. Sophie stood on the porch watering the hanging flower baskets with a garden hose.

She peered at Lacey. "Oh, it's you in that car. What happened to your convertible?"

"You mean you haven't heard?" Lacey climbed the steps and stood beside her. "You must be out of the loop."

Sophie moved the hose from one basket to the next in line. "I've been busy all day. One of our housekeepers is sick, and I filled in. Haven't had time to check my phone. What happened?"

Lacey told her about the Camaro's breakdown.

"Too bad," Sophie said, "but that's an older car for you. Hugh trades in ours every couple of years. 'Course, those old cars do have a certain allure. Rory thinks so, anyway."

"Yes, he's really into collecting. He seems to be making it a business."

They chatted for a few more minutes, and then Lacey said, "I'd better go in. I'd planned to do some work tonight."

Sophie put out her hand. "Hold on a sec. I was cleaning out the library bookshelf and I found some books on the town's history I thought you might be able to use."

"That's great, Sophie. I appreciate your thinking of me."

After Sophie shut off the water and coiled up the hose, they went inside and down the hall to the library. A guest, a middle-aged woman, sat in a wing chair paging through a magazine.

"Hi, Mrs. Peterson," Sophie said. "How'd your day go?"

Mrs. Peterson looked up and smiled. "Just lovely. We took a beautiful boat ride down the river. So glad we stopped here on our way east."

"We are, too." Sophie turned to Lacey. "The Petersons are from Seattle and are driving to the East Coast."

"Our son lives in Baltimore," Mrs. Peterson said. "We decided to drive instead of fly so that we could see the country."

"That should be an interesting trip," Lacey said.

A man appeared in the doorway. "Oh, here you are, Mabel. Time for our program."

"Oh, already?" She put down the magazine and stood. "See you tomorrow, Sophie. Looking forward to those pecan rolls we saw on the menu."

After the Petersons left, Sophie turned back to Lacey. "I do love this business. I meet so many interesting people."

"You're a good hostess, too. This was the right choice for you and Hugh."

"Yes, he was hard to convince, but now he's glad to be here, too."

She led Lacey to a table near the fireplace. "Here are the books, pamphlets and also some photos I found of your parents and Hugh and me when we went on a picnic. Thought you might like to have them." She indicated an envelope on top of the stack.

"Pictures? Yes, I would like to have them." Lacey picked up the envelope and pulled out the snapshots. In one picture, her mother and father stood under a cottonwood tree, their arms around each other, the river flowing in the background.

"Mom and Dad look really happy."

Sophie nodded. "They were—most of the time."

Lacy studied the photo. "Mom's wearing

her amethyst necklace, the one that belonged to Grandmother Whitfield."

"Yes, she loved that necklace. Rick used to tease her, saying he was going to steal it and pawn it. And she'd get really upset. That necklace meant a lot to her."

Pawn it. That was what Gram said Lacey's father had actually done, not just teased about.

"Do you know what happened to the necklace?" she asked Sophie.

Sophie shook her head. "Why, no. Did it go missing?"

"I read in her journal that she lost the necklace at The Owl, and that someone found it and was going to return it to her. The day of the murder, actually."

"Who found it? Did she say?" Sophie wrinkled her forehead.

"No, she didn't include the person's name."

"Was it Al? I don't remember anything about the necklace at the trial."

"I don't, either. I really need to find that necklace." Lacey tapped her finger on the photo.

"Why? Because it's a family heirloom?"

"Not just that. I need to find it because I

believe it's the key to what really happened that day."

Sophie took a step back and vigorously shook her head. "Lacey, don't. Don't go down that road. Leave it alone."

Surprised at Sophie's strong reaction, Lacey narrowed her eyes. "Do you know something you're not telling me?"

Sophie pressed her hand over her mouth. "I— No, of course not. But now I understand why you took Elton's job. Not because you want to do him and the town a favor, but because you want to poke around in the past. Trust me, that's a waste of time."

"How do you know that?" Lacey put down the photos and propped her hands on her hips.

"I just do." Sophie bit her lower lip and looked away. "And if you continue, I'm afraid you'll get hurt—more than you already are. You don't need more hurt, Lacey. You need to heal."

Later, in her room, Lacey sat at the table gazing out the window. Dusk had faded into night and, except for a few lights here and there, the landscape lay in darkness. She hugged her arms and sighed. She'd never felt so lonely in her life. So far, she'd met with nothing but resistance in her quest. Gram, Claire Roche and now Sophie had warned her to back off. Were they concerned for her welfare or was something else behind their warnings?

LACEY STOOD ON Main Street and studied the metal owl above the restaurant's door. The sculpture was beautiful, the feathers a shiny blue and green, the head gray and gold. The restaurant was closed now, but when it opened in a couple hours, one of the owl's eyes would wink and one wing would move up and down, beckoning customers inside.

Lacey had never frequented The Owl, not even when her mother worked there. The restaurant attracted older people. Older men, to be precise. Truckers passing through, construction workers and businessmen, too. Like A. J. Dalton and his son, Al Jr. When he had been in town, Lacey's father, Rick, was a customer. He came not so much to eat and drink but to join the card game in the back room. He hadn't been there for several days prior to the murder because he'd been working out of town. Maybe if he had, things might have turned out differently.

Today Lacey was here to interview The Owl's owner, Jorgen Miller, for the *Sentinel's* special edition. Sara Hoskins's list noted the restaurant had an interesting history.

However, knowing her mother had worked there, Lacey had a special interest in the place—and in the owner, who had been her mother's boss. Considering the reactions she'd had from people so far, though, she'd be careful talking about anything concerning her mother.

Lacey tore her gaze away from the owl and approached the door. A Closed sign hung in one window. Next to that was a menu. The fare hadn't changed much over the years: steak and mashed potatoes, chicken and dumplings, ham and beans. Guy food, with a few salads thrown in to please the wife or girlfriend.

Lacey knocked on the door and waited. Finally, the lock snapped, and a man opened the door. When he saw her, his jaw dropped.

"Mr. Miller? I'm Lacey Morgan, from the *Sentinel*. We have an appointment."

"Oh, sure. You gave me a start there for a second. You look so much like her."

"Like my mother? Yes, I know."

Jorgen Miller opened the door wider and stepped aside. "And I haven't seen you in a long while, other than a glimpse around town now and then."

Lacey crossed the threshold. "I don't stay in town long. This visit is different, since I've agreed to help Elton Watts."

"You mind talkin' in the bar?" He thumbed over his shoulder. "My bartender called in sick this morning, and I gotta get the place set up."

"No, I don't mind."

In his sixties, Jorgen was slender, with narrow shoulders and slim hips. He had a sun-weathered face, gray stubble, gray hair and wore rimless eyeglasses. The rolled-up sleeves of his white shirt exposed a tattoo of an owl on his right forearm.

He led Lacey through the restaurant's main dining room. Booths lined the walls on one side; on the other was a counter. Tables and chairs filled the center. An open door led to a brightly lit kitchen. Sounds of pots and pans clanging and the aroma of something spicy drifted along the air.

They went through a dark doorway into a dimly lit room. The bar ran the length of one wall. As in the dining room, here tables and chairs filled the center, and high-backed booths lined the far wall. A glass display case held a collection of owl figurines. She tried to imagine her mother working there, serving drinks and food, smiling and joking with the customers.

Spying a closed door at the far end, Lacey wondered if it led to the room where the card games were played. She wouldn't ask, though, at least, not before she began the interview.

"Have a seat." Jorgen waved to the bar stools.

Lacey set her purse on the counter and perched on a leather-covered stool. The smell of stale alcohol hung in the air.

Jorgen poured a cup of coffee from a glass carafe and set it in front of her. Then he began unloading glasses from the dishwasher and placing them on the shelf.

Lacey readied her tablet and tape recorder. Seeing Jorgen's frown, she said, "I hope you don't mind my taping the interview. I sometimes miss important information if I rely only on my note-taking."

"Okay—I guess."

Never mind his grudging tone; she'd interviewed tough subjects before. She could handle Jorgen Miller.

Lacey sipped her coffee. "As I told you

on the phone, Sara Hoskins had you on her
list for the newspaper's special edition. Her
note said your restaurant has an interesting
history."

"You might say so."

"Let's start with you. What got you into
this business?" Lacey poised her fingers over
the tablet.

Jorgen set another glass in place. "I was
a cook in the army. After I got out, I didn't
know what to do."

As Lacey expected, Jorgen's tone softened.
Like many people, he enjoyed talking about
himself.

"So you came home to Silver River."

"Not exactly. The town hadn't been my
home, but a cousin lived here. Danny O'Brien.
He's dead now." His expression sobered. "He
had most of the money to start this place. We
became partners. I cooked, and Danny was
out front with the customers. We rented the
place from A. J. Dalton. He owned the building. Still does."

Lacey wasn't surprised. Besides selling
property, A.J. owned a lot himself. "Is he a
good landlord?"

Jorgen raised an eyebrow. "You need that
for your story?"

"No, I was just curious."

"Then I'll skip the answer." He ducked his head to retrieve two more glasses from the dishwasher.

Lacey finished adding a note on her tablet. "Okay. Tell me how you chose the restaurant's name."

"There's an old stump behind the building." Jorgen rearranged the glasses to accommodate the new ones. "Used to be an owl sittin' there when I came to work in the morning. And sometimes when I'd leave at night he'd be there. Like he was watching over the place. I told my customers about it.

"One guy who heard the story was a local artist, a metal sculptor named Will Ersholz. He designed and made an owl and gave it to us. It's the one that's over the front door."

"I love that story," she said when he'd finished. "I'll be sure to use it in the article. Is Mr. Ersholz still in town? I'd like to talk to him, too."

Jorgen shook his head. "He moved away. Don't know where he went."

Lacey added the information to her notes and drank some more of her coffee. When she looked up, Jorgen had finished shelving the glasses and stood with his hands propped on his hips watching her. "You got enough now?"

Clearly, an invitation to leave.

She held up her forefinger. "Just a couple more things. Your restaurant started out as a family operation. After your cousin's death, did any other family members help out? Your wife? Children?"

"No."

Lacey wanted to ask more, but his "no" had a ring of finality to it. Okay. She switched off her tablet and tucked it into her purse.

She wasn't ready to go yet, though. Some off-the-record talking was yet to be done. She hoped.

"You've done a great job with the place," she said, gazing around. "I remember my mother saying how much she liked working here."

"Yeah? That didn't end so well, did it?"

Lacey winced, but doggedly went on. "You gave her a job when my family needed money."

Jorgen rubbed his forehead. "I gave her a job because she applied for it, and one of my waitresses recommended her."

"Bonnie, wasn't that her name?"

"Yeah, Bonnie Rosen. They were friends."

"Was my mother a good employee?"

He raised one eyebrow. "Well, she was friendly. Sometimes too friendly."

Lacey leaned forward. "Can you remember who she was friendly with?"

He made a sweeping gesture. "Every guy she waited on."

"Can you remember any names?"

Jorgen gripped the edge of the bar with both hands. "What's this about, Lacey? You got some agenda besides the articles you're writing for Elton Watts?"

"I'm, ah, thinking of writing my family history."

He narrowed his eyes. "Look, I had enough of your family ten years ago. Having my restaurant dragged into your father's trial nearly ruined my reputation. Your mother gave us a bad name with her…her flirting and her…her carrying on." His face turned red.

"But—"

"I don't know what your game is, but don't come around under the pretense of working for our town's celebration when you got another reason. You're asking for trouble."

"Trouble? What kind of trouble?"

His gaze fell on the tape recorder. "And turn that off!" He reached for the machine.

Lacey snatched up the recorder just as his

fingers grazed the top. She switched it off and thrust it into her purse. "There. Is there anything you want to say to me now?"

"Far's I'm concerned, we're done here." He grabbed her coffee cup and dumped what remained into the sink. Then he pulled a towel from the rack and swiped the counter.

"Jorgen!" someone called. "I'm here."

A woman stepped through the doorway into the bar. "Oh, I didn't know you were busy..." She squinted at Lacey as she came closer. "You're Lacey Morgan, aren't you? I haven't seen you in a lo-o-ng time. Do you remember me?"

Lacey studied the woman. "Yes, I believe I do. You're my mother's friend Bonnie—"

"Right. Bonnie Rosen."

Bonnie had short, reddish-blond hair cut in uneven lengths. Her short-sleeved blue blouse had an owl appliquéd on the pocket, and the matching flared skirt hit her legs just below the knees. High-topped black shoes completed her outfit.

"What brings you here?" Bonnie looked from Lacey to Jorgen.

Lacey explained her assignment. "Jorgen's been telling me the history of the restaurant." She glanced at Jorgen, who was still polishing the bar vigorously. When he didn't respond, she said, "I was just leaving. Oh, wait. I do want to take some pictures, especially of that tree stump where the original owl sat."

"I can show you where that is," Bonnie said.

"Great." Lacey jumped off the stool. "Thanks for seeing me today, Mr. Miller."

"Sure, sure," he said without looking up.

CHAPTER NINE

BONNIE LED LACEY from the bar, chattering about owls. Despite the clunky shoes, Bonnie moved with a fluid, gliding motion, undoubtedly acquired from all her years as a waitress.

They went through the kitchen, where the cook, a young man in his twenties wearing a white chef's hat, diced potatoes on a cutting board. He barked orders at three helpers, one stirring a pot on the stove, another slicing bread and a third stacking dinner plates on a shelf. The aromas of roast beef and tomatoes filled the air.

Bonnie waved at the chef as they went by. "Smells wonderful, Frankie."

"Everything I make is wonderful." Frankie grinned and tossed the potatoes into the steaming pot on the stove. Water splashed over the sides, sizzling as it hit the burner.

Outside, Lacey slipped on her sunglasses against the bright sunlight. Looking around, she quickly spotted a ceramic owl sitting in a clump of ivy twined around a tree trunk. "Great bird," she said.

"Yes, he's the best in the collection," Bonnie said. "Jorgen found him in an estate sale when he was looking for fixtures for the restaurant."

"Isn't he afraid someone might steal him?"

"He's cemented onto a post that's been driven into the center of the trunk and into the ground. He's secure."

Lacey pulled out her camera and photographed the owl from several angles. When she lowered her camera she caught Bonnie's worried look.

"Jorgen was hard on you."

"So you overheard."

"I didn't mean to eavesdrop, but I heard enough to get the gist."

Lacey slipped her camera into her tote. "The interview was going okay until I mentioned my mother."

Bonnie nodded. "That was a tough time for all of us."

"You were her friend."

"I was. I got her the job. And when she and Jorgen clashed, he blamed me."

"I'd like to hear about that."

Bonnie glanced at her wristwatch. "I've got a few minutes before I'm officially on the job. Let's sit and we'll talk." She nodded at a wrought-iron table and metal chairs.

Lacey sat and slid her hand into her tote again, intending to take out her tape recorder. Then she changed her mind and decided to keep their talk off the record.

"So, why didn't my mother and Jorgen get along?" she asked.

"He said she was too friendly with the customers—the male customers—and gave the place a bad rep."

"Was she too friendly?"

Bonnie tilted her head. "Your mom was, well, clueless. She'd never worked before. She didn't know she could get in trouble by acting that way with customers who might want to get to know her better, if you catch my drift."

"Like Al Jr.?"

"Yes, like Al." Bonnie nodded, her expression solemn. "He'd lost his wife when Rory was ten, you know, and never married again. I don't know why. He was such a nice man."

"Okay, but who else besides him was my mother friendly with?" Lacey leaned forward.

Bonnie made a sweeping gesture. "Everybody."

"Can you give me some names?"

Bonnie eyed her. "Hon, what's this all about? Why do you want to dig up all that old stuff?"

"I want to know my mother better. I was so young at the time—"

"And thick with Rory Dalton. He's still single, you know." She smiled, flashing a dimple in her left cheek.

Not wanting to go there, Lacey kept on task. "I read in Mother's journal that someone was following her home after work. Do you have any idea who?"

"Your mother kept a journal?" Bonnie widened her eyes.

Lacey realized her mistake too late. She waved dismissively. "Just a book where she wrote some poetry." True enough.

"I never knew anybody followed her home." Bonnie frowned. "But if so, maybe the person was watching out for her."

"I never thought of that. Maybe Jorgen?"

"Maybe. He was protective of her, like a dad or a big brother would be."

"Did he have any family besides his cousin? I asked him if a wife or children helped out in the restaurant, and he said no, but then clammed up. Like he didn't want to talk about anything personal."

"You're right about that. He's always been a very private man. But I know he did have a wife and a little girl, too. A couple years after he and Danny started the restaurant, she up and left him and took the girl with her. He said she left because she hated living here and wanted to go back East to live with her folks. He never wanted to talk about them, and so we didn't ask anymore."

"Thanks for telling me, Bonnie. I'll respect his privacy and not mention a wife and child in my article."

"No problem. But, Lacey, I still want to know, why all this interest in the past?"

Bonnie's sympathetic manner prompted Lacey to speak frankly. Besides, she'd already revealed the existence of the journal.

"Bonnie, do you really believe my father shot Al Jr. in the back in cold blood?"

Bonnie wrinkled her forehead. "The jury said he did."

"But what do *you* believe? You knew my father, didn't you?"

"Sure, I knew Rick. Me 'n' Tom went out to dinner with your mom and dad a few times."

"And?"

Bonnie shrugged. "I felt bad about him going to prison, and really, really bad about losing your mom. She was my friend. But if he did it, he did it."

"I don't believe he did. I've never accepted the jury's verdict. I want to find out the truth."

"What difference docs it make now? They're all dead."

Lacey straightened her spine. "But I'm not, and it makes a difference to me."

Bonnie shook her head. "Lacey, hon, stop wasting your time. Get on with your life."

"Bonnie!"

Jorgen stood in the restaurant's open back door, his feet spread apart and his hands propped on his hips. A scowl darkened his sun-weathered face.

"What are you doing out here?" he went on. "We open in fifteen minutes. You need to put the daily special sheets in the menus."

"Oh, right. Sorry."

Apology written across her face, Bonnie jumped up.

Lacey stood, too. "My fault. I was photographing the owl—" she gestured toward the tree trunk "—and Bonnie was telling me its history."

Jorgen swiped the air, as though swatting a fly. "We got a business to run here."

"Of course. I'm on my way."

"Nice seeing you again, Lacey, honey." Bonnie's gaze lingered on Lacey, and then she turned away and hurried toward the restaurant's back door. "Coming, boss."

LACEY'S NEXT APPOINTMENT was with Kristal Wilson and her aunt, Millie Nixon, at Millie's Boutique. A childless widow, Millie had adopted Kris after her parents drowned in a boating accident, and now they worked together in the store.

Lacey stopped to admire the window display of T-shirts with "Silver River Days" across the front and then stepped inside. Kris stood behind the counter wrapping a purchase for a customer. Millie swept by from the dressing rooms, her arms laden with clothing.

"Hello, Lacey. What do you think of this outfit?" Millie held up a blue linen jacket and matching slacks.

"Very nice. Probably not for me, though. I'm pretty much at home in my tights and tees."

"I know. But if you ever need to, ah, dress

up a little, keep this in mind. The color would be great on you." She hung the outfit on a nearby rack, adding the other items she carried.

Kris's customer left, and she joined Lacey and Millie. "Hey, Lacey, just in time for lunch."

"Uh-huh. But let me get some info on the raffle before we go." She pulled her tablet from her purse.

"The raffle was Kris's idea." Millie favored her niece with a fond smile.

"I thought a raffle would be a good way to get people into the stores," Kris said. "Each participating business will have their prizes on display and a jar or a box to collect the tickets."

"What are you offering?" Lacey tapped the tablet's keyboard.

"Several of my handbags. Come see."

Kris led Lacey to a window display featuring a large, barrel-shaped glass jar surrounded by several handbags.

"Beautiful." Lacey exchanged her tablet for her camera and snapped a picture.

"Aunt Millie thought we should offer the vinyl purses she ordered." She cast a covert glance at Millie, who had finished hanging up the clothing and was now tidying the counter. "She's not exactly onboard where my designs are concerned."

"I can't imagine any woman not wanting one of these." Lacey ran her fingers over a bag's brocaded fabric.

Kris laughed. "You have to say that. You're my friend."

"No. And to prove it, when I get my raffle tickets, I'll put them all in your jar."

Kris drew back and raised her eyebrows. "Then you're staying for the celebration? I hoped you would."

"Ah, no, I'm not. But do I have to be present to win?"

"No, but I wish you would be here, for lots of reasons."

Lacey sighed. "I don't even know if I'm doing the right thing by staying this long."

Kris looked at her wristwatch. "Let's continue that subject over lunch."

A few minutes later, seated in a cozy booth in the restaurant section at Abby's Bakery, and having given the waitress their orders, Kris and Lacey chatted about the upcoming celebration, Kris's new handbag designs and Lucas's day-camp experiences.

Visiting with her old friend gave Lacey a

warm feeling. She had friends in Boise, but no one had taken Kris's place. They'd been through a lot together.

After a lull in which they both were busy enjoying their roasted turkey salads, Kris leaned forward and in a low voice asked, "I have to know, Lacey. Are you and Rory getting back together?"

Lacey shook her head. "Not a chance. With our background, how could we?"

"Then why did you take the job with the *Sentinel*?"

Lacey plucked a roll from the basket and broke it in half. "I read something in my mother's journal that may prove my father's innocence."

Kris dropped her jaw. "What? Are you kidding?"

"No, I'm serious." She told Kris the story of the amethyst necklace. "I thought staying here awhile longer might help me with my personal quest. That doesn't mean I'm not interested in the job for Elton. I am. You know how I love history."

"I do, and I know you'll give it your all, but I don't see how a missing necklace proves your father's innocence."

"It doesn't—yet. But it might when I find out what happened to it."

Kris finished a bite of salad. "I think you're wasting your time."

Lacey bristled. "I don't consider my time wasted. I thought you, of all people, would understand."

"I'm sorry, but I think you'd be better off putting the past behind you and using your time to get back together with Rory."

"Oh, like you're getting back together with Sam?" Lacey bit her lip. She hadn't meant to sound so sarcastic, but too late to take back the comment now.

Kris's face turned red. "Our breakup was way different from yours and Rory's."

"Yes, as I recall, when Sam went off to college, you were going to wait for him. But while he was gone, you married Nolan instead."

"Sam and I argued and broke up before I started seeing Nolan. Besides, waiting wasn't my choice. It was Sam's."

"But you didn't want to leave Silver River to be with him, either."

"That's true," Kris admitted. "I wanted to stay here and work at the store. I owe Aunt Millie a lot."

"I know." Lacey's anger softened. "She's been a wonderful parent to you all these years. But Sam's here now, so what's keeping you two apart?"

Kris looked down at her plate. "It's too late for us. We really hurt each other."

"Does that mean you're never going to get married again?"

"No, I'm not saying that. But not to Sam."

Lacey waved a hand. "See? That's exactly what I'm talking about. Rory and I are in the same situation. Sometimes, the past just can't be healed."

A noisy group passed by on their way to the adjacent booth. After they were settled, Kris said, "I wonder if it's the same for Sharone and Jaxon? Remember the promise the six of us made when we were in high school? We were all going to be married and live in Silver River and be friends forever."

"We were young and naive. By the way, has anyone heard from Shar? Or Jax? Last I heard he was at the police academy."

"He finished that and took a job in Brighton. But no one's heard from Shar. I don't think even her parents know where she is. Her mom still has Flower Power, though."

"I know. I stopped there on my way into

town and bought some roses for Gram. I asked about Shar, but her mom just said she wasn't sure where she was. She acted like she didn't want to talk about it, so I didn't push."

They were silent a moment, and then Kris said, "Oh, Lacey, I don't want us to argue, but as your friend, I can't help worrying about you—and Rory, too. I care about both of you. And even if it's too late for me and Sam, it might not be for you and Rory."

"That's not what's on my mind," Lacey insisted. "Proving my father's innocence is what matters."

After they had finished lunch and gone their separate ways, Kris's last words lingered in Lacey's mind. She'd all but echoed Gram's accusation that Lacey had an ulterior motive for her inquiry into Al Jr.'s tragic murder. Well, they were wrong. She and Rory? Together again? No way. Nothing could be further from her mind.

RORY WAS POLISHING the rear fender of his '57 Chevy when Sam drove up in his Mustang. Sam stepped from his car and entered the garage. "That's tonight's project? Spit and polish?"

Rory dug his cloth into the polish can

and spread the wax over another section of fender. "Yeah, I'm getting her ready for the show. What's on your agenda?"

"New wipers. Not that I'm expecting it to rain anytime soon. But they came today, so might as well put them on. Part of the restoration."

"That's the name of the game, buddy. Bring 'er on in."

Sam pulled the Mustang into an empty bay. He selected the tools he needed from Rory's workbench and went to work. Rory returned to his polishing.

"How's Lacey doing with your loaner?" Sam asked after a few minutes of silence. "Bet she misses her Camaro."

"Don't know. Haven't talked to her since she drove off. Told her to call if she had any problems."

"She's probably busy with her assignment for Elton."

"No doubt." Rory stepped back and surveyed his progress. The polished finish shone under the overhead lights.

"You know any more about what's going on with her?"

"No, I haven't talked to anyone. The person I want to talk to is Remy."

"You still want that property."

"I want that house gone." Rory gave the front fender a vigorous swipe with his cloth.

"Can't blame you for that. But maybe she'd be more likely to sell if she knew what you were going to do with the property."

"If A.J. has his way, it'll be a subdivision. And since he's the financial backer, I don't have much choice. You got any ideas?"

Sam finished removing the wiper on the driver's side of the windshield, laid it on the workbench and picked up the new wiper. "Maybe a park, something like that, donated to the city."

Rory rubbed his jaw. "Do you think what happened there would put people off?"

Sam shrugged. "I don't know. Just a thought. Hey, can you give me a hand here? I got a question."

"Sure."

Rory put down his can of polish and went to Sam's side. A few minutes later both wipers were in place.

"Okay, what's next?" Rory asked.

Sam looked at his watch. "I've had my fix for tonight. Len and Jim said they'd be at Erv's about now. Why don't we head on over for a game of pool?"

Rory was about to agree. A night out with the guys at the popular sports bar sounded good. But then his gaze traveled to the Chevy. "Think I'll pass. I need to give the Chevy a run. She hasn't been out for a couple of weeks."

Sam nodded. "Okay, but on your way home, give Erv's a look. We might still be there."

After Sam left, Rory finished cleaning up and then turned out the lights and locked up the shop. The Chevy stood in the driveway now, waiting for him.

He drove down the hill and across the bridge to Main Street. The lights of establishments blinked on here and there. Beyond the town, the mountains glowed against a pale blue sky.

He turned off Main and cruised through the residential area, where cars were parked in the driveways and lights shone from the windows of the homes. He thought about going home himself, having taken the short ride he'd intended. But his house would be dark. No one waited for him there.

He could go to Erv's and meet up with the guys, but tonight that held no appeal, either.

He continued driving aimlessly for a while,

and then decided on a destination. Turning back onto Main Street, he headed out of town.

LACEY SIPPED HER TEA, glancing at Gram over the rim of her cup. Gram gazed into the distance, lost in her thoughts. Neither had said much since they'd come out to the patio to enjoy the evening. Although the heat of the day lingered, a light breeze swept off the foothills and through the cottonwood trees along the riverbank.

Lacey had brought her tablet, intending to review the notes she'd taken today, but it lay in her lap, yet to be turned on. Instead, she savored the peace of the evening and the comfort of a full stomach. The dining room had served up a wonderful dinner of baked chicken, sweet potatoes and a variety of salads. She'd enjoyed meeting and chatting with some of Gram's new friends.

Gram shifted in her chair and patted Lacey's arm. "I'm glad you're here."

"Me, too." Warmth filled Lacey. Despite their differences, she dearly loved her grandmother. Remy had been a steadying presence in her life, paying attention to her when her mother drifted off into her dream world and her father was working out of town. And of course, Gram was the mainstay in her life after both of Lacey's parents had died, seeing her through her college years and, even though she hadn't wanted Lacey to settle permanently in Boise, rooting for her when she was offered a job with the historical society.

"I really appreciate all the help with the move," Gram went on.

"I know."

"I wish—" Gram looked away.

"What? What do you wish?"

"Ah, that I was more able to help."

Gram's initial hesitation told Lacey that that wasn't what she really wanted to say. Before she could pursue the matter, her cell phone rang. She picked up the phone and looked at the incoming number. Local, but not one she recognized. She answered the call.

"Hello, Lacey," came the responding greeting.

The number she might not recognize, but no mistaking the deep male voice that rang in her ear. Her breath quickened.

"Hey, Rory," she said, striving to sound casual. "I hope you're calling to tell me the part for my car arrived."

"No, not yet."

"Then what—"

"I want to show you something. Come on out front."

"You're here?"

"Yeah, so come on out. You gotta see this."

"Can't you just tell me what it is?"

"No. I want you to see it."

At least, he wasn't asking to come in. "All right, just for a few minutes."

She punched off the call. "Rory's out front with something he wants to show me. I'll be back in a few minutes." She slipped her cell phone into her jacket pocket, picked up her tablet and stood.

"I'll see you tomorrow," Gram said.

Lacey shook her head. "No, in a few minutes."

"No, no. I feel the past rolling in on us, like the fog sometimes rolls off the river. Don't you remember? He'd call and off you'd go, and we wouldn't see you the rest of the evening. I'd hear the stairs creak late at night as you crept up to bed."

"The past is over, Gram, and we can't go back. Any association Rory Dalton and I have now is strictly business."

Gram just shook her head and waved Lacey off.

IN THE PARKING LOT, Lacey stopped and looked around, expecting to see Rory's truck, but it was nowhere in sight. Then a voice called, "Over here, Lacey."

She followed the voice and found Rory, arms folded, leaning against an older-model, two-toned green Chevrolet.

He straightened and made a sweeping gesture, as though introducing royalty. "Take a look at this."

"Wow. Is this the car you bought when we—"

"Were back in high school? Yep. You were with me when we found it in the scrap yard. Since then, I've bought other cars and restored them, too. But this is a favorite."

She ran her hand along the car's smooth, shiny fender. "It's beautiful. You did a great job."

He opened the passenger door. "Get in. Try 'er out."

She took a step back. "No, I—"

"Come on, Lacey. You know you want to." His voice teased.

He was right. She did want to. But was the car the temptation? Or the man? She looked at him standing there, eyes shining, a big grin on his face, and her heart skipped a beat.

"Oh, all right." Lacey slid onto the seat.

Rory shut the door and came around to the driver's side. "New upholstery, new finish on the dash, new carpets, the works," he said as he climbed behind the wheel.

He stuck a key in the ignition. The engine hummed to life, and before she realized what was happening, he backed out of the parking space.

"Wait! What are you doing?"

"We're going for a ride."

Lacey gripped the door handle. "No, I can't."

"Come on. You love classic cars as much as I do."

"That's beside the point. Gram's expecting me to spend the evening with her."

"I'll have you back in thirty minutes, tops."

They reached the end of the driveway. Rory stopped to check for traffic and then pulled onto the highway. He talked on about the car, what he'd done under the hood, in the trunk, in the interior. Lacey listened with only half her mind. The other half spun back ten years to when she and Rory took many rides such as this.

Twilight faded away, and Rory switched on the car's headlights. Familiar aromas drifted in the open windows: hay from passing farms, sage growing alongside the road. The whistle of a distant train drifted across the landscape.

Rory glanced at her. "How's your assignment for Elton going?"

"Good. Tomorrow, I'm interviewing Del Ford at the museum."

"I remember how much you liked history when we were in school. You were so good at remembering all those dates."

"So were you—after I coached you."

He made a face. "History. Ugh. Especially European History."

"Not exactly the most exciting subject," she agreed, gazing out her window in time to glimpse two people on horseback ambling along a trail. "But we made it through."

"Yep, I owe my passing grade in Mrs. Clemson's history class to you." His expression brightened. "The car repair class was a different story. That was something we both could get into."

"Uh-huh. Remember that old Ford someone towed in that Mr. Callahan said belonged to a movie star who was passing through town? And when the car quit on him he abandoned it?"

Rory laughed. "Yeah. And you and I fixed it. That was a sweet old car. Wonder what ever happened to it."

"Probably in a junkyard somewhere."

"I should track it down, add it to my collection."

Lacey turned back to him. "You're really serious about the classic cars, aren't you?"

"I am. It's my calling, like history is yours. My dream is to have a classic car museum, where fans can come to look and to buy, too... Ah, here we are."

"Here, where?"

"The turnoff to Linton Road."

"Oh, no, Rory. We don't want to go there." Linton Road led to a spot where they often went to be alone.

"Just enjoy the ride, Lacey, okay?"

They wound up into the hills, past lighted farmhouses where sensible people had settled in for the night, instead of riding around the countryside with someone...dangerous.

They rounded a bend, and there stood the tree they'd always parked under: a huge maple silhouetted against the darkening sky, its leaf-laden limbs outstretched like welcoming arms. The property belonged to someone, of course, but no one ever had bothered them when they came here, and she and Rory had considered the spot theirs.

Rory pulled the car under the tree, leaving the engine idle, a soft hum in the otherwise silent evening.

She turned to face him. "Rory, why are you doing this?"

"I wanted you to see the car. Honestly. There's no one I'd rather share it with than you, Lacey."

"Okay, but why come *here*? We're not teenagers anymore. The past is the past."

"Then we'll get out." Rory cut the engine, opened his door and jumped out. He came around, pulled open her door and held out his hand.

Lacey stared at his hand but didn't move. Not that she didn't trust him. *She* was the one she worried about.

"Lacey?"

With a resigned sigh, she grasped his hand and stepped from the car. A path circled the tree and then wandered off into the grassland, with the foothills and mountains in the distance.

"I come up here often." Rory drew her forward in a slow, easy walk. "This is a good place to think. But I've never brought anyone else up here. This is *our* place."

"Was," she corrected, as she fell into step beside him.

"Is," he said, just as emphatically.

"We can't go back, Rory. You know that."

"I know. But who says we can't go forward? When you came into the shop the other day and we were working together on your car, something inside me snapped, and I thought later, look at all you've lost in the past ten years."

"What happened wasn't our fault."

"That's just it. Not our fault. Why should we be punished for what our parents did?"

Or did not do. But she kept that thought to herself. "We were young…"

"And we did what we were told. But I don't want to go there."

"What do you want, then?" Her heart beat faster as she waited for his answer.

They'd reached the tree. Rory clasped her shoulders and turned her around. "What I want right now is this."

His eyes focused on her mouth, and then he leaned nearer. His body heat, his scent, surrounded her, filling her with memories—and desire. She closed her eyes just as his lips touched hers in a gentle kiss. After a few moments, he pulled her close and deepened the kiss. She wrapped her arms around his neck and threaded her fingers through his hair.

He trailed kisses across her cheek. "Oh, Lacey. Oh, honey, I've missed you so much."

"I've missed you, too, but—" she gently pushed against his chest, carving some distance between them "—but this is too much, after—"

"After ten years? We have a lot of time to make up for." He laughed softly and leaned toward her again.

She kept her hands firm against his chest. "No, Rory."

He sobered and drew back. "What's wrong? Oh, I get it. You're involved with someone in Boise."

"No, I'm not. But what about you?"

"There've been others. But none to take your place."

"Oh, Rory, don't talk that way. There's no future for us." Breaking away, she started walking back to the car.

He caught up with her. "There can be. Look. Once we get rid of that house, everything will change. You'll see. 'Out of sight, out of mind.'"

She whirled. "So, we're back to that. When will you understand that the fate of the house is not mine to decide?"

"Your grandmother would listen to you if you said you wanted it gone."

Lacey propped her hands on her hips. "Oh, really? Well, then, you don't know my grandmother. She has a mind of her own. Can we please go? I told Gram I'd be back in thirty minutes, and we're way over that now." She turned and marched toward the car.

"Sure, sure." He raced ahead of her and opened the passenger door.

Without meeting his eyes, she plopped down on the seat.

All the way back to Riverview she sat with her arms folded. He didn't try to make conversation and neither did she. But when they pulled into the driveway, she turned to him. "I'm sorry for the way things turned out."

He stopped at the front door and shifted the gearshift. "This evening or ten years ago?"

She lowered her gaze. "Both."

"Me, too. But tonight—well, I got to show you my car, anyway."

She had to smile. "You did. And a beautiful car it is."

LACEY HEADED UP the walk to the entrance of the Silver River Historical Museum at exactly ten o'clock, ready for her appointment with Del Ford, the museum's director. Of all her interviews, she looked forward to this one the most.

As far as her personal quest was concerned, she had no idea whether or not Del Ford could offer any help, but she'd be on the alert for any pertinent information.

Once inside the museum, she felt immediately at home. In school, when the other kids groaned about a field trip to a museum, Lacey cheered. Her interest led to being a history major in college and then to the position with the Boise Historical Society.

Del, a fiftyish man with white hair and matching mustache, stood behind the counter talking to a couple with two teenagers. While the kids played with their phones, the parents watched Del trace a route on a map spread on the counter.

Del gave Lacey a smile and a nod, and then went back to his guests.

Lacey wandered around, noting new exhibits since she'd been there last. A display of old fountain pens caught her eye, and one of World War II memorabilia. She took out her camera and snapped a few pictures.

The front doorbell tinkled, signaling the family's departure. Del put away the map and ambled over to Lacey.

"So you're working on Silver River Days," he said, hitching up his slacks and smoothing his Hawaiian print shirt over his stomach. "Does that mean you're moving back to town?"

"No, just helping Elton Watts while I'm getting Gram settled at Riverview."

"Heard about her accident. I thought she'd move to Boise to live near you. My son wants me to come to Milton, now Sybil's gone, but I don't want to give up my job here."

"You really like the museum, don't you?"

"I like old stuff."

"I do, too."

"I figured. You work for a museum in Boise, right?"

"Ah, right." She told him a little about her work. She didn't mention she had given up her job to take the one Elton had offered.

"Sounds interesting," he said. "Well, let me show you around our place." He led her through the exhibits in the main room, which included artifacts from the area's early pioneers and the tools used for silver and gold mining.

"Gotta show you our new wing," Del said. "Not exactly new, but renovated." He stopped at a wide doorway and gestured to the pile of lumber and empty display cases lined against one wall. "This is now known as the Trenton Wing. You know the family? 'Course you do. Everyone knows the Trentons, even though Cora's the only one left."

Lacey made a note on her tablet. "I remember when George Trenton was mayor. I was in high school and our history class took a field trip to his office. They had a son named Calvin, right?"

Del nodded, and led her into the room. "George and Cal are both gone now. George died of a heart attack, and Cal had a brain tumor." He grimaced. "Bad enough for Cora when George died, but then to lose her only child, too. She had such high hopes that Cal would follow in his father's footsteps and carry on the Trenton name."

"Giving this wing is a good memorial and very generous," Lacey said.

"She's not stopping with the wing. She wants the Clapton Building renamed after the family, and also City Park. What's wrong,

I ask you, with the name 'City Park'? But I keep my mouth shut. We're glad to have the renovation here."

Lacey gazed around. A few glass cases in the middle of the room held exhibits, but most were empty. One wall had a display of historical maps. She stepped closer to examine them.

"George's collection," Del said. "From the Civil War to the Westward Expansion. Some are replicas, but some are originals, too.

"We're still a work in progress," he added as they strolled the room. "Stuff comes in all the time. We got a basement full of boxes and bags. You got any extra time while you're here, I could use a hand. The ladies who usually do the sorting are busy with Silver River Days."

"I might have some time." Lacey thought of her grandmother's stored belongings. "Maybe Gram has some things she could donate. I'd have to do some arm-twisting, though. She hangs on to stuff."

"Lots of people do. But we're always looking."

They went downstairs, where Del showed her the workroom. As he said, the tables were piled high with boxes and paper bags full of donations that needed to be sorted. Shelving held items that were identified and tagged, and several mannequins waited to be dressed with clothing hanging from racks on wheels.

Back upstairs, Lacey stopped to make some more notes.

Del nodded at her tablet. "One of these years that's gonna be on display here."

She laughed. "At the rate technology moves, that day might come sooner than we think. So, what is the museum's role in the celebration?"

"Open house every day. Refreshments. Historical Society will be hosting. They'll all be in costume. Oh, and we're having a reenactment, too."

She looked up from her keypad. "A reenactment?"

"Yeah. Lewis and Clark's trail goes right through town."

"I remember learning that in school."

"So, they're going to trek through here again. Sacajawea will be there, too."

"That sounds fabulous."

"It will be. You'll see."

"Oh, I won't be around then."

"What? Doing all this work and not staying for the celebration? Oh, right. You probably have to get back to your job in Boise."

Lacey nodded, not about to admit she had no job there anymore. Cutting that tie had set her adrift. She had nothing to return to there, and she couldn't stay here. Where did she belong? Would she ever know?

CHAPTER TEN

"SO, WHEN AM I going to walk again?" Gram asked Dr. James Foster later that afternoon.

Sitting beside her grandmother in an exam room at the Silver River Medical Clinic, Lacey waited for the doctor's answer. She liked Dr. Foster. Despite being at least twenty years younger than Gram, he projected a fatherly attitude that showed a real caring for his patients.

Dr. Foster studied his computer screen, tapped the keys and then turned to face them. "I'm afraid I can't answer that right now. But today's X-rays show your bones are mending well. And you said your therapist at Riverview has you exercising with your walker every day."

Gram nodded. "Every single day. Up and down the hall. She has me programmed like a robot."

"And you're taking your supplements?"

"No way I could forget when my aide brings them to me on the dot."

Dr. Foster smiled. "Riverview sounds like a good place for you. Keep up your daily therapy, and I'll see you again in a month. If anything comes up in the meantime, give us a call."

In the outer office, Dr. Foster led them to a counter where a nurse monitored a computer and printer. She retrieved a newly printed sheet from the printer and handed it to the doctor, who in turn handed it to Lacey.

"Here's a summary of our visit today," he said.

"Thank you. We'll be sure to review it at home." Lacey tucked the paper into her purse.

"Good you could bring your grandmother today. Right, Remy?" He patted her shoulder.

"Lacey's the only family I have, 'cept for my cousin Bessie. She moved away to live with her son."

"Well, I'm glad Lacey can be with you now."

Outside in the parking lot, Lacey tucked Gram in the front seat of the car and then folded and stowed her wheelchair in the trunk.

As they left the lot, Gram said, "Will you drive us by the house on the way home?"

Lacey froze her grip on the steering wheel. "Are you sure you want to? Seeing the place might be upsetting."

"Not seeing it today would be more upsetting. Please, Lacey. I can picture the house in my mind, and I can look at photos, but neither is the same as actually being there."

Lacey sighed. "All right."

She knew that "going by" did not mean merely passing by as they drove along the highway. It meant turning onto the side road that led to the house. And so, when they came to the turnoff, she swung onto the road without being asked.

The road seemed to have even more potholes than when she'd traveled it on her last trip to Silver River. Although she wouldn't admit it to Gram, she, too, had a constant need to visit the house, and whenever she came to town, she drove down the road at least once. She never went in the house, though; that would be too painful.

In between dodging potholes, she shot Gram another glance. "Are you okay?"

"I'm fine."

Gram's vague tone told Lacey she'd already stepped into the past. Just being on the property cast a spell over her.

When they reached the house, Lacey idled the car at the path leading to the front door. She gazed at the peeling paint, the empty windows, the sagging roof and thought how sad and neglected it looked. When she had lived there as a child, her grandfather kept the house painted and the lawn mowed. Gram kept the garden weeded and full of flowers. They had all worked together to maintain the place—even Rick had joined in and shared the chores.

"Drive around back." Gram's voice broke into Lacey's thoughts. "I want to see the barn."

Lacey put the car in gear and continued on down the driveway to where it curved around the side of the house. Years ago, the driveway led all the way to the barn, but now the area was overgrown. Lacey pulled the car to a stop. She didn't want to risk damaging Rory's loaner car by hitting anything hidden by the grass.

The barn, too, looked lost and forlorn, with faded red paint exposing raw and naked boards underneath, and the door sagging on the hinges.

Her gaze traveled back along the overgrown driveway to the spot where Al Jr.'s shiny red sports car had been parked on that fateful day ten years ago.

That's my dad's car, Rory had said when he'd brought her home from school that day. Disbelief had colored his voice. *What's he doing here?*

Later, the speculation was that Al parked behind the house so that his car wouldn't be visible from the highway, and no one would know he was visiting Norella Morgan.

"I was pregnant when we started building the house," Gram mused.

"Yes, pregnant with Mom," Lacey said absently, still seeing Al Jr.'s red car in her mind's eye.

"No, not with Norella."

That caught Lacey's attention. "What?"

"I was pregnant before her," Gram whispered, looking down at her hands clasped in her lap.

Lacey patted Gram's shoulder. "I never knew that."

"Not many people did."

"So, what happened? Or do you not want to talk about it?"

"I need to talk about it, to make sure I don't forget. I don't remember like I used to.

Sometimes, I feel my life is slipping away, piece by piece."

"Oh, Gram, I'm so sorry. Please, do tell me what happened." Lacey shut off the car's engine and gave her full attention to her grandmother.

Remy leaned her head back against the seat and closed her eyes. "I found out about the baby at the same time we started building the house. We were so happy because we'd already waited several years to have a child."

"I knew you'd been married for a few years before you had Mom."

"Six years. Anyway, I wanted to help build our house. But your granddad didn't want me to. He was so protective. But I insisted. I did odd jobs, carrying boards and tools, cleaning up, besides keeping everyone fed and watered, same as the cows and chickens." She laughed.

That was so like Gram. She always had something cooking in the kitchen—a pot of stew on the stove, cookies or cake in the oven.

"Anyway, one day I brought out a basket of cookies I'd baked at the tiny apartment we were living in while we waited for our house to be built. I climbed over the foundation,

being very careful, as always. I stepped on
what appeared to be a solid piece of flooring.
But it wasn't solid. The boards split apart,
and I fell into the cellar."

Lacey gasped. "Oh, no. What happened
then?"

"I woke up in the hospital, your granddad
at my side. He broke the news that I'd lost
the baby."

Lacey's eyes filled with tears. She took
Gram's hand and squeezed it.

"Your granddad blamed himself," Remy
went on. "He couldn't go back to work on the
house. We both were torn with grief. Finally,
our friends who'd been helping us coaxed
him back. I wasn't allowed there, though.
When the house was finally finished, Jay
made a shelf in the basement and I put a cross
there, as a memorial."

"I think I know the shelf you mean. But I
don't remember a cross."

"Long before you arrived, I took the cross
away. I just didn't want to explain about it to
people who might see it and not know the
story. But I could imagine the cross there
whenever I wanted to, and think of my lost
child."

"I'm so sorry, Gram, that you lost your

baby. That must have made you love Norella all the more."

Gram nodded, and her eyes misted. "It did—and then to lose her, too…"

Lacey put her arms around Gram's frail shoulders. Gram returned her hug, and they sat there for long moments in painful silence.

A few minutes later, when they were on their way out, Gram's gaze lingered on the house. Then she turned to Lacey. "Thank you for bringing me here today."

"You're welcome."

"Do you understand, just a little?"

"I do."

"As long as the house stands and I can visit once in a while and remember—the good and the bad—my world is complete. If it were gone, such a big part of my life would go with it that I doubt I could survive."

How different Gram's view of the house was from Rory's, Lacey thought. For Rory, the house reminded him only of pain and sadness, which would go away—or so he thought—if the place were torn down. For Gram, the house's existence preserved both her good and bad memories.

For Lacey, whether or not the house continued to stand was not as important as proving her father's innocence. What would Rory say if he knew of her quest? Would he try to dissuade her? Probably. Didn't matter, though, because she wasn't going to tell him.

"Hey, Rory!" Jorgen Miller waved to Rory as he entered The Owl Restaurant.

"Jorgen. What's today's lunch special?"

"We got steak tartare."

"Say what?" Rory laughed and slid onto a stool at the counter.

"Something our cook wanted to try." Jorgen poured a cup of coffee from the carafe on the hot plate and set it in front of Rory. "He went to a fancy French cooking school, ya know."

"Trying to give the place a little class, huh? I'll stick to a burger. Hold the onions."

"You got it."

Rory wasn't one of The Owl's regular customers. Not that the place didn't have good food. The main reason he'd stayed away was because the restaurant reeked of bad memories, which had always made enjoying his meal difficult. His father had come here frequently, and his grandfather, too. So had Lacey's father, Rick Morgan. This was where Norella Morgan worked at the time of her death.

After the tragedy, The Owl became known as the place where "they" met. "They" being Lacey's mother and Rory's father. The illegal card room that Jorgen had allowed had been exposed, and he'd almost lost the place. Rory wasn't quite sure why he didn't, but he suspected his grandfather, who owned the building and knew people in high places, had something to do with that.

Now, ten years later, the restaurant thrived. Jorgen had painted the walls, recovered the booths and stools, and put down new flooring. He'd quit doing the cooking and hired the French-trained cook.

The ghosts lingered, though—at least in Rory's mind they did.

He sipped his coffee, his thoughts jumping to the times he'd spent recently with Lacey, especially the ride they'd taken to their special spot. Although the evening had ended on a sour note, he'd enjoyed her companionship and especially the kiss they'd shared. For the last ten years she'd popped in and out of town, never staying more than a few days. They'd done no more than nod or say a curt "hello" when their paths crossed.

Why on this visit had they started talking to each other again? Okay, her assignment for Elton and then her car trouble necessitated communication. Still, a long-closed door had edged open. But did that mean anything? Or would the door slam shut once again when she finally returned to Boise?

Jorgen reappeared, coffee carafe in hand. He refilled Rory's cup. "You gettin' your classic car show organized?"

"I sure am. You gonna join us?"

"Thinkin' 'bout it." Jorgen poured himself a cup of coffee and took a sip. "If I can get that old Ford to run long enough to get there."

"Bring it by. We'll give it a tune-up."

They talked about the upcoming festival, and then, after a pause, Jorgen slanted him a look and said, "Lacey Morgan was here the other day."

"That right?"

"Never expected her to be hanging around town. She's usually in and out in a coupla days."

Rory nodded. "This time, she's helping her grandmother move into Riverview and doing a job for Elton at the newspaper."

"Right. But there's more to her hanging around than that."

Rory frowned. Was Jorgen referring to him and Lacey being seen around town together? No surprise that word had reached his ears. "What do you mean?" he asked, and braced himself for questions.

Jorgen turned away to replace the coffee carafe on the hot plate, and for a moment Rory thought he planned to ignore his question.

But then he faced Rory again, his brows knit into a frown. "Okay, she came around to interview me. Fine. I'm all for contributing to the newspaper Elton wants to publish. And so she and I talked about the history of the restaurant, the owl on the stump and the one over the front door. You know the stories."

He'd heard them often enough from his father and his grandfather. "I do. Great stories."

"But then she starts on the past, the time her mother worked here. Who Norella knew, who she was seen with." Indignation edged Jorgen's voice.

Rory sat up straight. "She's not going to write about my dad's murder, is she?"

Jorgen's mouth twisted into a grimace. "I don't know. But I don't want to drag out that stuff again. Nobody does. The town wants to forget that awful time. We've moved on."

"We have," Rory agreed. *Well, sort of. Except for the house.*

"Then why can't she leave it alone?"

"I don't know." Rory set his jaw. "But I intend to find out."

LACEY STOOD AT the doorway of City Hall's conference room and peered in. Today was a meeting of all those involved in planning the Silver River Days celebration. Not wanting to call attention to herself, when Elton had invited her to attend, she'd declined. He'd insisted, though, and so here she was. Her stomach churned at the thought of mingling with the townspeople. What would those who believed her father to be a murderer think about her involvement with their celebration?

The room was set up with a head table facing rows of folding chairs. The American flag and the Idaho flag occupied one corner. On a counter along one wall sat coffee urns and water pitchers, cups and glasses. The aroma of freshly brewed coffee filled the air. Some attendees stood chatting in small groups while others had already claimed seats.

A few people passed her on their way in,

but no one paid her any special attention. Still, she didn't want to be there. If she left now…

She turned to find Elton behind her.

"Hello, Lacey. Good timing. The meeting's just about to start."

"I can't stay, Elton. Gram—"

"—is playing bridge this afternoon. I know that because my sis-in-law's in the group. Come on, I need you to be here."

Her stomach still protesting, Lacey followed Elton into the room. They stopped at the coffee urn, and he poured them both mugs of coffee. Then he led them to the table.

"Can't I sit in the audience?" she asked.

"No, because you're part of the planning committee. We sit up front."

"I won't have to say anything, will I?"

"Not unless you want to. I'll introduce you, though. So be prepared at least to wave."

He pulled out a chair for her and one for himself, and they sat. A man Lacey didn't know approached, and while he and Elton conversed, she sipped her coffee and took out her tablet.

She looked up to see Rory enter the room and felt her heart skip a beat. She hadn't expected him to be here. And yet why not? As organizer of the classic car show, he, too, would be involved in the planning.

His gaze roved the room, zeroing in on her. He nodded and headed her way. She expected him to take one of the empty seats on her other side, but instead, he sat at the far end of the table. Not surprising, considering how their ride the other night had ended.

The tap of a gavel caught her attention. Marshall Tolliver, the committee's chairman, had stepped to the lectern.

"Meeting come to order, please," Marshall announced.

The crowd quieted.

"All stand for the Pledge of Allegiance."

Marshall raised both hands, palms up, much as a preacher might when leading his flock.

After they were seated again, he made a few introductory remarks and then asked for committee reports. Lacey focused on listening and taking notes. When Elton's turn came and he left her side to approach the lectern, her nerves knotted.

Elton cleared his throat and adjusted his bolo tie. "When Sara Hoskins had to give up writing the *Sentinel's* special edition, I didn't know who would take her place. Then Lacey

Morgan came to town to help her grand-mother move into Riverview. Most of you know Remy Whitfield…"

A few people put their heads together and whispered behind their hands. Lacey clenched her teeth and clutched her tablet. She glanced at the door, wishing more than ever that she could bolt.

Marshall tapped his gavel. "Quiet, please."

"We're lucky to have Lacey," Elton contin-ued when the audience quieted. "She writes for the Boise Historical Society and comes well qualified. I'm sure our special edition will be one of the highlights of our celebra-tion." He nodded at Lacey.

Lacey smiled and waved, but even with Elton as her champion, chose not to speak.

Elton said a few more words about the news-paper's special edition and then reclaimed his seat. "That wasn't so bad, was it?" he whis-pered to Lacey. Then he added, "Okay, so there were a few rude people. Don't pay them any mind."

"Thanks, Elton," Lacey said, grateful for his support.

After several more speakers, Rory stepped to the podium. "There's still time to enter the classic car show," he said. "So, spread the word."

Cora Trenton followed Rory. Lacey recalled her conversation with Del Ford about the Trentons. Cora's husband, George, who'd been the town's mayor some years ago, had died of a heart attack, and their only child, Calvin, passed away from a brain tumor.

Wearing a stylish blue pants suit and with every gray hair sprayed into place, Cora stepped to the lectern with her head held high.

"Plans are underway for the dedication of the Trenton building," she said. "We'll have a ribbon-cutting ceremony and speeches. Mayor Palmer will give the keynote, and a reception will follow."

Elton whispered to Lacey, "She'd rename the town after her family, if she could."

"And, the new Trenton Wing in the museum will be ready for a grand opening during our celebration," Cora went on. "Isn't that right, Del?" She looked at the museum's director, who also sat at the table.

Del nodded. "You betcha."

When the meeting ended, Elton stepped away to speak to Marshall Tolliver. No one paid Lacey any attention. Now would be a good time to leave.

Then her gaze landed on Cora Trenton. Cora was on her list to interview. Lacey really should use this opportunity to set up an appointment. Picking up her purse and tablet, she stood and approached the woman.

"Mrs. Trenton?"

Cora turned. "Yes? You wanted to speak to me?"

Her condescending tone grated. Lacey took a deep breath and in her best professional voice, said, "I'd like to interview you for the newspaper's special edition. When can we get together?"

"Ah, the newspaper." Cora's thin lips curved into a smile. "I do want to make sure our family is accurately represented. George's ancestors were pioneers here, you know. And I have some photos I'd like to see included. Hmm." She pressed a finger to her chin. "I suppose you could come to Wildwood."

Was that an invitation? Or not?

"Wherever you want to meet is fine."

"Wildwood would be best. Then I won't have to pack up the photos. I'm free tomorrow at two."

"So am I. I'll see you then."

"Do you need directions? Probably not. Everyone knows where Wildwood is."

"I'm sure I can find it."

Cora peered over Lacey's shoulder. "Oh, there's Harriet Horton. I must see her about the dedication. Harriet!" She stepped around Lacey and hurried off.

Intent on making a quick exit, Lacey pushed open the outside door and almost collided with someone. "Excuse me," she said and looked up.

Rory.

"I need to talk to you," he said.

His serious tone put her on alert. "About my car? Are you having trouble getting the part?"

"No, the part's been shipped. This is about something else." His brow wrinkled.

"Can it wait? I have an interview in fifteen minutes, and then Elton and I are meeting at the newspaper office." Lacey turned her steps toward the parking lot. She hoped he would wait. Her morning had been stressful enough.

Rory kept up with her. "I'll make it quick. I had lunch at The Owl…"

"Oh?"

"And Jorgen said you were asking questions about your mother and when she worked there."

Lacey's grip on her purse tightened. "And what if I was?"

"Why, Lacey? What are you trying to prove by digging up the past?"

She stopped on the path and waited until several people passed by. Taking a deep breath, she said, "If you must know, I intend to prove my father's innocence." There, she'd finally told him.

"What?" Rory stepped back and stared. "But that's impossible."

"I don't think so."

"I should have known you weren't—" He looked away.

"You thought I was staying in town because I wanted us to get back together? Oh, Rory, no. I mean, I—"

He raised a hand. "I get the picture. But you're wasting your time, and you'll upset a lot of people. Let it go." He moved to stand in front of her, blocking her way to the parking lot.

Pushing away the doubts he'd raised, she lifted her chin. "I need to go to my appointment now. Could you call me when my car is ready?"

Rory remained rooted to the spot a few

moments longer before standing aside. "Sure, sure. You'll be the first to know."

After conducting her interview, Lacey returned to the *Sentinel's* office. Learning from Clio that Elton was still out, she retreated down the hall. After her troublesome morning, her office offered a comforting protection. She settled into her chair and took out her tablet.

Her mind drifted to her confrontation with Rory. Yes, a confrontation. But, in a way, a good thing, for now her motive for staying in Silver River was out in the open. Neither of them would have any false expectations about their future.

CHAPTER ELEVEN

RORY TIGHTENED THE fan belt on Jorgen Miller's 1950 Ford and straightened up from under the hood. There, that ought to fix Jorgen's old car just fine and allow him to join their car rally. He pulled out a handkerchief and wiped the sweat from his forehead. Man, it was hot today. Grabbing a bottle of water, he stepped outside to catch the breeze.

A brown UPS truck pulled into the driveway and parked. After rummaging in the back, the uniformed driver, package and clipboard in hand, jumped to the ground.

Rory went to meet him. "Hey, Marty."

"Rory. How's it goin'?"

"Good, good." Rory took the package Marty held out. A glance at the return label confirmed it was the part for Lacey's car.

Marty offered a clipboard with a delivery confirmation for him to sign. "Next paycheck, I want to do some serious talking about that '64 Olds you fixed up."

Rory nodded as he signed his name. "It's at my place, waiting for you."

Marty left, and Rory returned to the garage. He set the package on the worktable and started an oil and lube job. The package still sat there, unopened, when Sam dropped by an hour later.

"Whatcha got here?" Sam pointed to the package. "The part for Lacey's car, I bet."

"Right." Rory tossed an empty oilcan into the trash.

"Gonna let her help you install it? Like old times?"

Rory shook his head. "Those times are best forgotten." He picked up a knife and slit the box's wrapping.

"I thought you two were getting reacquainted. I know you said your association was all business, but I gotta say, I wasn't buying it." Sam pulled a couple of wrenches from their hooks on the wall and tossed them onto the table. "These ought to work."

"Turns out you were right. She's got an agenda." He opened the box and removed the cylinder. He turned it over in his hands, checking to make sure it was in fact the part he ordered. It was.

"So how'd you find out?" Sam added a couple screwdrivers to the wrenches.

"Jorgen Miller told me that when she was interviewing him she also asked a lot of questions about when her mother worked at The Owl. When I asked her why, she said she plans to prove her father's innocence." Rory slammed his palm on the workbench. "Can you beat that? After all these years?"

"That's a long shot, all right."

"A long shot? It's impossible. A jury convicted him. It's a done deal."

"True enough. But he wouldn't be the first person to be sent up for a crime he didn't do."

"Okay, but he was guilty. You saw the trial."

"I did. And the evidence was convincing. But Lacey must have some reason for believing he was innocent. Maybe she's uncovered some new evidence."

Rory folded his arms. "I don't know. I didn't ask."

"Well, maybe you should."

After Sam left, Rory picked up the new switch assembly and the screwdrivers and wrenches. Time to get to work.

As he ducked under the Camaro's hood to disconnect the battery, part of his mind lingered on Sam's suggestion that he find out if Lacey had uncovered any evidence of her father's innocence.

But even if she did, would she trust him enough to share it?

LACEY DROVE THROUGH the open wrought-iron gate marking the entrance to Wildwood and continued along a winding road to a beautifully landscaped lawn. A circular driveway led to the home's front door. She parked and turned off the engine.

Instead of getting out, she sat there anticipating what she might face once she was admitted to the house. Although Cora was receptive to being interviewed about her family, of which she obviously was proud, what if she had heard about Lacey's interest in the past? Jorgen had told Rory, and perhaps the word had reached Cora's ears, as well. Lacey would have to be on guard while still pursuing her purpose.

She took a deep breath, grabbed her purse and stepped from the car. Overhead, branches of the tall pine trees swayed in the breeze, casting wavy shadows on the ground.

She gazed at the two-story house, an elegant structure with peaked roofs, bay windows and ivy climbing up the side. Then she approached the double doors and rang the doorbell. Inside, chimes resonated.

She expected a servant to open the door, but instead Cora appeared. Her long skirt and a wraparound top in shades of violet gave her a casual look, rather than the business-like demeanor she'd presented at yesterday's meeting.

"Come in, Lacey."

Cora's smile appeared genuine, and as Lacey stepped inside, some of her tension eased. Not all, though. There was something intimidating about Cora that kept her nerves thrumming.

Lacey turned her attention to the home's interior. The two-story-high ceiling, from which a clear glass chandelier hung, gave the place a spacious feeling. Directly ahead, a circular stairway climbed to a balcony with doors leading to second floor rooms.

"I want to show you some things first," Cora said, not wasting any time on small talk, "and then we'll have tea."

Cora led Lacey past the stairs and down two carpeted steps to a sunken living room. Floor-to-ceiling windows faced a stone patio and a swimming pool.

"Your home is lovely," Lacey remarked as she gazed around.

Cora nodded. "The original house was remodeled and renovated so many times over the years, by George's parents and his grandfather before them, that we finally decided to start over. Oscar Fields was our architect. You've heard of him?"

"Yes, I have. Didn't he design the governor's home?"

"Very good," Cora said. "Oscar and George went to school together. Another of George's schoolmates, Harry Leonard, became an artist. He painted this portrait of George." She gestured at the picture hanging over the stone fireplace.

Lacey stepped closer and gazed up at the painting. With his piercing blue eyes, unsmiling lips and rigid pose, George Trenton looked like a man who took himself and his job seriously. She'd bet he and his wife had made a good team.

"I remember when he was mayor," Lacey said.

"Two terms." Cora held up two fingers. "He would've had a third term, if he'd lived. He was the best mayor this town ever had.

But come, I have so much more to show you. We'll go upstairs."

The second-floor room they entered might have been one of the museum's rooms. Photographs lined the wall, shelves were stocked with books and glass cases displayed various objects.

"We'll start here with our family portrait." Cora pointed to a photograph of her and George and their son, Calvin, who appeared to be in his early twenties.

In contrast to his parents, who both stood tall and unsmiling, Calvin had a slouch and a sly grin on his face.

"This was taken just after Cal graduated from Yale," Cora said. "We sent him to the best schools. He was to carry on the family name, but that didn't happen." Her voice cracked, and she glanced away.

"I remember hearing about his illness a few years ago when I was in town visiting Gram."

"Glioblastoma," Cora said. "A brain tumor of the worst kind."

"I'm so sorry. He never married, did he?"

Cora shook her head. "No. I always hoped he would. I would've loved to have grandchildren. But he never found anyone suitable."

Lacey wondered who exactly was in charge of determining suitability, Cal or his mother. She'd put her money on Cora.

Cora moved on to the next photo. "Here, look at the rest of the Trentons. I've traced the line all the way back to the Mayflower. Such a prestigious family."

"Agnes and Jed Trenton came here by covered wagon, didn't they?" Lacey said.

Cora's eyebrows peaked. "Ah, you've done your homework."

"I have. Elton has quite a library, and so does the museum."

As they perused the glass display cases, Cora told Lacey more stories about the family. When they finished they went back downstairs. Cora settled Lacey on the patio and went to get their tea.

Lacey sat back in her chair, admiring the well-kept grounds and the view of the mountains in the distance. She congratulated herself on the way the interview was progressing. So far, although not overly friendly, Cora had not been hostile, either. But then, the focus had been on the Trentons, clearly a subject dear to her heart.

Cora returned with a tray holding a pitcher of

iced tea and ice-filled glasses. She set the tray on a glass-topped table and poured their tea.

"What about your own family?" Lacey asked, realizing she hadn't heard anything about Cora's origin.

Cora handed Lacey her tea. "My father died when I was seven. I had three brothers and two sisters. My mother worked hard to raise us and keep our family together."

"How did you meet George?"

Cora slipped into a chair across from Lacey. "He came into the place where I was working… You're not going to put that in your story, are you?"

"I hadn't thought that far ahead yet. I'm just gathering information now."

"Well, don't." Her voice was sharp. "I want the story you write to focus on the Trentons and how important they've been to this town. I want their legacy carried on."

"But you are a Trenton," Lacey pointed out.

Cora drew herself up. "Yes, I am. But how I came to be one isn't important."

Cora filled the rest of the interview with more stories about George and his side of the family. Lacey listened politely, asking questions and taking notes.

"I could go on all day," Cora said after a half hour had passed, "but I'm sure you have other things to do."

Taking the hint, Lacey nodded. "This assignment is keeping me busy."

Cora stood. "Del tells me you volunteered to help sort donations at the museum."

"Yes, I thought I would." Lacey turned off her tablet and tape recorder and tucked them into her purse.

"I'll be bringing in some things for the Trenton wing."

"I'll look forward to that." Seizing the opportunity, she added, "My grandmother might have some donations, too. Some things she's kept of my mother's."

She slanted Cora a glance, but she had turned away to pick up their empty glasses. Lacey waited a second or two and then added, "You knew my parents, didn't you?"

"Knew them? Hardly. We knew who they were, especially after…" The glasses clinked together as she set them on the tray.

Lacey squeezed her purse strap. "Oh. I thought Calvin also played cards at The Owl."

Cora's lips thinned. "Why would Calvin

be gambling at The Owl? Card rooms were illegal."

"I know, but Jorgen allowed the game, anyway. My mother worked there then."

"You're not planning to write anything about that…that unfortunate incident involving your father, are you?"

"For the special edition? No, although—"

Cora waved a hand, cutting her off. "Good. That was a time best forgotten. Focus on the people who've done good deeds, like—"

"—the Trentons," Lacey finished.

Cora smiled. "Yes, like the Trentons."

"WE'LL ADD YOUR grandmother's donations to the rest of the stuff that needs sorting." Del Ford put the cardboard box on the table in the museum's basement workroom. "Nice of her to think of us," he added.

Lacey set her carton next to his. "I'm pleased she was able to let go of at least some of her belongings."

"I remember you said she hangs on. How'd you convince her?"

"I pointed out that these treasures would be on display here where she could see them whenever she wanted. And that others could appreciate them, too."

He gave her an admiring glance. "Hey, pretty smart."

Lacey grinned. "It worked, anyway." She placed her hands on her hips and surveyed the worktable loaded with bags and boxes. "What's the procedure?"

"Log in each item." He pointed to the computer on a nearby table. "The clothing goes on those racks, the books on the shelves and small, miscellaneous items on the carts."

"Your committee is well organized."

"They are. But like I said, they've been busy with Silver River Days and haven't had time to do much sorting. I'm sure they'll appreciate your help."

"I'm happy to lend a hand."

"Okay, go for it. I'll be upstairs if you need me."

Del left, his footsteps echoing along the cement hallway.

Lacey turned her attention to the table. As she'd told Del, she was glad to help. She volunteered because she truly enjoyed anything that had to do with the past, considering herself a historian. Besides, she liked Del Ford.

He'd been helpful and accommodating when she interviewed him for the *Sentinel*, offering the museum's resources as well as his own knowledge.

So this was going to be fun. And maybe she'd find something that would help her own personal search, too.

"How're you doing, Lacey?"

"What?" Lacey looked up to see Del standing in the workroom doorway.

"Sorry. Didn't mean to startle you." He stepped into the room.

"That's okay. What time is it?" She checked her wristwatch. "Have I been here two hours already?"

"You have. Any treasures so far?"

"Lots. Look at this baby doll from the Cooper family." She held up the doll she'd been examining. "They donated several dolls, and this one dates back to the early 1900s. She's in great condition."

She patted the doll's painted-on brown hair, and then tipped her back and forth to show how her blue eyes opened and closed with the movement.

Del hitched up his trousers. "I bet that doll

belonged to Nettie. She was quite the lady. My great-grandfather courted her but lost out to Eddie Peabody. Eddie owned the hardware store, and she wanted to live in town and not on my ancestor's farm. Anyway, the Coopers have been generous to us."

Lacey smoothed the doll's pink cotton dress. "She would be perfect in the doll carriage upstairs."

"Good idea."

Lacey put down the doll and picked up a red chiffon dress. "This is from Cora Trenton. It's from the '20s."

"As you know, Cora's one of our big donors. If you have time, you could dress a couple mannequins in the clothes she brought and stick 'em in the Trenton wing. That should make her happy."

"I'll do that. Speaking of Cora, I went to Wildwood the other day to interview her for the paper's special edition. She has her own museum."

He nodded. "I've been there. Quite a place. It's too bad she's all alone now."

"I know how she feels. 'Course, I still have Gram, but everyone else in my family is gone."

He wrinkled his forehead. "What happened with your dad and Rory's dad was a bad scene. Shocked everybody. Al Jr. was well liked around town."

Lacey stiffened. "And my father wasn't."

"He had problems. 'Specially where money was concerned."

"Money matters to a lot of people." Lacey sorted through a pile of scarves, picked out one and held it against the dress. A perfect match. She laid the scarf aside.

"Sure, money's important, but most of us don't commit murder over it."

Lacey folded her arms and gave Del her full attention. "What do you mean? Was there a money issue between my father and Rory's father?"

"I think there was. I was in on some of those poker games with them in the back room at The Owl."

"Who else was there? Do you remember? I want to know everything I can about my father and his life, including his friends…"

"I wouldn't call any of the other players his friends. But, okay, let me think." He rubbed his chin and looked at the ceiling. "Besides Al and me, there was Hugh Bennett—"

"Sophie's husband?"

He shot her a glance. "Yes, why?"

"I'm surprised he gambled. Sophie says he's tight with his money."

"He is. But at that time, Sophie was bugging him to buy the B and B. They had money from the sale of their farm, but not enough."

"Did he win much?"

"Not that I ever saw. But I wasn't there for every game, mind you."

"Okay, please, go on. Who else?"

He ticked off the names on his fingers. "Clint Roche. He and Claire almost got divorced over his gambling, so I heard."

Claire Roche, the woman Lacey suspected of placing the pansies on the graves.

"Elton Watts was another player."

"Elton? That surprises me. I can't see him involved in anything illegal."

"That was when his wife was sick. He had doctor bills insurance didn't cover."

"I guess that would be a motivator. Any others?"

"Bonnie Rosen's husband, Tom. She was a waitress at The Owl, along with your mother. Still is. I suppose he came the closest to being

a friend of your dad's. They went fishing together."

"And Bonnie told me the two couples spent
time together, too."

"I wouldn't know about that, but like I
said, your dad had a temper. One time, he
accused Al Jr. of cheating. And he threat-
ened him."

"With a gun?"

"Well, not that we could see. But we all
knew he carried. Al won the pot that night,
too."

IN HER ROOM at Sophie's that evening, Lacey
took out her mother's journal. She'd been so
busy lately that she hadn't taken the time to
read any more entries. Kicking off her shoes
and plumping up the pillows, she settled on
the bed, opened the book and read more of
the entries, focusing on those made after
Norella began working at The Owl.

She found nothing about any gambling in
the restaurant's back room. Nor was there
any mention of the necklace, until she'd lost
it. Lacey still thought the necklace was the
key to everything. If only she could find out
what happened to it. Gram had speculated

that if Lacey's father took it, he'd pawned it. Suppose that were true. If so, what happened to the necklace after that? He wouldn't have had the opportunity to reclaim it after he was arrested.

If the police didn't know about the necklace's existence, they wouldn't have searched for it. So, if Rick had pawned the jewelry, it was long gone by now, either sold to someone else or perhaps melted down for the gold. Lacey grimaced. She hated to think of the beautiful keepsake being destroyed.

Pawnbrokers kept records of their customers, but for how long? Even if they were kept for ten years or more, privacy laws might protect the identity of the person who'd brought in the necklace.

Was attempting to find the necklace a waste of time? Or a chance to find the true killer?

Lacey slipped off the bed and took out Sophie's photo of her mother wearing the necklace. She took it and a sheet of paper and a pencil to the table, where she sat and drew a picture of the necklace.

Her mother had told her the piece was unique, having been designed for her grandmother by a jeweler who was a family friend.

Her parents had commissioned it for her twenty-first birthday. Amethyst was her birthstone. There were five of the stones, each in a gold filigree setting, suspended from a gold filigree chain.

Lacey finished the sketch and tucked it away in the journal. Maybe tomorrow she'd know what to do next.

CHAPTER TWELVE

"YOUR CAR'S READY to go," Rory told Lacey during their call the following day. She was in her office at the *Sentinel*, surrounded by books and journals and microfiche, deep in research for the newspaper's special edition. She and Rory hadn't spoken since their discussion after the committee meeting. She'd thought about him a lot, though, and was both pleased and dismayed by how good hearing his voice made her feel.

"Wonderful. I didn't even know you'd received the part."

"When it arrived, I went ahead and installed it. You weren't expecting to help, were you?"

"No, I'm busy with my job for Elton. I'm glad you could do it."

"I'll bring your car into town, and we can exchange cars. When's a good time?"

"I'm at the *Sentinel* now, but not for long. I have a couple of interviews this morning and then lunch with Gram. This afternoon I'm working at the museum."

"Busy lady. I'll catch up with you at the museum."

"I'll look for you."

Later, in the museum's sorting room, Lacey searched a box of vintage hats for just the right one to match the mannequin's tweed jacket. She finally chose one of gray felt and set it on the model's red-wigged head. She stepped back and surveyed the effect. No, the hat needed more color, maybe blue, to pick up the blue in the jacket.

She sighed, pulled off the hat and tossed it back in the box. She dug through the hats again but finally gave up. Her mind wasn't on her job today. Her appointment with Rory this afternoon kept her nerves on edge. Telling herself their meeting would be brief, with only the exchange of her Camaro for his loaner, hadn't done much good.

Half an hour later, Rory arrived.

"Del told me where to find you," he said, stepping into the room.

Lacey made a sweeping gesture. "This is where I've been hanging out."

"You've got company, I see." He nodded at the mannequins.

His teasing tone took the edge off her tension.

"Yeah, but they're not much for conversation."

He tipped back his head and laughed. "Maybe that's a good thing."

"Maybe."

"So, what does this have to do with your job for Elton?"

"Nothing. When Del mentioned that the ladies who usually sort were busy with the celebration, I volunteered to help out."

"That was nice of you."

"My motive was purely selfish. You know how I love history and old stuff."

"I know that very well," he said, his tone serious. He let a beat go by and then added, "Your car's out front, so whenever…"

Lacey waved a hand. "Now's good, so let's get our business over with."

The last words came out sharper than she'd intended.

He raised his eyebrows, but then nodded and turned to lead the way.

On the main floor, Del was showing visitors around the exhibits. He took a moment to exchange waves with Lacey and Rory before they went out the front door.

Outside, Lacey's gaze landed on her car sitting at the curb. The top was down and the white paint shone in the sunlight. "Wow, my car looks beautiful."

"Wynn Walker's gas station and car wash is down the hill from the shop. Only took a few minutes to fill up the tank and run her through the wash."

"I hope it runs as good as it looks."

"I guarantee it does. Want to try it out?"

"I'll take your word for it."

He grinned. "You trust me, huh?"

"Where cars are concerned."

His smile faded. "Lacey, I need to talk to you—about the other day at the committee meeting…"

"Oh, Rory, talking won't change anything. You have your opinions, and I have mine."

"I still need to talk to you. I'm not handing over your keys until that happens."

Lacey puffed her cheeks and exhaled. "You are a stubborn man."

"I am. You should know that."

Behind them, the museum door opened, and a group spilled out and headed down the ramp. As Lacey stepped aside to let them pass, she glanced over her shoulder and saw

Del peering out the window. He gave a sheep-ish grin, waved and ducked out of sight.

She turned back to Rory. "Well…I do need to write you a check. Where do you suggest we go?"

"How about Dugan's?" He pointed to the café across the street.

"It's so public. People will see us together there."

"It's way too late to worry about that."

DESPITE LACEY'S CONCERN, none of the customers paid her and Rory any attention when they entered the café and chose a table by the window. The waitress gave them a friendly but impersonal greeting and took their orders for coffee without further comment.

Lacey pulled her checkbook from her purse. "Let's take care of the bill first."

Rory took some papers from his shirt pocket, unfolded them and slid them across the table.

Lacey perused the invoice and then looked up. "I don't see any charge for labor."

He waved dismissively. "I threw that in."

"Why? I don't want your charity."

"Not charity. And no strings attached. Just something I wanted to do."

His firm tone told her arguing would be useless. She wrote out a check and handed it to him. "Thanks for fixing my car," she said with sincerity.

"You're welcome. It's what I do." A smile played across his lips.

"I know. And you do it very well."

Their coffees came, and they picked up their cups and drank. The silence between them grew awkward. Overhead, the ceiling fans hummed, and across the way a table of teenagers laughed and joked. The aroma of frying hamburgers drifted from the restaurant's kitchen.

Finally, Rory spoke. "Lacey, I need to apologize for what I said at the meeting the other day—"

"You don't have to—"

He raised a hand. "Hear me out, please. When Jorgen told me about the questions you asked him, I got angry. I want to put the past behind me. I want to move on."

"I do, too. I live every day with the belief that my father is considered a murderer."

"Is a murderer."

Lacey slapped her palm on the table. "See? That's where you and I part company."

"If you could only accept it—"

"This conversation is over." Lacey reached for her purse.

Rory laid a hand on her arm. "No, it's not. I'm not finished."

Lacey briefly closed her eyes. Her stomach churned. "All right. Say your piece and then let me go."

"Okay. If you're so determined to do this, then I want to help you."

Lacey dropped her jaw. "What?"

"You heard me. I want to help you."

"Why? You don't believe in my father's innocence. You just confirmed that a few minutes ago. Why would you want to get involved?"

"Because, although I don't agree with you, I understand what proving his innocence means to you. And if that's possible, I want to help you make it happen."

"Oh, Rory—"

"Look. Ten years ago, I abandoned you. We never spoke after that day."

"I know," she said, and pressed her stomach as the old pain surfaced.

"I should have stood by you."

"But I abandoned you, too. We both did what our families told us to do. We were young—"

"Eighteen is old enough to take a stand. I didn't." He looked out the window. "Maybe if I had, things between us would have turned out differently. But I want to move forward. You want to prove his innocence. Have you found anything that might do that?"

Lacey bit her lip. "I can't say."

Rory leaned forward. "Yes, you can. You can trust me. This is me, Rory, you're talking to." He pointed a thumb at his chest. "We used to tell each other everything."

"I know, but that was then, and this is now."

He leveled her a look. "I'm the same old Rory. You could trust me before, and you can trust me now."

Lacey took a deep breath. "All right, I did find something."

"Tell me. I've got time…"

She put out a hand. "No, Rory. Not now. This is a big step for me to take, and I need to be sure taking you into my confidence is the right thing to do. I'll let you know tomorrow."

Rory furrowed his brow. "But—"

"Don't push. Please."

"Okay, I'll wait until tomorrow. But don't forget, Lacey, I'm in this with you, whether you like it or not."

AT TEN O'CLOCK the following morning, Lacey's cell phone rang. She picked it up and checked the screen. Rory's number.

"Good morning, Rory," she said into the phone.

"I'm outside in the parking lot."

She couldn't help laughing. "Eager, are you?"

"You bet. Didn't know whether or not to come in."

"I'll be out in a few minutes."

"Good. Have you made your decision?"

Her gaze strayed to her mother's journal lying on the round table. She'd spent a restless night making up her mind.

"You'll find out in a few minutes," she said.

"I know you're choosing in my favor."

"Such confidence."

"I do have confidence in you, Lacey. See you in a few minutes."

Lacey switched off the phone. She stared at the journal a moment more and then walked over, picked it up and tucked it into her purse.

In the parking lot, he had the passenger door to his truck open, and she climbed onto the seat beside him.

"Where do you want to go?" he asked.

"Let's sit here while I tell you what I have. When you hear, you may not want to go anywhere."

Half an hour later, after sharing her mother's journal and the drawing she'd made of the necklace, Lacey sat back and asked, "So, what do you think?"

Rory tapped his fingers on the steering wheel. "You may be on to something. The necklace was never mentioned in the investigation or the trial."

"That's just it. What happened to it?"

"You're sure my father was returning the necklace to your mother on the day he was shot?"

"No, because she didn't name the person." Lacey rifled the journal's pages. "But your father was the one who came, so I'm assuming he was bringing the necklace to her."

"And you think checking the pawnshops in the area might give us the answer? After ten years?"

She shrugged. "I know it's a long shot, but it's all I have."

"What if you find out your father was the one who pawned it—if in fact it was pawned?"

Lacey lifted her chin. "That isn't going to

happen. But you don't have to get involved in this—"

"Like I told you yesterday, I am involved. And if you want to check out the pawnshops, I'll go with you. John can manage the shop today."

"All right. I'm ready now." Lacey consulted her list. "We might as well start with the one in town—Mel's Pawnshop."

Rory drove to the entrance to the highway, but instead of turning left, toward town, he turned right.

"Where are you going?" Lacey asked. "Mel's is in the other direction."

"I know. But there's something I want to do first."

"What's that?" Judging by the set of his jaw, the mission was a serious one.

"I want to go by the farmhouse."

"Why would you want to do that when you hate it being there? I'd think you'd want to avoid it whenever possible."

"Huh. Pretty hard to do when the house is right off the highway. No, I want to go there—with you. We haven't been there together since that day."

"We haven't done anything together since

that day. Except this trip. But, no, I can't…
We can't." She clenched her hands in her lap.

He placed his hand briefly over hers. "Just
for a few minutes. You have my word we'll
leave whenever you want. But, please, give
it a try."

Since they were already on the way, Lacey
gave up her protests. But her stomach churned,
and the moment she glimpsed the house's roof
peeking through the willow trees a lump rose
in her throat.

"I remember that day like it was yesterday," Rory said as he turned onto the road
leading to the farm. "I brought you home
from school, as usual. We saw the flashing
lights from the highway, and when we drove
down this road the sheriff's deputy stopped
us—"

"—and said there'd been a sh-shooting,"
Lacey said, her voice quavering. "When we
asked who, he said he didn't know."

"But then I spotted my father's sports car
behind the house, on the driveway leading
to the barn. Right over there." Rory slowed
and pointed to the overgrown grass shielding
the old driveway. "At first, I thought I must
be mistaken. Why would Dad be here? But

I knew the car was his. No one else in town drove a red Corvette."

"I can never come here without seeing your dad's car in my mind's eye," Lacey said.

Rory drove on, past the willow trees, to the house's front door, where he pulled to a stop. Lacey leaned around him to look out his window. The place appeared the same as always—walkway overgrown with weeds, sagging screen door, peeling paint. Lonely and sad.

She let a few moments pass and then said, "Okay, we've seen it. Now we can leave…"

"I want to go inside."

Lacey leaned back and shook her head. "No, no—not possible."

"Why not? I'm betting you have a key."

"I do," she admitted. "They're always on my key ring when I'm in town. Gram often wants me to bring her here, and sometimes I come by myself. We don't go in, but I carry the keys, just in case."

"Then you can give them to me now." He turned and held out his hand. "I'm going in. You can stay here."

Lacey stared at his open palm and then raised her gaze to his face. His eyes were slightly narrowed and his mouth was set. The look that meant there was no use arguing with him. Better to let him have his way and get it over with.

"All right, but I'll go, too." She opened her purse and pulled out her key ring.

They got out of the truck and, Rory in the lead, went up the weed-infested walk. At the door, he stepped aside.

Lacey stared at the screen door, full of holes and rotting wood, and swallowed hard. "Are you sure you want to do this?"

He nodded. "I'm sure."

He held open the screen while she unlocked the door, and they stepped inside. The air smelled of mold and dust and made her choke. She let her eyes adjust to the dim light of rooms long hidden behind drawn blinds and then stepped into the living room, where an overstuffed chair with torn upholstery, a scarred end table and a couple of straight chairs were the only remnants of occupancy.

They went down a hall to the kitchen. Sunshine peeking through a torn blind splashed liquid gold across the floor, an incongruous bit of cheer in the otherwise dark room. A hole gaped where the refrigerator once stood. The dishwasher and stove were still in place, the stove with the oven door hanging open.

Lacey went over and shut the door, although she wasn't sure why. No one used the oven anymore, nor would they ever again.

Back in the hallway, they approached the stairs leading to the second floor. Rory stopped and looked up toward the landing.

"No," Lacey said. "You don't want to go up there."

"I do. I want to see the room where it happened. All these years, I've only imagined what the room was like. Now I want to be there. Stay here, if you'd like. Or wait in the truck."

"Okay, if you're going up, I'll go."

Gulping down a shaky breath, she climbed the steps, Rory behind her. When they reached the second floor, Lacey paused again and then started down the hallway. She barely glanced at the other rooms, including the one that had been hers, but headed straight for the last bedroom.

"This was my parents' room."

She opened the door, and they walked in.

The room was as she remembered it. A brick fireplace with an arched opening and a raised hearth dominated one wall. The furniture included a double bed, with only a bare mattress on its frame, an oak dresser with a mirror, an armchair covered in a faded blue fabric and a small, round table.

Two walls had windows, one overlooking the side yard, the other the backyard. Lacey pointed to the window facing the backyard. "The shots were fired out this window."

His face grim, Rory crossed to the window and looked out. "My father was on his way to his car when he was shot."

"That's what came out in the trial."

"The trial. All we know about that day is from the trial, isn't it?"

"Except for what I read in the journal."

Rory turned away from the window and began to pace. "Let's piece it together, what we heard at the trial and what you found out from the journal."

Lacey took a deep breath. "Okay. My mother lost her necklace at work."

"And others knew this."

"Yes, she asked people to look for it. Then she came down with a bad cold. She stayed home from work for several days. Sometime during that time, someone—I'm assuming it was your father—told her he found the necklace. That's from the journal."

"Told her? How? Called her on the phone?"

Lacey dug into her purse and took out the

book. She opened it and flipped through the pages. "Here it is. There's just a line in place of the name." She showed him and then read aloud: "'The one who found my necklace wants to bring it to me here at home.'"

"So, according to the journal, he came here to give her the necklace."

"Yes, but no one knew that. It wasn't mentioned in the trial. The prosecutor contended your father came here because he and my mother were having an affair—or about to start one. Evidence proved he was in this room. His fingerprints were found on the door and on the bedpost."

Lacey closed the journal. "Supposedly, my father came home and saw your father's car parked behind the house. He flipped out, grabbed his rifle and came upstairs. He found your father and my mother here in the bedroom.

"Your father managed to escape. Maybe Rick ordered him out. We don't know. Whatever, Al Jr. left, and on his way to his car, my father shot at him. Three times. Two shots missed him, but the third—"

She swallowed and cast a glance at Rory. His face was pale. "We shouldn't be doing this. It's hard on you, too."

Rory passed a hand over his forehead. "No, I'm okay. Keep going. Then what happened?"

"The prosecutor contended that my father went after my mother, who was in bed. She managed to get out of bed but got tangled in the sheets. Either he pushed her or she fell on her own and hit her head on the fireplace's raised hearth." Lacey walked over to the fireplace, gazed down at the brick hearth and shuddered.

"She went into a coma," Rory said dully.

"And never woke up. My grandmother finally had her taken off life support." Tears burned Lacey's eyes, and she blinked hard to hold them back.

"Your father said he was at Forksville, right?"

Lacey hugged her arms and turned away from the fireplace. "Yes, he was at a job site there, which was verified. He came home around lunchtime to see if a check he was expecting had come in the mail. It had. Gram testified that the mailman arrived just as she was leaving to go to her bridge game. She put the mail, including the check, on the table in the entry. The check was gone when she came home."

"She's the one who found my father, wasn't she?"

"Uh-huh. When she drove around behind the house to park her car, she saw him lying in the driveway." Lacey walked to the window again. She looked out at the spot and swallowed hard.

"Go on, please," Rory said in a strained voice.

Lacey heaved a breath. "Gram came upstairs and found my mother unconscious here on the floor. She called the aid car and the police."

"As I recall, the police picked up your father in Forksville."

"Right. He admitted coming home to get the check. He said he came upstairs to look in on my mother. She was asleep, and he didn't wake her. He left and went back to Forksville. His boss confirmed he was there."

"And the murder weapon?"

"My father's rifle. The police found it over there." She pointed to the doorway. "Most of the fingerprints had been wiped off, but what remained were his." Her lips trembled, and a tear rolled down her cheek. She looked up and met Rory's bleak eyes.

"Oh, Lacey, honey."

Rory put his arms around her and gathered her close. Unable to resist any longer, she let the tears freely flow. As he lowered his head to pull her tighter, his cheek, wet with his own tears, brushed hers, which made her cry all the harder.

CHAPTER THIRTEEN

SITTING NEXT TO Rory in his truck, Lacey leaned back against the seat and took a deep breath. They hadn't spoken since they'd ended their embrace and left the house.

She glanced at him. He stared straight ahead out the windshield, as though lost in his thoughts.

"Rory?" she said tentatively.

He turned and their eyes met. His were bleak.

"Are you glad we talked about what we know of that night?"

He gave a harsh laugh. "Not sure *glad* is the right word, but, yeah, I needed to do that. Needed it for a long time. Hard on both of us, though."

"Yes, it was." She looked away for a moment but then turned back to him and straightened her shoulders. "But do you see now that the murderer could have been someone else? Someone who took the necklace?"

"And pawned it because it was incriminating evidence?"

"Only it really wasn't, because no one knew Al was returning it to my mother."

Rory slowly shook his head. "I gotta say, that's a stretch."

She shrugged, palms up. "It's all I have right now. But if you don't want to waste your time on this—"

"I said I wanted to help you, and I meant it, Lacey."

At his sharp tone, she lowered her hands and bit her lip. "Sorry I'm so touchy. I want so badly for my theory to be true."

"I know you do," he said, his voice softer. "And if your father didn't kill mine, I sure want to know who did. So, okay, onward to the pawnshops to see what we can find."

FIFTEEN MINUTES LATER, they pulled up in front of Mel's Pawnshop, located on Sandstone Avenue between Goldilock's Hair Salon and Ben's Variety Store. A bell on the door announced their arrival. A tall, skinny man stood behind a counter arranging wristwatches in a tray. He looked up, his gaze landing first on Lacey and then on Rory.

"Well, hello, Rory. You bring me a new customer?"

"Maybe. This is Lacey Morgan." He took Lacey's hand and led them to the counter.

Mel frowned. "Morgan…as in Rick Morgan?"

Lacey nodded. "My father." Anticipating his negative response, she tensed.

"You don't live here anymore." Mel idly fingered one of the watches.

"I moved to Boise, but I come back to visit. My grandmother still lives here. Remylon Whitfield."

"I seen you around town now and then. And sure, I know the Whitfields. My dad and Jay went to school together. So, what can I do for ya?"

"Lacey's trying to track down a piece of jewelry." Rory leaned one elbow on the counter. "A family heirloom."

"That right?" Mel put the watch in the tray and shoved it to one side.

"I don't have a photo, but here's a drawing." Lacey took a copy of the drawing from her purse and handed it to Mel.

She held her breath while he studied the drawing.

"Hmm, looks like a nice piece," he said.

"Amethysts, it says here." He tapped the paper with his forefinger.

"Yes, and the gold is twenty-four karat."

Mel looked up and shrugged. "I dunno. I might have seen it. Might not. A lotta stuff comes through here. How long ago you figure it was lost?"

"Ten years ago."

"Right around the time of the shooting." He cast an apologetic look at Rory. "Sorry about that, Rory. You father was a good man."

Rory acknowledged the comment with a solemn nod. "Could you check your records for the necklace?"

Mel shook his head. "Don't keep records that far back. Even if we did and I found one on this here, I couldn't tell you who brought it in. Privacy law, you know."

"But say the seller was Lacey's father. He's dead now."

Mel nodded. "Died in prison, I heard."

"So would the privacy law still apply?" Lacey asked.

"That's a good question and one I can't answer."

Rory straightened and propped his hands

on his hips. "Sure appreciate it if you could help us out. This is really important to Lacey."

"The necklace belonged to my great-grandmother, Jay's mother," Lacey said. "I'd really like to have it back."

"Yeah, yeah, I know. I hear that story all the time." Mel folded his long, thin arms close to his chest.

"I'm sure you do," Rory said. "But isn't there something you can tell us? You knew Lacey's father, didn't you?"

"Sure, I knew him. He worked for the outfit that remodeled Goldie's next door." He pointed a thumb in that direction.

"Did you know him as a customer?" Lacey asked, encouraged that they might be getting somewhere.

He gave her a long look and then said, "Okay, yeah, he was a customer. I'll tell you that much."

Mel's admission didn't surprise Lacey. Money slipped through Rick's fingers like sand. "But you don't remember if he brought in the necklace."

Mel's frown deepened as he looked from Lacey to Rory. "What's going on here? I get the feeling you two are digging for more than the necklace. You're asking questions like you're the cops or something. What gives?"

Rory stepped back and raised both hands. "We're just hoping to find Lacey's necklace, that's all."

"Thought it was your grandmother's."

"Originally, it was. It was passed down to my mother, and eventually was supposed to be mine."

"So, how did it get lost?"

"I don't know. It just disappeared," Lacey said.

"Sorry, I can't help you." Mel held the drawing out to Lacey.

"Please, keep it," she said. "And I'd appreciate a call if you remember anything you think would help me."

Mel shrugged his narrow shoulders. "Okay, but don't hold your breath waitin'."

"Do you think he knew more than he was letting on?" Lacey asked Rory when they were back on the street.

"Hard to say." Rory took her elbow and guided her to his truck parked at the curb. "He's been in the business a long time, and he's undoubtedly used to being questioned. Can't blame him for protecting himself. And, he did finally admit your father was a customer."

"I still felt he was prejudiced against me."

"Really? I didn't notice anything. Do you think you might be overreacting?"

Lacey stopped walking and pulled away. "No, I don't think I'm overreacting. You don't understand, and you never will. Maybe I should do this alone."

He wrinkled his brow. "Please, don't get upset. That was a dumb remark."

She turned her head away so that he wouldn't see the tears burning her eyes. She hated being vulnerable. That was why she was on this search. One reason, anyway. Once she proved her father's innocence, she would no longer be vulnerable. She would be able to hold up her head wherever she went.

"Lacey…" Rory lightly touched her cheek with his forefinger. "I'm sorry."

She took a deep breath and mustered a tremulous smile. "Okay, apology accepted."

"Good. Now, what's next on our list?"

For the next couple of hours, they traveled the highway to neighboring towns, locating the pawnshops on Lacey's list. No one knew anything about the necklace. If they did, they didn't admit it. At noon, Rory and

Lacey ate lunch at a roadside café. At two, as they emerged from yet another shop with no luck, Lacey said, "Maybe we should give up for today. You probably need to get back to work."

"No. Like I said, John's in charge. Besides, there's only one more shop on your list."

"I could come back tomorrow by myself."

He placed his hand over hers. "I want to do this with you. Don't you get it yet?"

She sighed and briefly closed her eyes. "All right. I do appreciate your help."

Lacey spoke the truth. Despite their upsetting visit to the house, without Rory by her side, today's search would have been lonely indeed. Accepting his help had been a difficult decision, but so far, she was glad to have him by her side.

The last pawnshop was in Milton, a town ten miles up the highway from Silver River. While the proprietor finished helping a man choose a guitar from a shelf of musical instruments, Lacey and Rory wandered around. Like all the other stores they'd visited, shelves lined the walls, filled with everything from cameras to musical instruments to computers and other electronic equipment. Glass cases displayed smaller items such as coins, watches and jewelry.

At last, the customer left with a guitar slung over his shoulder and a big grin on his face.

The proprietor approached Rory and Lacey. She looked to be in her fifties, with dyed red hair, dangling turquoise earrings and a ring on nearly every finger.

"Howdy, folks. I'm Midge. What can I do you for today?"

Her friendly tone encouraged Lacey, and she stepped up to the counter and launched into a speech that, having been given several times today, rolled readily off her tongue.

Then she handed Midge the sketch of the necklace.

Midge studied the drawing, tracing the outline with her forefinger.

Lacy held her breath.

Rory paced.

Midge looked up. "I sure do remember this piece."

Expecting to hear the usual "no," Lacey stared. "You do?"

"You betcha. I'd never seen anything like it."

"Do you remember who brought it in?"

Midge shook her head. "I wasn't here that day. My father was here by himself. But when I came in the next day and saw this pretty thing, I knew I wanted it."

Hope flared in Lacey's chest. "Do you have the necklace?"

"Oh, no. Someone claimed it the day after that."

"The same person who brought it in?" Rory asked.

"I don't know. Again, I wasn't here."

"Do you have records?" Lacey asked. "Or can we speak to your father?"

"I wish." Midge's mouth turned down. "Dad died five years ago. I run the place by myself now, 'cept for my son, who helps out now and then. And no records, either. Not that far back."

"Is there anything else you can tell us about the necklace?" Rory asked. "Anything at all."

"Nothing I can think of at the moment." Midge shook her head. "I'm sorry. I can understand why you'd like to have that beautiful necklace again."

"If you think of something, my number's on the drawing." Lacey pointed to the paper Midge held.

"You betcha. I'll call you first thing."

"So how do you feel now?" Rory asked Lacey when they were on their way back to Silver River.

"That I'm on the right track. Just like I thought, the real murderer pawned the necklace."

"Okay, let's say you're right. If he—or she—pawned the necklace to get rid of it as evidence, why would they go back a couple days later and get it?"

Lacey idly gazed at the mountains in the distance, where low clouds touched their peaks. "Maybe someone else reclaimed it."

"Wouldn't they need to have the ticket?"

"I'd think so."

"So, are two people involved? Or just one?" Rory braked for a stop sign at an intersection and then turned onto the highway. A couple cars in the fast lane whizzed by.

"We don't know."

They rode in silence the rest of the way to Sophie's. Rory pulled into the parking lot and turned to Lacey. "It's been quite a day."

"It has." Lacey grasped her purse and prepared to get out of the truck. "And I do appreciate your help. But tell me, did being in the farmhouse change your mind about wanting to destroy it?"

"No," he said without hesitation. "If anything, I'm more determined than ever. And if you were honest with me—or with yourself—you'd admit that's what you want, too."

IN HER ROOM at Sophie's, Lacey kicked off her shoes and plopped down on her bed. She was exhausted, physically and emotionally. The events of the day, especially her and Rory's trip to the farmhouse, had taken a toll. If anyone had told her she and Rory would ever visit the scene of the crime together, she would have declared him crazy. Rory's continued determination to destroy the house disappointed her, though, and she still needed to protect Gram.

Learning her mother's necklace had been pawned, as she'd suspected, told her she was on the right track in proving her father's innocence. All in all, the day had been successful.

Perhaps most astonishing of all was Rory's participation. Despite his wanting the house destroyed, she believed his offer to help her was sincere. And the emotion they'd shared made her feel close to him, much like the old days, when they were in love and planning to spend the rest of their lives together.

Not that she expected them to ever be together again. No, that wasn't possible.

She opened her purse and took out the journal. She rifled through the pages, thinking of her mother and the hours she'd spent writing about her life. Discovering the journal had allowed Lacey to begin a quest she'd long dreamed about but had never until this trip believed was something she could actually do. "Thank you, Mom," she whispered as she closed the book and laid it on the nightstand.

Would her search lead to the outcome she hoped for? she wondered as she prepared for bed. Or would it lead only to disaster? And what was the next step to take?

"*S-T-A-B-L-E.*" GRAM PLACED each Scrabble tile on the board. "Stable. I'm out." She high-fived her partner, Hal Jacobson.

"All r-i-ght," Hal said. "That makes us the winners."

Lacey and the other onlookers gathered in Riverview's activity room cheered. The losing couple made mock sour faces. "We'll win the next one," the man said.

While the crowd drifted away, Lacey stood and approached the game table. "Good job, you two."

"She's quite a player."

A smile lit Hal's round face. The sleeves of his white shirt were rolled up to the elbows, and suspenders held up his brown trousers. Lacey judged him to be near Gram's age.

Gram scooped up a handful of tiles and dropped them into a cloth bag. "I always thought bridge was my game, but now I'm beginning to wonder."

When the tiles and board were stowed away on a shelf with other games, Hal said, "How 'bout we all have a drink?" He nodded to the open doorway leading to the café, where residents enjoyed snacks and drinks between meals.

Lacey had a mind to excuse herself and leave the two alone, but Hal's invitation included her, and she was curious about him. Gram had mentioned Hal a few days ago, adding that he had asked her to be his Scrabble tournament partner.

"A drink sounds like a good idea." Lacey approached Gram's wheelchair, intending to grasp the handles.

Hal reached the chair first. "I can take her."

"Well…sure." Lacey stepped away and let Hal take over.

In the café, Hal settled them at one of the round, glass-topped tables and then went off to get their drinks. He soon returned with iced tea for Lacey and Gram and a cup of coffee for himself. They talked about the Scrabble game for a few minutes, and then Lacey turned to Hal. "Gram says you're new here at Riverview, too."

Hal nodded. "I'm from Kettle Falls. I stayed in my house for a few months after my wife, Lucille, passed, but my kids, who'd moved here to Silver River, wanted me to live here, too."

"How many children do you have?"

"Two daughters and four grands. I don't see 'em much, though. They're a busy bunch."

"I didn't see Lacey much, either," Gram put in, "till I had my accident."

Hal laughed. "So that's what it takes to get attention from your family."

"Well, I wouldn't recommend it." Gram sighed. "I'll be sooo glad when I can walk again."

"You were stepping pretty lively this morning on your walker."

Gram widened her eyes. "You were watching?"

"I happened down the hallway where you and your therapist were. You two were busy talking when I slipped by."

"Hmm, I'll have to show off a little if I have an audience."

Hal put out a warning hand. "Now, now, Remy. No overdoing it. You'll be walking soon enough."

After they finished their drinks and decided to leave, Hal insisted on wheeling Remy to her apartment. They said good-night at the door.

"I'll look for you at breakfast," Hal said.

When the door closed behind them, Lacey took over and wheeled Gram into the living room. "For a minute there, I thought he was going to insist on tucking you in," she teased.

"Lacey! Such talk." Gram's cheeks turned as pink as her blouse.

"Seriously, he's a very nice man. I'm glad you have him for a friend."

"Scrabble partner," Remy corrected.

"Mmm-hmm." Lacey hid a smile.

Later, when she was on her way to Sophie's to settle in for the night, Lacey thought about Gram and her new friend. Hal appeared to be truly interested in her grandmother, and she seemed to return the interest. Lacey hoped their friendship would flourish and grow. At least they didn't have a painful past to deal with, like she and Rory had.

CHAPTER FOURTEEN

LACEY STEPPED FROM the *Sentinel* office into the sunshine of another summer day, on her way to interview the woman who was organizing the Silver River Days' children's activities. She was almost finished with her interviews. One of her articles had already appeared in the newspaper, and the commemorative issue was well underway, too.

As she headed down the sidewalk, she heard someone call her name. Turning, she saw Toni Young, her long ponytail swinging as she hurried toward her. Toni was an old high school classmate, one of the many she'd lost touch with after leaving town.

Toni skidded to a stop and pressed a hand to her chest as she caught her breath. "Glad I ran into you, Lacey. I wanted to call, but don't have your number."

"Nice to see you, Toni. You're looking good."

Toni laughed and patted her stomach.

"Thanks. Finally got my figure back after being pregnant again."

"You have two children now, right?"

"Right. Loni's our oldest. She's seven. And Skylar's three. Anyway, I heard you were staying in town longer this trip—seems I always miss you when you're in and out so fast. Jim and I are having our annual barbecue this coming Saturday and would love for you to come."

"Why, I, ah, that's really nice of you, but—"

"It's not all couples, if that's what you're worried about. Kris is coming and some other singles we know. It is a family occasion, too, though, and kids will be running around. But do come. It'll be a good opportunity for you to catch up with some of the old high school gang."

Toni kept her gaze on Lacey, hardly giving her time to think. Finally, she said, "Well... okay, yes, I'll come."

"Great!"

Toni gave Lacey all the particulars before they parted company. Lacey continued on to her interview, her mind whirling. Although Toni's invitation took her by surprise, she'd agreed because when she thought about it, she would like to see how her classmates had fared. Kris kept her up-to-date on important news, but secondhand was never as good as firsthand. And, maybe she and Kris could go to the party together.

As the day wore on, though, Lacey began to have misgivings. Would everyone be as welcoming as Toni? Some of her classmates, especially those who were friends with Rory, had sided with him at the time of the murder. Would they have forgotten old loyalties by now?

Thinking of Rory brought to mind the possibility that he would be at the party, too. He and Jim Young had been on the high school football team together, and according to Kris, their friendship had endured. Well, so what if he was? It wasn't as though they weren't speaking to each other. But what if he brought someone? How would she feel about seeing him with another woman? *Perfectly fine*, she told herself. *Perfectly fine*.

That evening, settled for the night in her room at Sophie's, Lacey picked up her phone intending to call Kris to see if they could ride together to the Youngs' party. Before she could speed dial her friend's number, she received an incoming call. Rory. What did he want? She was tempted to let it go to voice mail, but in the end answered it.

"Heard you're coming to the Youngs' barbecue Saturday," he said.

"The news is out already? Wow."

He chuckled. "Jim and I played racquet ball at the health club after work today."

"Ah. Who won?"

"I did, but I didn't call to brag or to spread that news around. I called to say I'm going to the party, too, and I'll pick you up on my way."

"What? You think I'm going to be out on the road hitchhiking?"

"Noooo, I'm giving you door-to-door service. Be ready by five thirty. They're early partiers."

"I know what time the party starts, but I don't think our going together is a good idea. Thanks, though." Her tone turned serious.

"Wait. Why not?"

"Because people might think—"

"We're together again? It's already out that we've been seen together. They'll think it strange if I don't bring you."

"But—"

"It's just a ride, Lacey. Once we get there,

you can ignore me for the rest of the evening."

Yeah, like that would happen.

She thought about telling him she'd already arranged to go with Kris, but that wouldn't be true, and she wasn't in the habit of lying, even little white ones.

"I'll look for you on Sophie's front porch, five thirty."

"I might not be there."

"You will be."

She ended the call, not knowing whether to be furious or amused. Maybe a little of both. Next, she called Kris and explained the situation. "I'd rather go with you," she added.

"I'm not going, after all. I got my dates mixed up, and Lucas has a birthday party to go to that night. But you and Rory will do fine. You'll have a good time. I'm glad you're going."

"Thanks. Wish I had your enthusiasm, but I'll give it my best."

LYING ON HIS back on the trolley on wheels, better known as "the creeper," Rory rolled out from underneath the Honda, where he'd been installing new brake pads. He stood and, with one foot, pushed the creeper out of the way and then rubbed the back of his neck, working out the kinks.

Hearing the sound of a car's engine, he looked around to see Sam's truck pull to a stop in the driveway. Sam got out and came into the garage.

"Hey, buddy," Rory said. "I think you spend more time here than you do in your office. What's the matter? Out of court cases to try?"

"Huh. Not likely. Just checking up on you, see how you're doing. You look like you're in pain. Back bothering you again?"

Rory arched his back. "Nah. I just get a little stiff, sometimes."

Sam grinned. "I've got a remedy for that." He went to the open shelves lining the back wall and grabbed a football. "Here you go." He lobbed the ball over the Honda's hood.

Rory jumped back and raised his arms for the catch, but not fast enough. The ball hit him in the stomach and dropped to the floor. It bounced a few times before he scooped it up.

"You're out of practice," Sam said. "C'mon, let's hit the field."

"Like that will solve all my problems."

Sam shrugged. "Can't hurt."

"Okay, okay." Rory turned toward the office, where John stood behind the counter. "Catch the phone, will you, John? I'm out back, if you need me."

"No problem." John gave a salute.

Rory followed Sam around the corner of the building to the backyard. The breeze coming off the mountains stirred the sun-dried grass and the leaves on the trees. He took a deep breath, feeling better already.

They spread out, facing each other, and Sam tossed him the ball. This time, Rory caught it, fingers spread, gripping the ball the way he'd learned when he was on the Silver River High team.

The ball felt good in his hands. And for a second he didn't want to let it go. But Sam waited to receive the pass. Rory lobbed him the ball. Sam caught it and tossed it back. For the next few minutes, Rory concentrated on catching and returning Sam's passes.

Finally, Sam cupped his hands around his mouth and yelled, "Time out."

Holding the ball against his chest, Rory jogged to the picnic table. "Who's out of condition now?" he teased as he flopped down on the bench.

Sam sank onto the bench beside him. He

pulled out a handkerchief and wiped his fore-head. "Not me. It's you I'm worried about."

They sat there for a few minutes catching their breaths, and then Rory said, "Remember the time we played Milton High and the score was tied right up to the last five seconds?"

"How could I forget the highlight of my career?" Sam laughed. "'Course I had a little help from my friends in making that touch-down."

"The crowd went wild." Rory leaned back and propped his elbows on the table.

"And the party afterward was awesome."

They lapsed into silence. Finally, Rory said, "It seemed so simple then."

Sam snorted. "Simple? Winning a game?"

"No. Our futures. Me and Lacey. You and Kristal. Jax and Sharone. What happened?"

"Life happened. Things don't always work out according to our plans. How're you and Lacey doing, by the way?"

"We went to the farmhouse together."

Sam raised his eyebrows. "*The* farmhouse? As in Whitfields'? That must've been tough. Why'd you do a thing like that?"

Rory shrugged. "I'm not sure. I wanted to go there, and I wanted to go there with her."

"So, did your experience change anything?"

"Not that I'm certain of. I still want to tear the place down."

"And she doesn't."

"No. She's determined to protect her grand-mother."

"So, did your search of the pawnshops turn up anything?"

Rory gave him a summary of his and Lacey's visits to the pawnshops, including the last one where Midge recognized the necklace.

"No kidding? Maybe there's something to Lacey's theory, after all."

"Maybe. I still think it's a long shot, though. But then, after Jim told me they'd invited her to their barbecue, I called her and said I'd pick her up. Am I crazy or what?"

"What'd she say?"

"We're going. By the way, will you be there?"

"Nah, I'm out of town this weekend. One of my law school buddies is getting married, so I'm off to Boise."

"Married. Wonder what that's like."

Sam laughed. "Not like winning a football game, I'll bet."

"Or a court case."

"You got that right. Come on, we've rested

long enough. We'll toss a few more and then I gotta take off."

Fifteen minutes later, Rory was back in the shop and Sam's truck had disappeared down the hill. John stepped from the office and handed him a slip of paper. "Miz Simmons wants you to call her about her van. The one she uses for her day care."

"Thanks, John. I'm on it." He pulled out his cell phone and punched in Alice Simmons's number.

CHAPTER FIFTEEN

LACEY STOOD ON the porch at Sophie's, waiting for Rory to pick her up to go to the Youngs' barbecue. Her misgivings about accepting both the Youngs' and Rory's invitations had haunted her all week. For the past ten years, she'd kept herself aloof when it came to her old high school acquaintances, and now here she was, showing up at their party. Wouldn't they wonder why Rory, of all people, had brought her? The worst worry of all, of course, was that someone would mention her past.

Too late to change her mind now, though. She was stuck.

She expected Rory to be driving his truck, but instead he arrived in a shiny red Chevrolet Impala. He pulled to a stop, jumped out and hurried around to open the passenger door.

He looked up to the porch. "Your chariot awaits, madam." He made a sweeping gesture.

Taking a deep breath, Lacey went down the porch stairs and climbed into the seat. "Another beautiful car. What year is it?"

"A '78. Not quite a classic, but a gem nonetheless."

She waited until he was behind the wheel again and then asked, "You must have quite a collection now."

"I have a few. Ties up a chunk of change, but like I told you, I want to open a classic car museum." Rory guided the car back down the driveway, earning admiring looks from a couple strolling the walkway.

"Any idea where that will be?" she asked.

"Not at the moment."

"With you and your grandfather in the property business, I'd think you'd have several options."

"Maybe. But I'm not ready yet, anyway. Juggling two jobs is about all I can handle right now."

After driving several miles down the highway, Rory turned off and drove through stone pillars marking the entrance to Mountain View Estates, and after winding around several streets, they reached the Youngs' mini-ranch. Rory pulled up alongside other vehicles parked at the side of the house. Their arrival immediately caught the attention of the guests gathered in the backyard.

"Hey," someone called. "Rory's here."

The men swarmed around the Impala like bees to honey, and Lacey had barely exchanged greetings with them and exited the car before the hood was up and the car's innards were under scrutiny. Despite her nervousness, she had to smile.

Toni followed in the men's wake. Today, instead of a ponytail, her hair was loose, almost reaching her waist, and blue shorts showed off her long legs.

"Crazy, aren't they?" Toni nodded at the men gathered around the Impala. "But leave them to their fun and come meet the other women."

Lacey fell into step beside Toni as she led them to the backyard, which had a barn painted a traditional red, a garden where cornstalks waved in the breeze and beyond that a grove of apple trees. "What a nice place you have," she said.

"We love it. Plenty of space to raise kids and only a few miles from Jim's job. He works for Bennett's Building Supply, you know. Or maybe you didn't."

"No, I didn't. I've lost track of...so many people here." Suddenly awkward, she looked away.

"Hey, my memory isn't so great, either. We were in at least one class together, though, weren't we?"

"We were. English, I think."

Toni snapped her fingers. "Okay, now I remember. Mrs. Doakes and the Friday essay. You always wrote about a famous historical person."

"And you always wrote about those fabulous vacations your family took."

Toni laughed. "My mom's a travel agent, and she always had a deal for us."

They reached a stone patio, where the women guests sat in a semicircle. Two children sat on their mothers' laps while several older children played with a ball nearby. A black Lab and a dachshund lay on the grass, idly watching the action. The aroma of barbecue drifted from the barbecue pit at the patio's far end.

Toni poured Lacey a glass of wine from a keg sitting on a table, and then brought her to the group. "Most of you remember Lacey Morgan. Have a seat, Lacey." She indicated an empty chair.

Lacey sat and waved as she looked around at the familiar faces. "Hi, everyone."

"Hi, Lacey."

"Good to see you."

"Long time, Lacey."

"I don't think you know Beth Markey." Toni nodded toward a dark-haired woman. "Her husband, George, works with Jim at Bennett's."

Beth and Lacey greeted each other, and the women resumed their discussion. Not surprisingly, talk centered on their children.

"Keesha will be in preschool this fall," Beth said with a sigh. "Seems like only yesterday we were bringing her home from the hospital."

"They do grow up fast." Lorna Phillips bounced her baby boy on her knee. "But she'll love it. Tyler likes school so much he wants to stay there all day."

Beth frowned. "Keesha's clingy. She hasn't adjusted to our move here."

"Give her time," Sara North put in.

Lacey nodded and smiled politely, all the while feeling very much the outsider. She glanced over her shoulder to see that the men had migrated from the Impala to the barbecue pit. Bottles of beer in hand, they gathered around chef Jim, wearing a long white apron and traditional chef's hat.

"What about you, Lacey?"

Startled to hear her name, Lacey turned back to the group. Beth had spoken, and she was looking at Lacey with raised eyebrows.

"Me?" Lacey pressed a hand to her chest.

"Do you have children?"

"No, I don't. Too busy working, I guess."

"We're old high school friends," Toni explained. "After graduation, Lacey went off to college in Boise and stayed there to work."

"So you didn't want to live in a small town anymore?" Beth said.

The other women exchanged glances. Then all eyes focused on Lacey.

Lacey twisted her fingers together. "I, ah, the historical society there made me an offer I couldn't refuse."

"Time to eat!" Jim called from the barbecue pit.

Toni jumped up. "I'd better get the salads on the table."

"I'll help," Sara North said.

"Me, too," Tammy Schulz put in.

Glad for the interruption, Lacey expelled a relieved breath. No telling where that conversation would have led.

When all the food had been brought to the buffet table, Rory caught up with Lacey to fill their plates. The guests sat at one long table, with the children at card tables nearby. Tails wagging, the dogs roamed, looking for handouts.

"Are you doing okay?" Rory asked Lacey as he slipped onto the bench beside her.

"I'm fine."

Except for the tense moments when Beth had questioned her motive for leaving Silver River, Lacey was surviving better than she'd expected.

"These ribs are the best, Jim," one of the men said.

"Thanks." Jim stood and took a bow.

Toni grinned at her husband. "I keep telling him he should quit selling lumber and open a restaurant."

The talk jumped from subject to subject, finally landing on Silver River Days. Anna Thompson looked down the table at Lacey and asked, "How's your job with the newspaper going, Lacey?"

Lacey finished a bite of potato salad. "It's interesting. I do love writing about history."

Beth's brow wrinkled. "You have a job here, Lacey? I thought you worked in Boise."

"The one here is temporary," Lacey explained. "I'm helping our newspaper's editor with publicity for Silver River Days."

Anna's husband, Len, spoke up. "You ought to move back, Lacey. What happened ten years ago wasn't your fault. Or Rory's."

Anna elbowed him. "Len!"

Len dropped his fork and raised both hands. "Sorry!"

The others exchanged looks.

Rory cleared his throat. "Who's going to join me in the car show?" he asked, and much to Lacey's relief, the conversation took a new turn.

After dinner, Lacey helped the other women clean up and put away the leftover food. As she entered the kitchen with a bowl of potato salad, she saw Beth and Anna at the sink, rinsing dishes. Their conversation floated to her ears:

"—her father killed Rory's father," Anna was saying. "Shot him in the back in cold blood. Can you imagine?"

"And he's with her now?" Beth pressed her fingers to her lips.

Anna looked around and saw Lacey. Her face turned red. "Oh, Lacey, I'm sorry. Beth being new and all—"

Lacey placed the bowl on the counter. "It's all right, Anna. But, no, Rory and I aren't together. He just gave me a ride to the party." Then she wheeled around and walked out.

Lacey kept going all the way across the lawn to the apple trees, where she stood gazing at the distant mountains. Her heart was pounding, and her face felt hot. She took a few deep breaths and concentrated on the calm, peaceful scene before her. Presently, she calmed down, too. A glance over her shoulder told her no one had noticed her absence. The women were either occupied with their children or helping to clean up, and the men were following Jim into the barn to inspect something there. Still, she waited a few minutes more before returning to the party.

LATER, ON THE way home, after Lacey had not uttered a word, Rory said, "Len has a big mouth, but he didn't mean to hurt you."

"He said what everyone was thinking. Everyone except Beth and her husband. And now she knows the story. When I was helping to put the food away, I walked into the kitchen while Anna was filling her in."

"I'm sorry you had to hear their gossip."

"My past will always be the proverbial 'elephant in the room.'"

"Do you have to let it be?"

His voice had an impatient edge she found irritating. "I can't imagine you like being reminded, either."

"No, I don't, but I want to move on."

Lacey folded her arms. "I'll be able to move on when I prove my father's innocence."

"So, we're back to that again. Well, for me, it'll be when that house is no longer standing."

Neither spoke. A mile or so went by, and then Rory turned off the road.

"Now where are we going?" she asked, not bothering to hide her annoyance.

"Thought we'd take a little side trip."

Rory followed the road until they reached the river and a park with picnic tables and benches. He pulled into a space reserved for vehicles. "I need to stretch my legs. How about a walk by the river?"

"I don't know—" Lacey gazed out the window at the water flowing by, a soft silver in the shadows from trees on the opposite bank.

"C'mon, a walk'll do us both good."

He got out of the truck, came around to her side and opened the door. Held out his hand.

She looked at his hand and then raised her gaze to his face. He smiled and said softly, "You know you want to."

She sighed and put her hand in his. "Okay, but not for long."

They stepped onto the path along the bank. The warm air carried the scents of earth and trees and the wildflowers growing nearby. On the other side of the water, the roofs of farmhouses and barns peeked through the cottonwood trees.

"This *is* pleasant," she conceded after they'd strolled for a few minutes. "I've always loved the river."

"So have I. Hey, there's a bench. We'll sit for a few minutes."

"I thought you wanted to stretch your legs," she teased.

"I do. But right now, I want to take a break."

When they were seated, he placed his arm casually along the back of the bench. They talked some more, and before she knew it, he'd lowered his arm to grasp her shoulder and pull her close.

"Rory—"

"Just relax, okay? Holding you feels so good."

With a sigh, she nestled against him. Being

close to him did feel good, more than she wanted to admit.

"Lacey…"

She half turned, just in time for him to gently grasp her chin, lift her face to his and kiss her lips.

With a sigh, Lacey returned his kiss. Being in his arms felt wonderful. After a while, though, she came to her senses and drew back. "Oh, Rory… We shouldn't… We can't…"

"Yes, we can. We're still good together, Lace."

"No, no. I shouldn't have let you help me search for the necklace. I shouldn't have come with you tonight."

"But you did, and here we are. And you want this as much as I do."

"What I want doesn't matter. It's what I have to do while I'm here in Silver River that's important. But right now, I need to go—" she'd almost said "home" before she remembered she didn't have a home here anymore "—to Sophie's," she finished.

LACEY AND RORY both were quiet on the drive to the B and B. Lacey searched her mind for something to say that would end the evening on, if not a positive, at least a neutral note.

At last, Rory turned onto the lamp-lighted driveway leading to the old Victorian. As they passed the guests' parking lot, Lacey automatically glanced at the spot where she knew her car was parked. Yes, there it was. Then she noticed a zigzagging light. A flashlight? Another guest checking on his car? Or a prowler?

"Rory, I think someone's over there by my car." She pointed.

Rory slowed the Impala and craned his neck. "Yeah, I see a light. We'll check it out." He turned his car down the row.

Keeping her eyes on the moving light, Lacey soon discerned a shadowy figure in front of her Camaro. "There *is* someone by my car."

Rory braked to a stop. He switched off the ignition and the lights. "You stay here. I'll find out what's going on."

"I'm coming, too."

"No, it could be dangerous. Stay here." He opened his door and jumped out.

Lacey climbed from the car and followed him.

A dark-clothed figure knelt by Lacey's car. "Hey, you!" Rory yelled.

The person looked up, froze and then

jumped up and ran. Rory followed, with Lacey close behind. They trailed him down another row of cars, but then he disappeared. They searched the rest of the parking lot and then the area beyond without finding any sign of the intruder. Finally, Rory stopped, planted his hands on his hips and shook his head. "We might as well give up. He got away."

Lacey pressed a hand to her chest and blew out a breath. "Probably out to the highway by now."

Rory nodded. "We'll check your car, see if he did any damage."

They traced their steps back to Lacey's car. "He slashed the tire." Rory pointed to the right rear tire.

Sure enough, the tire was flat and had a long gash in the side. They examined the other three tires and found all of them cut and flat.

Lacey pressed her lips together in anger. She'd had her car back for only a few days and now this.

"Anything else?" Rory said.

Lacey pulled on the front door handle. It didn't budge. "Still locked."

Further examination showed no broken windows and no tears in the top.

"At least, he didn't get inside," she said, and then looked around. "Did he slash just my tires, or others, too?"

An inspection of the cars parked nearby revealed none had their tires—or anything else—destroyed.

"Maybe he was just getting started," Lacey said. "And he happened to pick on me first."

"Maybe. Whatever, we'd better call the police."

"WE'VE NEVER HAD a problem with vandalism," Sophie told the guests assembled in the B and B's parlor the following morning.

"Were hers the only tires slashed?" A middle-aged man nodded at Lacey.

The others turned in her direction.

Lacey shifted in her chair, uncomfortable under everyone's scrutiny. But she didn't blame Sophie for calling this meeting. Some of the guests had witnessed the arrival of the police last night, and word had spread that there'd been trouble in the parking lot.

"As far as we know, Lacey's tires were the only ones," Sophie said from her post by the fireplace. "Has anyone else found any damage or evidence of a break-in?" Her gaze wandered over the group.

People shook their heads and murmured, "No."

Another man turned to Lacey. "Do you know who might have done that to your car?"

"No, I don't," Lacey said. Which was true. If she had been specifically targeted, though, it might have something to do with her inquiries around town, but of course she wasn't about to bring up that subject with strangers.

"I don't know if I want to stay here if it's not safe," a woman said.

A few others nodded and murmured their agreement.

"The police are investigating." Sophie fingered the blue scarf around her neck. "And Hugh is looking into hiring a security guard as we speak. But if anyone wants to cancel their stay, I'll certainly understand."

The guests exchanged looks, but no one accepted Sophie's offer. After answering a few more questions, Sophie said, "We'll let you know if we hear any more. And now, please, help yourself to coffee and tea and raspberry scones in the dining room."

As the guests left for the dining room, Sophie approached Lacey. "Can I talk to you for a minute?"

"Sure."

Sophie's smile faded to a frown. "Maybe what happened to your tires has something to do with all the questions you've been asking about what happened ten years ago."

"That occurred to me, too. But if so, then I'm on to something."

Sophie propped her hands on her hips. "Honey, Al Jr.'s gone, your father's gone and so is your mother. I've asked you before, and I'll ask you again. Why can't you leave the past alone?"

"Because justice was not served. My father was innocent."

"As far as I'm concerned, justice *was* served. You're the only one who won't accept that."

Lacey spread her hands. "But, Sophie, if someone did target my car as a warning, doesn't that indicate they're scared I'll prove my father wasn't the shooter, after all? That someone else was?"

Sophie sighed and folded her arms. "Okay, you make a point. But why put yourself—and our guests—in danger?"

Lacey sobered. "You're right. I don't want to do that. I'll leave. I'll pack up right now and be out within the hour." She started for the stairs.

Sophie hurried to her side. "Oh, hon, no. I

love having you here, and I want you to stay. I'm worried enough about you now, and if you left, I'd really worry. Please, stay."

Just then, Rory came in. "Your tires are all changed, Lacey. You're good to go now."

"Thanks, Rory," Lacey said. "I'll get the insurance forms filled out."

He nodded and held up his dirt-smudged hands. "Can you steer me to a place where I can wash up?"

"Down the hall and on the right." Sophie pointed the way. "And then there's coffee and scones in the dining room."

"That'll hit the spot." Rory grinned and headed down the hall.

A few minutes later, Lacey and Rory sat at a corner table in the dining room. "How did everyone respond to Sophie's talk?" Rory asked.

"They're concerned, but I think bringing everyone together and stopping rumors helped. I told her I'd move, though."

He raised his eyebrows. "Move where?"

She shrugged. "To one of the motels outside of town."

"You could stay with me." His eyes sparkled with teasing.

"Oh, now there's a good idea." Lacey didn't

bother to hide her sarcasm. "Like the town isn't talking enough about us already."

"Let them talk."

Lacey sipped her coffee. "Rory, you can't be serious about me staying with you."

He looked down at his hands gripping his cup. "I might be."

Lacey kept her tone light. "Thanks for the offer, but there's really no need. Sophie doesn't want me to leave."

He looked up. "Oh? What does she want?"

"For me to give up my search."

"Sophie's concerned about you. And maybe you should be, too."

"No. There's no proof I was targeted. But if I was, and the vandalism does have to do with the murder, then I'm all the more determined to continue my search for the true killer."

"DID YOU HAVE a good time at the party last night?" Gram asked Lacey.

"The party was…nice." Lacey kept her gaze averted as she rinsed their teacups in the kitchen sink. After the meeting at Sophie's, she'd spent the rest of the day at the *Sentinel's* office working on her projects. Then, as she did most days, she stopped at Riverview to check on her grandmother.

"Nice?" Gram snorted. "What does that mean?"

"Seeing some of the kids from high school was interesting. Well, they're not kids anymore. Now they have children of their own."

A knock sounded on the front door.

"That must be Mitzi," Gram said, "coming by to go to dinner."

"Not Hal?" Lacey asked with a smirk.

Gram shook her head. "He's visiting his daughters and grands. I'll see him tomorrow for Scrabble."

Lacey hung up the dish towel and went to the door. As Gram speculated, her neighbor Mitzi stood there, both hands propped on her cane.

"Hello, Lacey, time for dinner. According to the menu, we're having roast beef." She peered around Lacey. "You ready, Remy?"

"Soon's I run a comb through my hair." Gram wheeled herself toward the bathroom.

"You're coming, too, Lacey?" Mitzi asked.

"I, ah…"

"She's coming," Gram called from the bathroom.

"Guess I am," Lacey said with a laugh.

In the dining room, they joined two other women, Annabel and Edna, whom Lacey had met on another occasion. After they settled at a table for four, covered with a white tablecloth and with a centerpiece of fresh chrysanthemums, Mitzi turned to Lacey. "Did you get your tires fixed okay?"

Lacey stopped unfolding her napkin and stared at Mitzi. She'd expected word to spread, but not this fast.

"Tires?" Gram frowned. "What about your tires?"

Annabel and Edna leaned forward to listen.

"My tires were slashed last night at Sophie's," Lacey said. "But how did you hear about it, Mitzi?"

Mitzi sipped her water. "My cousin and her husband from Spokane are staying there. They phoned me this morning."

"Did they catch who did it?" Annabel wrinkled her brow and looked from Mitzi to Lacey.

Lacey finished spreading her napkin on her lap. "Not that I know of."

"Were your tires the only ones?" Gram asked.

"Apparently so."

Gram's sharp eyes bored into Lacey. "So you were targeted."

Lacey laid a hand on Gram's arm. "We don't know that for sure. Rory and I saw someone with a flashlight and chased him, but he got away. He may have just been getting started and planned to do more."

"I wonder if our cars are safe here at Riverview?" Edna sat back and gripped her elbows.

A waitress served their meals, plates of roast beef, mashed potatoes and green beans, and conversation ceased while they turned their attention to eating.

"The roast is wonderful," Annabel said after a few minutes. "I love the mushroom gravy."

"I always added a bit of sour cream to my gravies," Edna said.

"I sometimes made mine with beef broth," Mitzi put in.

While the other women continued talking about recipes, Gram turned to Lacey. "You never said one word about your tires. When were you going to tell me? Or were you?" she added in an accusing tone.

Lacey sighed. "I was. Eventually. I should

have known this town's gossip mill would spread the word."

"I'm glad for the gossip. We need to know what goes on so we can protect ourselves."

Lacey spread butter on her sourdough roll. "I suppose there's something to that. But, please, don't worry, Gram. There's no proof the vandal was targeting me."

She wanted Gram to believe that—even if she didn't believe it herself.

CHAPTER SIXTEEN

IN HER OFFICE at the *Sentinel*, Lacey searched through a box of old photos, looking for pictures to illustrate the commemorative newspaper. The text was shaping up nicely, but needed to be enlivened with more visual content.

Elton came in and peered over her shoulder. "Find anything useful?"

"A few." She pointed to a stack of pictures she'd set aside. "Right now, I'm looking for some of The Owl Restaurant."

"Should be some there, as I recall." He slipped into the empty chair beside her and held out a sheet of paper. "But take a look at this. Clio just finished writing up Police Beat."

Lacey took the paper and read the weekly list. "I see my tire slashing here. Is that why you're showing it to me?"

"Just thought you might be interested. Doesn't actually name you, though."

"Like everybody in town doesn't already know it was my car. I don't know why you bother publishing a newspaper," she added, only half teasing.

"We get the facts straight. Sometimes the grapevine doesn't."

"That's a point," she conceded. She turned back to the photos again, and one caught her eye. "Oh, here's what I'm looking for." She picked up the picture and held it out to Elton.

Elton adjusted his glasses and peered at the photo. "Yes, this was taken shortly after Jorgen bought the place. Look at that grin on his face." He pointed to the smiling man standing with feet spread and hands planted on his hips. "He was proud as all get-out."

"He still is. The place has an interesting history—including the card club Jorgen had in the back room."

Elton raised his eyebrows. "He told you about that?"

"Well, no. When I was at the museum, Del talked about the games that went on at The Owl."

Elton nodded. "Probably not a guy in town who didn't sit in at one time or another."

She raised an eyebrow. "Even you?"

"Even me. I never had much luck at cards,

though." Elton set the photo on top of the stack.

"How did Jorgen get away with it? Gambling in this state was illegal by then."

"Paid somebody to look the other way. Happens all the time. There's always somebody willing to take a bribe if you look hard enough."

"Del said that one night when my father was there, he accused Al Jr. of cheating. Maybe you were there that night?" She idly straightened the pile of photos and then looked up at him.

Elton met her gaze with a stern one of his own. "Lacey, let it be, will you? Let your poor dad rest in peace."

"I can't, Elton."

"No, not can't. Won't. Look, we hired you in good faith to write articles for our celebration, not to dig up old bones. Stop trying to prove your father's innocence. No one cares."

"I care."

Elton frowned and pressed his lips together. "I sure don't like what I'm hearing around town about the questions you're asking."

Lacey's shoulders tensed. "Do you want

me to quit the project?" she asked in a low voice.

"No, especially not at this late date. You're a darn good writer and a good historian. Your work so far is right on target, and I expect the finished work will be just as good."

Some of her tension seeped away. "Thanks, Elton. I appreciate the confidence."

"So, are we straight on everything?"

"Sorry, I can't make any promises."

Elton blew out an exasperated breath. "Well, at least you're honest." He stood, turned to go and then stopped. "Oh, and just so we don't need to have this conversation again, at one time or another, your dad accused everyone of cheating—even me."

"THEY CAUGHT THE guy who slashed your tires," Rory said over the phone two days later.

Lacey sat at the round table in her room at Sophie's, working on her computer. "Caught the guy? Who is he?"

"A teenaged kid from town."

"How'd they catch him?"

"Long story. Needs to be told in person. Good excuse for getting together, huh?" He laughed.

"Tonight?" She looked at her wristwatch.

Nearly seven. She'd had dinner with Gram, as usual, but then, needing to work, had begged off a game of Scrabble and come to her room.

"It's early yet."

"Well...okay. I'll meet you somewhere."

"Nah. I'll come pick you up."

She waited outside the B and B in the gathering dusk, the air still warm, expecting him to arrive in one of his classic cars. Instead, he pulled up in his truck. "Dugan's is still open," he said as she climbed in beside him. "It's a good place to talk."

At the diner, they sat in the same booth they'd occupied before. Instead of the teenaged waitress, though, an older woman served. She knew Rory, and they exchanged a few remarks as she poured their coffee.

After she left, Rory said to Lacey, "I suppose you'll worry now about Alma spreading gossip about us."

Lacey threw up her hands. "No, I'm giving up. I honestly don't know why Elton Watts bothers to report the news when everyone else does it for him."

"One of the hazards of small-town living. But okay, down to business. The kid's name is Alfie Mullen. He's fourteen years old. Lives with his mother and a couple sibs in the housing development by the fertilizer plant."

Lacey sipped her coffee. "So how do they know he's the one?"

"He finally confessed. Maybe I should start at the beginning. He went to Johnson's Electronics, picked out an expensive game and flashed a wad of money. Told Johnson he got a job but wouldn't say where."

Rory sat back and folded his arms. "Johnson told his cop buddy, Dave, who knows the family. Alfie's been in trouble before at school, stealing a kid's lunch money. His teachers have been trying to get him into a Big Brothers program, but no luck so far.

"So, Dave talks to Alfie's mom, who's worried because Alfie won't tell her where he got the money. He wanted to give her some, but she refused unless he told her where it came from. Bottom line, they do an intervention with Alfie, and he finally confesses."

"Confesses what?"

"That somebody paid him to slash your tires."

Lacey gripped her coffee cup and leaned forward. "Who?"

Rory shrugged. "That's the big question.

He doesn't know who. A guy he'd never seen before offered him a hundred dollars if he'd slash the tires of a white Camaro convertible, parked at Sophie's B and B."

Lacey frowned. "So, what will happen to him?"

"Don't know. Dave—or someone else from the PD—will contact you."

Lacey sat back. "Well, mystery solved."

"Not quite. We still don't know who hired Alfie. But we might know why."

"Because he—or she—doesn't like me stirring up the past."

"That'd be my guess."

"So that tells me I'm right about my father's innocence."

"No, it doesn't," Rory said in a reproving tone. "The person behind the tire vandalism might have a reason that has nothing to do with what your father did."

Lacey sighed. They were back to the same old argument. "I don't care what you say, I'll keep believing my father is innocent."

Rory folded his arms and heaved a breath. "O-kay, let's say you're right. Your father did not shoot my father. Someone else did. And you're willing to risk your own life to prove that?"

Lacey stared him in the eye. "I guess I am."

"I know you believe in your father's innocence," he said with studied patience, "and I'm willing to concede it's possible. But we haven't found any proof. Give up your obsession, so we can move on."

"I can't."

"You keep saying that. But I believe you could if you really wanted to."

"You don't understand."

"I'm trying my best. I wish I could convince you to see my point of view."

"You might as well stop trying, Rory, because even though I might be discouraged, I'm not giving up."

DRIVING ALONG THE highway on Saturday night, lost in thought, Rory was a mile down the road before he realized he'd missed the turnoff. He wheeled around and drove back, looking for the road leading to his grandfather's house. Yep, there it was, coming up around the bend.

Temptation to bypass the road again nudged him. He didn't really want to go to A.J.'s party. He'd rather spend the time with Lacey. Since she'd returned to town and they'd been together, the chains of the past that held them prisoner seemed to have slipped away—at least for him. Judging by her response to his kisses, she felt the same way.

Still, although he'd suggested they move forward, she was adamant in her refusal to focus on anything but proving her father's innocence.

Rory followed the winding road through the pine trees and scrub brush and finally reached A.J.'s house, a sprawling rambler sheltered by maple trees. The thirty acres included a barn, not for horses or livestock, but storage for golf carts and a couple of boats. A nearby shed housed an older-model pickup, a tractor and, last time he'd looked, an old, abandoned Pontiac.

Rory parked next to some other vehicles, climbed from the truck and entered the backyard. This year, A.J.'s Silver River Days party was bigger than ever. At least a hundred guests filled the brick patio and well-tended lawn. In addition to A.J.'s employees, there were also those he did business with—or hoped to.

"Well, Rory! We've been waiting for you." Leetha Parsons, all decked out in a frilly blouse, denim skirt, red boots and cowboy hat, hurried toward him.

Leetha and A.J.'s wife, Beryl, had been best friends. The passing of Beryl and then Leetha's husband, Edgar, drew her and A.J. together. She made a good hostess when A.J. needed one, and he provided the same for her.

Rory had always liked Leetha. He had good memories of her and Beryl taking him and Leetha's grandchildren, Bud and Sara, on picnics in City Park and to the movies at the Grand Theater.

"Hey, Leetha, how are you?" Rory opened his arms to receive her hug.

"Can't complain." She drew back and looked him up and down. "You're not in costume. Go grab a hat." She pointed to a stack of cowboy hats on a nearby table."

"Okay, if it'll make you happy."

She gave a wry grin. "It'll make A.J. happy."

Rory grabbed a black Stetson and plopped it on his head.

"See you later, hon. I need to check on the food situation." Leetha waved him toward the patio and then went into the house.

Rory looked around. A.J. stood at the barbecue pit, looking over the chef's shoulder. Probably giving him pointers. Nobody knew barbecue better than his grandfather, and why he'd bothered to hire a chef was a mystery.

The aroma of the sizzling ribs filled the air, and Rory's stomach rumbled. Lunch seemed a long time ago. He grabbed a beer from an ice-filled tub and a handful of chips from a basket on the buffet table.

"Hey, Rory." Stuart MacKenzie stepped to Rory's side.

"Evenin', Stu."

Stu wore a leather vest over a plaid shirt, a belt with a big silver buckle, cowboy boots and, of course, a Stetson. But then Stuart jumped through all of A.J.'s hoops.

And yet, Rory held no grudge against his grandfather's loyal employee. He liked Stuart and felt Stuart liked him, too.

"This is Hank Ebberly." Stu nodded to the man with him. "He's from Milton."

"Ah, Ebberly Construction." Rory shifted his beer so they could shake hands.

"Been lookin' at property for a subdivision," Hank said.

"I showed him the Whitfield farm," Stu said.

"Which we don't own yet," Rory reminded him.

"Right. But A.J. says you're about to close the deal."

"No date's been set. In the meantime, what about those fifty acres up on Sagebrush Hill?"

Stu looked at Hank.

Hank shrugged. "No harm in looking. But I sure do like what I saw at the Whitfield farm."

After Stu and Hank moved on, A.J. caught up with him, clapped him on the back and introduced him to some people he hadn't met. He sampled the ribs and salads and switched to coffee.

Finally, deciding he'd stayed long enough, he left the party.

On the way to his truck, Rory passed the outbuildings. As his gaze landed on the shed, he thought about the old car stored inside. He glanced over his shoulder. No one was in sight. A quick look wouldn't hurt.

The shed's door was unlocked. He turned the handle and went in, leaving the door ajar. The interior was dark and shadowy, but he could make out the object of his visit. The blue paint had faded, rust spots showed here and there and the tires were flat, but the '61 Dodge Polara still had character and style. He ran his fingers along the fin on the back fender and then stuck his head in the open driver's-side window. Steering wheel and gearshift looked okay, but what about the engine? Maybe he'd take a quick look…

"Thought you were in a hurry to leave."

Rory backed out of the car's window and, without facing his grandfather, said, "Just thought I'd see if you still had this baby."

When there was no reply, Rory turned and saw the sad look on A.J.'s face. In an instant the look vanished, replaced with a frown directed at Rory.

"Why don't you let me fix this up for you?" Rory said.

"And give you one more excuse to stay away from the office? I don't think so."

"But what good is this car doing sitting here? You could be driving it, enjoying it."

"Maybe I like it just the way it is."

"I remember Grandma telling me you gave her this car for her birthday."

The pained look crossed A.J.'s face again. "I don't need you to remind me of the car's history," he said, his tone gruff. "I need you to stop fooling around with cars and put your efforts into the business."

Rory folded his arms and shook his head. "You never change, do you?"

A.J. set his jaw. "I see no reason to."

"And I see no reason to change the way I am. So, I guess we're stuck, as usual."

Later, on the way home at last, Rory fumed. More often than not, he and his grandfather were at odds with each other. The Dodge was an old conflict. Something else that rankled was A.J.'s assuming the Whitfield property would be sold to a developer. The more Rory thought about that, the less he liked the idea. At first, he hadn't cared what happened to the property, only that the house was destroyed. Now, he found himself protective of the entire acreage.

When he reached town, on impulse he by-passed his street and continued on. Once he hit the highway, he watched for the Whitfield place, and when he reached the road, he turned onto it. He bumped along, his car's headlights cutting a swath of light in the darkness. At the house, he pulled to a stop, got out and gazed up at the derelict structure. He walked around to the back, his feet crunching in the dry grass. He gazed up at the bedroom window, and it dawned on him that that was all it was: a window. Not *the* window anymore, but *a* window.

The day he and Lacey had come here together, as painful as that was, had changed him. He still wasn't sure exactly how, or why, or what it meant, but it had.

It wasn't until he retraced his way along the highway to home that a plan began to form in his mind.

"WHERE'S RORY LATELY?" Gram asked a few days later while she and Lacey were enjoying their evening tea on the patio. A brief rainstorm left the air cool and refreshing, and rays from the setting sun glistened on the still-wet grass and the leaves of nearby cottonwood trees.

"Oh, he's around." Lacey kept her tone casual.

Gram sipped her tea, studying Lacey over the rim of her teacup. "Maybe so, but not so much around *you*."

"I saw him at yesterday's committee meeting. He gave me a photo to use for the article about the classic car show."

He hadn't mentioned helping her anymore, though. But, then, Lacey was at a loss for what to do next, anyway. What she had learned so far indicated her father made a lot of enemies, mainly through gambling. The mean side of him was difficult to accept because, to her, he'd always been kind and lov-

ing. And as far as she knew, he'd been kind
to her mother, too.

She'd read more of Norella's journal and
found nothing to indicate she feared her husband. If anything, she wanted more attention from him. Lacey believed her mother's
neediness made her vulnerable to the atten-
tions of other men, including Rory's father.
Still, none of that proved anything, one way
or the other.

"I always liked Rory," Gram mused, cap-
turing Lacey's attention again. "His father
was okay, too. But the grandfather, that A.J.,
bossy as all get-out." Gram folded her arms
and vigorously shook her head. "And I'll
never, so long as I live, sell him the farm
for a housing development or whatever. And
you've got to promise me that after I die, you
won't, either."

Lacey sighed. "I promise, but I know you'll
be around for a long time yet, so I don't have
to worry about that."

They sat in silence for a few minutes, and
then Gram said, "Do you think you and Rory
will ever get together again?"

"No. That's so not going to happen. Ever.
Why would you even think such a thing?"

Gram studied her fingernails, a bright pink, freshly painted during a visit to the in-house beauty salon. "Oh, I don't know. You've spent time together this trip. Not like the other times you've visited and did not say a word to each other."

"I know, but we can never regain what we lost, Gram. You, of all people, should understand that. You lost a lot, too."

Gram folded her hands in her lap and gazed into the distance. "I know. But I've been thinking that maybe a person shouldn't put so much effort into gaining back what's been lost. Maybe the goal should be moving on and creating something new."

Moving on. That was what Rory wanted them to do. But was that possible when such an important part of the past—her father's innocence—was yet to be proven? How could she give up that goal? And yet she had to admit to daydreaming more than once about reconciling with Rory. Fortunately, she always came to her senses before agreeing to something she'd later regret.

But Gram's mentioning moving on wasn't something she'd ever said before. She opened her mouth to ask her more about that, but before she could, Gram hugged her arms and said, "Let's go in now. It's a bit chilly out here."

AT DALTON'S AUTO REPAIR, Rory flipped the sign on the front from Open to Closed. It was five thirty, and John had already gone home. Rory went back to his office to straighten up. Well, sort of. He shut down the computer and stuffed a stack of invoices into a drawer. He'd finish up with those tomorrow.

His gaze strayed to the photos on the wall. His gallery. Growing all the time as he added new cars to his collection. He focused on the '57 Chevy, his favorite for so many reasons.

He pulled the photo from the wall and sat in his desk chair, looking at the picture, recalling the day he and Lacey had found the car at Stan's Auto Salvage. He'd talked his dad into having the car towed home, where it sat in the garage. He'd worked on it, bit by bit, piece by piece, learning as he went along. More often than not, his dad would be with him, lending a hand or just providing moral support and father-son companionship.

When the tragedy happened and his grandfather forbade him to see Lacey anymore, he didn't want to have anything to do with the Chevy, either, because it reminded him so much of her, and of his dad, too, and he missed them both so much. When he moved to A.J's rambler—his grandmother was still alive then—he'd put the car into the shed with A.J.'s old Dodge. He'd made occasional visits while attending college. After opening his auto shop, he'd brought the car over and picked up where he'd left off in the restoration.

His chest tightened at the thought of ever letting the Chevy go. He needed the car, needed it to help keep the memories alive. He didn't ever want to forget the happy times with Lacey—and with his father. Whenever he looked at the car or drove it, the past lived again.

Wait. Wasn't that the same reason Remy Whitfield wanted to keep the farmhouse standing? She needed the house to help keep her memories alive, just as he needed the car.

And he wanted to tear the house down. A sinking feeling hit his stomach. He blew out a breath and sagged back in the chair. What to do… What to do.

He leaned forward again and put his head in his hands. And as he sat there, an idea came to him. A plan that would work for everyone, for him, and for Lacey and Remy. He straightened, turned on the computer again and pulled up his accounts. Savings, a few stocks, a couple of CDs and the balance in his checking account. He tapped the numbers into his calculator. Added an estimation of the amount he figured Stan Levy at the bank would loan him. The bottom line wasn't as much as he'd hoped. Okay, he could sell some of his cars. But not the '57 Chevy. Never that one.

He needed something to show Lacey and Remy. He grabbed a piece of paper and made some doodles. He was no artist, though. Not with pencil and paper, anyway. He needed a professional.

Kane Peters, an architect who worked with Dalton Properties, came to mind. He picked up his phone and located Kane's number. A minute later, he had him on the line.

"Hey, Kane, I got a job for you. No, not for Dalton Properties. For me. I'm going solo on this one."

"HAPPY BIRTHDAY TO YOU…" Lacey joined the chorus. That Gram was seventy-three didn't seem possible, but she was. Her once lustrous black hair was mostly gray now, and her once strong body frail and confined to a wheelchair; but her blue eyes still had their sparkle and her smile beamed as wide as ever.

The Riverview staff had helped Lacey organize the party. They'd provided the cake and other refreshments and the balloons and streamers hanging from the ceiling.

In addition to Gram's new friends—including Hal Jacobson—Lacey invited some people from town. Seeing how much her grandmother was loved warmed Lacey's heart.

In truth, she'd had misgivings about attending the party herself because, like with the Youngs' barbecue, she risked the whispers and sidelong looks of those who remembered the murder. But when the home's activity director had approached Lacey with the idea, assuring her birthday celebrations were one of the services they provided for their residents, how could she refuse? She knew Gram would be thrilled to be honored on her birthday by all her friends, both old and new.

When the song was over, everyone clapped and cheered. Gram beamed as she gazed around the room. "Thank you, thank you," she said when the applause died down. "What a wonderful surprise. One of the best presents is having my granddaughter, Lacey, here with me to celebrate." She gestured to Lacey, who stood behind her.

Lacey leaned down to give Gram a hug. "I'm glad I could be here, too."

After they'd finished their cake and ice cream, Lacey picked up Gram's empty coffee cup. "I'll get you a refill."

"I can do that," Hal said.

Lacey shook her head. "No, Hal, I've got it. I'll get some for you, too." Before he could protest, she snatched up his cup and hurried toward the coffee cart. She smiled to herself. Hal had hardly left Gram's side all evening.

While Lacey filled one of the cups, Eleanor Higby, from her grandmother's bridge club, stepped to the cart.

"Lovely you could be here for your grandmother's birthday." Eleanor said.

Lacey set the filled cup aside and held the other one under the urn's spigot. "I'm glad the timing worked out."

Eleanor pursed her lips and shook her head. "Too bad your father's crime chased you away. Living with that all these years must be tough."

Lacey's stomach clenched, and she was about to mumble something and hurry away. Instead, she took a deep breath, lifted her chin and looked Eleanor in the eye. "It's true. I did leave town because of my father's *alleged* crime. But my circumstances have changed now, and…and I just might come back to Silver River."

"Why, that would be wonderful. I'd love to see you around town again. And I'm sure your grandmother would be thrilled." Her eyes twinkled. "But a certain old flame wouldn't have anything to do with your decision, would he?"

Lacey had to smile at "old flame."

"I have been renewing some friendships on this trip, but if I do move back, it will be just for me."

"I hope it works out for you, dear."

"Why, thanks, Eleanor. I appreciate your support."

Lacey returned to Gram and Hal, pleased with her and Eleanor's exchange. Voicing her belief in her father's innocence did not intimidate her anymore. She had more confidence now.

Then it dawned on her that she'd also told Eleanor she might return to Silver River. Where had that come from? Was she honestly considering coming home to stay?

CHAPTER SEVENTEEN

"COME ON, SON, you can't tell me you're surprised I'm planning a subdivision for the Whitfield property." A.J. gripped his putter and tapped the golf ball. The ball rolled along the green felt runway stretched across his office floor and dropped into the metal cup with a clink. He looked up at Rory and frowned. "You are going to seal the deal with Remy, aren't you?"

Rory shifted in his chair. "I plan to, but not as a representative of Dalton Properties."

A.J. dropped his jaw and stared. "What are you talking about?"

"I won't pressure her into selling her land for something she doesn't want."

"Hah. She might want the money. But don't tell me you're planning to buy the property yourself. No way you could swing a deal like that."

Rory avoided his grandfather's eyes but

kept his voice steady. "I haven't worked out all the details yet."

A.J. coaxed another ball into position with his putter. "You're not forgetting I own the property your shop sits on. Prime land like that would go in the blink of an eye."

"Go ahead and sell it. I can find another location."

A.J. shook his head. "I don't want you to find another location. I want you to come to your senses and give up that hobby and work full-time here, where you belong."

Rory stiffened. "You know this isn't what I want to do with my life."

"Have you ever given this business a real chance?" Without waiting for a reply, A.J. smacked the ball. It followed a straight path for a couple seconds and then veered off and missed the cup. "Drat!"

"I worked here summers while going to college and part-time since then," Rory said. "That's enough to know whether or not this is something I want to do."

"You've put in time, but your heart hasn't been in it."

"That's exactly the problem. My heart's not in it."

A.J. walked to his desk and propped the

putter against the side. "We'll plan on you being here full-time by—" he leaned over to flip the pages of his calendar "—October first."

"No."

"You're not giving up this business, son." A.J. leveled him a stern look.

Rory gritted his teeth. "Please, don't call me 'son.' Your son is dead."

A.J. drew a sharp breath.

Realizing how cruel his words sounded, Rory wished he could take them back. But A.J. had pushed him into a corner.

A.J. let a few seconds elapse and then said in a calm tone, "You don't need to remind me. Not a day goes by I don't miss him. But you are like a son to me. And so like your father."

"No, I'm not like him. I'm not the same as either of you. I am my own person."

"Of course," A.J. said soothingly. "And you can be your own person—right here. You can still play with your cars, as a hobby. I have my golf—" he held up his putter "—and you have your cars."

Rory stared at the floor.

"I don't understand you, Rory. Any other grandson would be grateful to have a livelihood like this handed to him. This is what your father would want. If you think so much of him, honor his memory."

"I'll find some other way to honor him." Rory clamped his jaw shut and folded his arms.

Neither spoke for several minutes. Then A.J. said in clipped tones, "Okay, enough for now. There are some accounts on your desk to go over."

Rory stood. "Sure. I'll take care of them. And you'll have my resignation by the end of the day."

Rory headed down the hall to his office in a daze. Although he'd long dreamed of resigning from his job at Dalton Properties, he never expected it to happen like this. He felt as though he were stepping off a ledge with the ground nowhere in sight.

And yet, a few hours later, when he placed his resignation on his grandfather's desk— thankfully, A.J. had already left for the day—and walked out into the sunlight, he felt better than he had in a long, long time.

"HOW'RE YOU DOING down here?" Del asked Lacey the following Tuesday.

Lacey surveyed the array of clothing,

jewelry, old dolls, kitchen utensils and other items on the workroom's table. "I think every family in town must have cleaned house and made a donation."

He laughed. "We sure got a good response to the request we ran in the *Sentinel*. This is a lot of work for you, though, and all this doesn't have to be sorted now. As soon as Silver River Days are over, the ladies who usually do this will be back on the job."

"I know. But I enjoy it. I at least want to get the mannequins into costumes. They'll add a lot to the displays."

He wandered to the table. "What's this?" He pointed to a box of rocks.

"From the Martin family. The rocks were found on their farm, which is near an old silver mine. Some of them have veins of silver."

"I see that." Del picked up a rock and turned it over in his hands. "We can add these to the display on mining."

"That's what I thought. I'll make a card for them."

"I'd appreciate that, Lacey." He replaced the rock and looked at his wristwatch. "Just about closing time now, though."

"I know, but would you mind if I stayed for a while?"

Del frowned and rubbed his chin. "I don't know… Maybe not such a good idea."

"Why not? I'm safe here. No one can get in, right?"

"We had a break-in a coupla months ago. The alarm went off, but the thieves got away with a bunch of gold coins before the cops got here."

"What time did the break-in occur?"

"About 2:00 a.m."

"I won't be staying that late. I'll leave before dark, if that will make you feel any better."

"Well…okay. I'll get out of your way, then."

His steps echoed down the hallway and then faded away.

Lacey picked up the skirt she'd chosen for the '50s model. She slipped the blue felt over the mannequin's head and positioned it so that the red hibiscus appliqué was in the front.

A noise, like a door closing, drifted down the stairwell. She raised her head, ears alert. Maybe Del forgot something and had returned. She remained still but heard nothing more. She picked up the red blouse she'd chosen to go with the skirt.

As she slipped the blouse over the model's head, footsteps sounded in the hallway. She looked up, expecting to see Del, but a woman entered the room. Cora Trenton, carrying a large cardboard box.

"Oh, Mrs. Trenton. I thought you were Del."

"He said you were working late this evening, so I thought I'd bring over a few more donations. I have my own key. I often drop in after hours to attend to our new wing."

"Yes, the one honoring your family. Well, this is nice of you." Lacey took the box from Cora and set it on the table. "I'm sure the museum appreciates your generosity."

Cora straightened the jacket to her beige pantsuit and secured her tapestry purse over her arm. "I am on the museum board. So in a sense, I am the museum."

"Yes, of course," Lacey said, determined to be polite. "Because of you and all the others who so generously give, the Silver River Museum is one of the best around."

"Is that right? And you've seen a lot of museums, I suppose?"

The woman's challenging tone grated, yet Lacey kept her voice even. "As an historian, yes, I have visited a lot of museums."

When Cora made no move to leave, Lacey said, "Thanks again for your donation. I'd better get back to work."

Cora stood her ground. Her gaze cut away from Lacey and landed on the mannequins. "What are you working on?"

"An exhibit from the '50s. Did you happen to bring any clothing from that decade?" She nodded at Cora's box.

Cora shook her head. "Not this time. What I brought tonight belonged to Cal. I've had a difficult time going through his things since he left us, but now that we have the Trenton wing, I want him represented there."

Hearing the catch in Cora's voice, Lacey softened. Cora had lost people she loved, just as she had, and the memories lived on. The circumstances of death didn't alter the fact that they were loved and missed.

Lacey nodded at the box. "May I take a look?"

"Of course. You're in charge."

Lacey doubted Cora believed that but smiled politely. She opened the box and pulled out a manila envelope stuffed with photographs.

"Cal took a lot of pictures," Cora said. "That bunch includes some of the dam project and wildlife he saw while hiking in the mountains."

"Wonderful. We have a display on the dam and one of wild animals, too."

"I know," she said dryly.

"Of course you do. What was I thinking?" Lacey set the photos aside and reached into the box again. This time she pulled out an army jacket. As she unfolded it, the odor of mothballs floated into the air.

Cora snapped her fingers. "Oh, I forgot I put that jacket in, too. It's from the '50s. George wore it in the Korean War. After he passed away, Cal wore it on occasion. He worshiped his father."

Lacey held up the jacket. "This will be great for the male '50s model. I'm almost finished with the female." She gestured to the half-dressed mannequin.

"You'll make sure the display includes Cal's name, now, won't you?"

"Absolutely." Lacey laid the jacket on the table and pulled the trousers from the box. They, too, reeked of mothballs.

Cora slanted her a glance. "I suppose you'll be leaving town once the celebration is over."

Lacey folded the trousers and placed them

on top of the jacket. "I'm not sure," she said, keeping her tone casual.

Cora idly fingered a silk scarf lying on the table. "You have a job in Boise, don't you? Surely, you don't want to give that up to move back here."

"Gram's been wanting me to come back for a long time. I miss Silver River. I miss it a lot."

"I can't imagine you'd ever want to live here again, considering what your father did. And, frankly, the town doesn't need the kind of churning up you've been doing. Bad enough your father's in our cemetery to remind us. Whenever I go to visit Cal and George, I have to pass your father's grave." She put down the scarf, hugged her arms and shuddered.

"I'm sorry that bothers you."

"Why are you asking so many questions around town about Al Jr.'s murder? You don't need that kind of information for the *Sentinel*. No one wants to remember that awful time, or the man who did such a horrible thing."

Lacey winced. Cora was certainly testing her tonight. But enough was enough.

She looked Cora in the eye. "I don't believe my father was the one who shot Al Jr."

Cora narrowed her eyes. "I thought that might be the reason. But that's ridiculous. He was tried and convicted."

"Mistakes are made in trials. He wouldn't be the first man sent to prison for a crime he didn't commit."

Cora propped her hands on her hips. "What could possibly make you think your father wasn't the killer?"

"I have my reasons. But tonight, I'm here to dress the mannequins." Lacey reached into the box and pulled out a folder containing a coin collection, and a square leather box. She held up the box. "What's in this?"

Cora's frown turned into a smile. "Cal's cuff links and tie clasps. He was quite the dresser. He always wore a suit and tie to his job at City Hall. He planned to run for mayor, you know, like his father. He would've won, too," she added on a wistful note.

"I'm looking for cuff links for the shirt my '40s model is wearing."

"I'm sure you'll find a set of Cal's that will work. And with a tie clasp to match."

"I'll take a look." Lacey popped the box's snap and lifted the lid. The container held about a dozen pairs of cuff links and as many tie clasps. Some had stones, some had his initials and some were plain.

"Nice collection," Lacey said.

"Cal had good taste."

"I like this one." Lacey held up a silver cuff link engraved with curlicues.

"Choose whatever you wish." Cora waved dismissively.

"I need to find the other link." Lacey poked around in the box.

"It's in there. Cal was very careful about his things."

Footsteps sounded in the hallway. Lacey turned toward the door just as Del stepped into the room.

"Hello, ladies." Del looked from Cora to Lacey. "Got all the way home and realized I forgot the book I'm reading, a new one on the Civil War. Saw your car out front, Cora. Didn't see you upstairs, so figured you were down here with Lacey. Thought I'd say hello."

"I brought some donations for the displays." Cora gestured to the worktable. "Mostly Cal's things."

"Isn't she somethin', Lacey? She's done more for this town than anyone I know. She 'n' George, and Cal, too, rest their souls. We're lucky to have you, Cora."

"Yes, we are lucky," Lacey said with a touch of irony. Then she realized she'd said "we," as though she were a part of the town, too, and smiled to herself.

"My pleasure." Cora beamed.

They chatted a few more minutes about the museum displays, and then Cora looked at her wristwatch. "I should be getting back to Wildwood."

"I'll walk out with you," Del said. "I have some questions about tomorrow's committee meeting." He turned to Lacey and waggled a finger. "Don't you stay too late, now, you hear? Your grandma's probably waitin' for you to come and play Scrabble."

"I'll leave soon," Lacey promised. "I'll put these cuff links Cora brought on the model's shirt, straighten up a bit and then I'll be done."

After Del and Cora left, Lacey finished dressing the female mannequin with stockings and high heels. A white pearl necklace and earrings and a red patent leather shoulder bag completed her outfit.

Now, to finish the '40s male mannequin. She picked up Cal's leather cuff-link box and, after poking around a bit, spotted the link that matched the one she'd chosen earlier. But when she grasped it between thumb and forefinger, it wouldn't budge. Then she saw that part of it was stuck underneath the pad in the bottom. She tugged harder and the link popped free. At the same time, the pad came loose, with a force that sent links and tie clasps flying.

Lacey was about to push the pad back into place and retrieve the jewelry from the floor when something gold underneath the pad caught her eye. Another cuff link or a tie clasp? No, too delicate. She pulled the object free and held it up. Amethyst stones in filigree settings glittered in the overhead light. A necklace. Not just any necklace— her mother's necklace.

Lacey dropped her jaw and stared, unable to believe her eyes. But, yes, the necklace was Norella's. She'd know it anywhere.

Her thoughts whirled. Had Cal stolen it? Was he Al Jr.'s killer? And what about her mother? Did Cal have anything to do with her death?

She must tell someone, but who? Not Gram. Not yet. Rory? Could she trust him? Of course she could. They may have their differences, but he would never betray her.

She picked up the cuff-link box, intending
to replace the pad. Then she saw the corner
of a piece of paper. There was more hidden?

She freed the paper, a folded square small
enough to be concealed in the bottom of the
box. Holding it gingerly between her thumbs
and forefingers, she unfolded it. The size of a
sheet of notebook paper, one edge was ragged
where torn from its source. Small, cramped
handwriting covered both sides. One side had
a date in the upper right-hand corner.

Lacey gasped.

The note had been written ten years ago,
on the day Al Jr. was shot and her father was
arrested.

She swallowed hard and began to read…

CHAPTER EIGHTEEN

"'I DID SOMETHING bad today. I shot Al Dalton, Jr. Shot him dead.'" Rory read aloud the opening words of the note Lacey found in Cal Trenton's cuff-link box. He turned to look at Lacey. "Unbelievable."

Lacey shifted her position on the hard bench. "That's what I thought, too."

She'd wanted to call him last night but feared the hour was too late. And so, after a restless sleep, she'd phoned him early this morning and told him of her discovery. He came over to Sophie's, but instead of sitting in the parlor, where they might be overheard, they went down to the river and sat on one of the benches along the bank.

"Read on," Lacey said. Maybe hearing the words aloud would make Cal's confession more real.

Rory cleared his throat and continued.

"I couldn't let Al be with Norella. I followed him to her house, crept in after him

and saw him go up to her room. I grabbed Rick's rifle from the mudroom, where I knew he kept it and went up the stairs. I heard their voices in one of the bedrooms.

"I burst in. Al stood at the foot of the bed. Norella was in bed under the covers.

"'Get out!' I ordered and pointed the rifle at Al. He turned and saw me. 'Cal! What the hell are you doin'?'

"'Get out,' I told him again.

"'Go,' Norella told him. 'He won't hurt me. Will you, Cal?'

"'Of course I won't,' I said.

"Al ran past me and out the door. Something he'd been holding fell to the floor, but I was too busy wanting him gone to bother with it just then.

"'I'll be watching to see you get in your car,' I said. Ordering him out like that felt good. He thought he was such a big shot.

"I went to the window and waited till I saw him on the driveway walking to his car. But then he pulled out his cell phone. That made me mad, and before he could make the call, I shot him.

"Norella screamed. She jumped out of bed, all tangled in the bedclothes. 'Keep away from me!' she shouted.

"That made me mad again. I saved her, and she wanted to get away from me. I meant it when I said I wouldn't hurt her. Of course I wouldn't. I love her.

"I went to help her. But before I could catch her, she fell and hit her head on the fireplace hearth. She didn't move. I didn't know if she was dead or just knocked out.

"I guess I panicked. I grabbed a corner of the sheet and wiped off the rifle. Then I saw what Al had dropped. Her necklace. The one she said she lost. He must have found it and was returning it. I picked up the necklace and put it in my pocket. I ran out.

"I got scared and pawned the necklace. Then I went back the next day and took it back. I had to have something of hers. I loved her.

"It all seems like a dream now. That's why I had to write it down."

Still clutching the note, Rory sat back. "It's signed 'Cal Trenton.' And you found this with the necklace. I— This is so hard to believe." He looked at her, his eyes bleak.

"I know, but, yes, I found both hidden in Cal's cuff-link box. Lacey held out the necklace, which had been lying in her lap."

Rory took the jewelry and held it up. The

gold setting and purple stones glistened in the sunlight. "This is an impressive piece, and it looks like the drawing you made. But are you sure it's your mother's?"

"I'm positive."

"Cora doesn't know about the necklace or the note. If she did, she'd have destroyed them."

"Right. She never would have brought them to the museum."

Rory turned to her, his eyes shining now. "This is the evidence you've been looking for. Not just the necklace, but a confession, too. What a find."

Lacey nodded. "I guess."

"Lacey, what's the matter? I'd think you'd be shouting for joy. You're going to take them both to the police, of course. Want me to go with you?" He handed her the necklace.

Lacey fingered the stones, idly watching the river flowing past. The water breaking over the rocks sent silver droplets floating into the air. "I don't know what to do."

"What?" Rory sat upright. "Why not?"

"Like Cora said, they're all dead now. And the Trentons have done a lot for the town. Built buildings, given the wing to the museum, scholarships to the junior college.

Okay, she's pompous and overbearing, but, still… Do I want to ruin all the good the family has done?"

Rory nodded solemnly. "I see what you mean. But the truth is important, too, Lacey. I have to admit I'm in a bit of a shock after believing all these years that your father killed mine—" He puffed his cheeks and blew out a breath. "But now that we know the true killer's identity, don't you think the world should know? Set the record straight?"

Lacey ran a hand over her forehead. "I'm so confused right now."

"Think about it for a while. You don't have to decide today. But I want you to know that I'll go along with whatever you decide."

"Even if it means people will never know your father's true killer?"

"Yes. Since you've come back this time, I've changed my thinking about a lot of things."

LACEY DROVE THROUGH the gates to the Rest-lawn Cemetery and followed the familiar route to her mother's and her grandfather's graves. She parked, took the tub of flowers from the floor of the front seat and walked across a freshly mowed lawn to the familiar markers.

She hoped her visit today would help her decide what to do about her discovery. Rory had offered to accompany her, but she wanted to make this trip alone.

When Lacey reached her mother's and her grandfather's markers, she saw that the flower vases once again were filled with pansies. This time, the blossoms were fresh, indicating a recent visit. Lacey tucked some of the flowers she'd brought into the vases. She said a prayer and crossed the lawn to her father's grave. The fountain burbled softly, and birds twittered in the trees. She expected to find pansies in her father's vase, and sure enough, purple blossoms peeked from the buried container.

She knelt to add her flowers and then sat back. "Dad, what should I do?" she whispered. "Shall I expose the killer and clear your name? Or let well enough alone so that the town continues to benefit from the Trentons?" She bowed her head and waited, but no answer came. Finally, she closed her eyes and whispered a prayer.

As she was leaving, she noticed a woman sitting on the bench surrounding the fountain. A straw hat hid her features. Curious, Lacey approached her. When the woman looked up, Lacey recognized Claire Roche. Somehow, she wasn't surprised.

"Hello, Lacey," Claire said. "I saw you earlier, but I didn't want to interrupt your privacy."

"I didn't see any other cars around."

"I parked down the road. I always like to walk a bit when I visit."

"You are the one who puts pansies on the graves. Isn't that true?"

Claire looked down at her hands clasped in her lap. "Yes, I'm the one."

"Why, Claire?"

"Sit down, and I'll tell you." She patted the seat beside her.

Lacey stepped onto the cement platform and sat beside Claire.

"First of all," Claire said, "I want you to know there was never anything romantic between your father and me."

"Okay…"

"He was devoted to your mother. He loved her very much."

"I always thought so, but it's good to hear you confirm that."

Claire crossed her ankles and smoothed

her skirt. "I had a cat named Mosey. He followed me everywhere. One day when I was cleaning the attic, he got himself stuck in a cubbyhole. I mean, really stuck. I couldn't get him out for the life of me.

"Clint and I were separated at the time, and I was living in the house alone. I didn't know what to do. I was frantic. Then I remembered your dad was building new kitchen cupboards for the Martins next door. I ran over there and asked him if he could help me.

"He packed up his toolbox and came over. He spent over an hour removing the boards, but, finally, he got Mosey out of the hole. Then he had to put the cubbyhole back together. He wanted to board it up, but I said no, because I didn't want Clint to know about Rick having been there. Clint was—and still is—a jealous man. So, instead, Rick stuffed some cardboard in the hole.

"He said he'd take Mosey to the vet if I wanted him checked over, but as far as I could see, the cat was fine. I gave your dad a cup of coffee and a piece of cake and we had a nice chat."

Lacey shook her head in wonder. "He never told me that story."

"Clint and I got back together. And when

Rick was arrested for Al's murder, I couldn't believe it, but the evidence was so strong..."

"It was," Lacey agreed.

"Maybe I could have been a character witness, but I was afraid because I'd never told Clint about that day, so I kept quiet. And then when your dad died in prison, well, I felt terrible. I've been sorry all these years... But I didn't think about putting pansies on the graves until last summer."

Lacey let a few moments of silence elapse and then said, "What if my father's innocence could be proven, even after all these years? But what if having the truth known would affect the town?"

Claire gazed off into the distance. "I'd vote for revealing the truth, even if there's a price to pay. You owe it to your father, and to Rory's dad, too, to set things right."

They talked a bit more, and then Claire said, "Well, I'd better get back to my garden."

"I'm ready to leave, too," Lacey said.

"Do you want me to stop bringing the flowers?" Claire asked as they stepped onto the grass and began walking.

Lacey put out a hand. "Oh, no, no. Please, continue as long as you like. I know how much you love your flowers, and sharing them with my family is a wonderful gesture."

They reached the turnoff to Lacey's car. "Thanks for your story about my father." Lacey gave Claire a hug.

"You're welcome," Claire said, with a sad smile. "He was a good man."

IN HER ROOM at Sophie's, Lacey took out the envelope containing her mother's necklace and Cal's confession. Pulling out the necklace, she looked at it for long moments, fingering the stones and the delicate filigree setting. She thought about her mother and her father, and about Al Jr., and Cal, and how their lives had become so entwined and, in the end, so tragic. She wondered what would have happened if her mother had not lost her necklace and Al Jr. hadn't been returning it to her that day. Would Cal eventually have found them together and done his dirty deed?

Of course, she would never know the answers to those questions. But now she knew the truth about what had happened that day. She thought about what Claire said about the importance of truth and at last knew what she had to do.

Half an hour later, she parked in front of

the Silver River police station. Inside, she approached the receptionist behind the counter.

"Can I help you?" the woman asked.

Lacey took a deep breath. "Yes, you can. I want to see Chief Barnett."

BACK IN HER room once again, Lacey called Rory and told him of her visit to the police station.

"I can imagine the look on Barnett's face," Rory said.

"He was shocked, all right. But he said he'd look into it, and if Cal's confession proved authentic—from handwriting experts, I suppose—he'll make a public announcement."

"That would set things right for you—and your father, wouldn't it?"

"It would, but if that turns out to be the case, I asked him to please wait till after the celebration. I don't want anything to spoil that for the town. Everyone's worked so hard to make it a success."

"Including you."

She gave a short laugh. "Yes, I guess I can be included."

"So that means you'll be here, too. You can ride with me in the car rally and we'll go to the street dance."

"Wait a minute, Rory. You make it sound like, well, like we're together, or something…" Her voice trailed off.

A moment of silence followed, and then he said in a low voice, "We are together, Lacey. For now."

After they ended the call, Lacey walked to the window and gazed out. Together *for now*, he'd said. What would happen after the celebration? What would happen after Chief Barnett revealed the outcome of his investigation? Would they still be together then? Or had they been apart too long?

Her roving gaze landed on the copse of trees marking the Whitfield farm, where the old house still stood. The house that Rory hated and wanted to destroy. Wouldn't the fate of the house always come between them?

"THAT'S THE LAST ONE." Lacey sealed the envelope, put on a stamp, and added the envelope to the stack of outgoing mail on the corner of Gram's desk.

"All the bills are paid, then?" Gram asked.

"Yes, and the thank-you notes to everyone who helped with your birthday party are written, too. Do you want to write a note to Cousin Bessie?"

"No. We've been emailing and talking on the phone. She's doing fine. I still miss her, though. Maybe we could visit her someday?"

Lacey smiled and replaced Gram's pen in its holder. "Maybe. Montana's not that far away."

She was tucking Gram's checkbook and mailing supplies into the desk drawer when someone knocked on the front door.

"Could you get that, please, honey?" Gram said.

"Of course."

Lacey shut the drawer, went to the door and opened it. She frowned when she saw who stood there. "Rory?"

"Hey, Lacey." He took a step forward.

She moved to block his way. "What are you doing here?"

"I have an appointment to see Remy."

Lacey narrowed her eyes and kept a tight grip on the doorknob. "Appointment? What about? If you're here to nag her into—"

"It's all right, Lacey," Gram called from the living room. "Let Rory come in."

"Well…all right." Lacey stood aside while Rory entered the apartment. He was casually dressed in jeans and a blue cotton shirt with the sleeves rolled up to the elbows. A leather briefcase slung over his shoulder was the only indication he might be there on business.

She followed on his heels. "If you think you're going to badger Gram about the farm…"

Gram held up her hand. "Please, Lacey. Rory called and said he wanted to talk to me, and, yes, it's about the farm. I said I'd been thinking about the place, too, and maybe the time had come to have another discussion."

"Why didn't you tell me?"

"Because I didn't want you to tell him he couldn't come. Have a seat, Rory, and let's hear what you have to say." Gram gestured to one of the easy chairs grouped around the coffee table.

Rory sat and placed his briefcase on the coffee table. Gram rolled up her wheelchair across from him. Lacey went to Gram's side but remained standing. She folded her arms and waited, her muscles tense.

"First of all," Rory began, "I want you to know I'm not here as a representative of Dalton Properties. I turned in my resignation and no longer work for them."

"What?" Shock rippled through Lacey.

Gram leaned forward in her chair. "Rory, you didn't."

"I did, Mrs. Whitfield. I've been doing a lot of thinking. About everything." He looked up at Lacey and then focused on Remy again. "And I have in mind what I would like to do."

"Uh-huh," Lacey said, coming back to her senses again and allowing sarcasm to creep into her voice.

Rory spread his hands. "Hear me out, please."

"Lacey, hush," Gram said.

"First, I want to tell you what you might expect if you sell the property with Dalton Properties as your representative." He opened his briefcase and took out some papers. "There's a builder in Milton who's very interested." He spread the papers on the coffee table. "This is what he wants to do."

Gram leaned over to look. "A subdivision."

"Of course," Lacey said.

"Yes. And here's his offer." Rory pointed to a figure on one of the papers.

Gram gasped. "That much?"

Lacey looked over her shoulder and when she saw the amount, she sucked in a breath.

"Yes, that much," Rory said. "But I have something else in mind."

"You want to buy the land yourself," Gram said.

"I would, yes. But even if you don't want to sell it to me, I want to restore the house."

Gram pressed a hand to her chest. "Why would you want to do that?"

"Because I understand how much the house means to you, how it helps you to remember the happy times as well as the sad times. And I thought if the house were brought to life again, well, maybe it would help you to have more happy memories than sad ones."

Gram handed the paper back to Rory. She looked up at Lacey. "What do you think?"

"Why, I don't know. This is all so sudden. But it's what *you* want, Gram."

Gram clasped her hands together. "I don't know what to say, either, Rory. This is such a surprise. But if I did sell the property to you, what would you do with the rest of it?"

"I have some ideas, but they're not fully worked out yet. I'll show you the plans when they're finished. But I wouldn't build subdivisions. I give you my promise on that."

"And who would live in the house, once it's restored?"

Rory shrugged. "You might want to sell it so that some other family can enjoy it, like you did. Or, you might want to live there yourself."

"I am going to walk again." Gram straightened her spine and lifted her chin.

"You don't have to make a decision right now," Rory said. "Just think about it."

Later, after Rory left, Lacey joined Gram on the patio. They sat in silence. Lacey looked out across the lawn to the path by the river, but her thoughts lingered on Rory and his startling proposal. Who would've thought…

Gram broke the silence. "I don't know what I will decide about Rory's offer, but I do know one thing."

"What's that?"

"He is a very, very nice man. I've told you often enough that I've always liked him. But I've never liked him more than I do today."

"It's HERE, LACEY." Elton Watts greeted Lacey as she entered the *Sentinel's* office two days later. He picked up the top copy from a stack of newspapers on the counter and handed it to her.

Silver River Sentinel Special Edition blazed

in fancy script across the top. Below that was the byline, "Written by Lacey Morgan." She took a deep breath and savored the moment. Seeing her name on something she'd authored was always a thrill.

Elton's daughter, Clio, left her desk and came to join them. "The paper looks really good, Lacey."

"I knew you'd come through with a winner." Elton beamed.

"Thanks, Clio, Elton." Lacey spread the paper on the counter and turned the pages. "It does look good. You two deserve credit, too, though, for soliciting the advertising and doing the layout."

"That's mostly Clio." Elton gestured at his daughter.

Clio grinned and took a little bow. "Glad to help."

"The paper will be on sale all over town during the celebration," Elton said, "and Del wants it for a special display at the museum. He wants you to be there. At least for opening day." He looked at her over his glasses. "You are sticking around, aren't you?"

Lacey looked up. "I, ah, guess I am."

"Oh, you have to stay." Clio clapped her hands.

Elton nodded. "You are a part of this celebration, Lacey. And, you're still a part of this town. You might as well accept that and take your rightful place."

Her rightful place. What exactly did that mean?

"I'M SO PLEASED to have this." Grace Patch clutched a copy of the *Silver River Sentinel Special Edition* to her chest and smiled at Lacey.

Sitting behind a display of the newspaper at the historical museum, Lacey returned Grace's smile. "Your ancestors are included in one of the articles. They were some of the area's earliest pioneers."

"I know. I'm going to save this for my grandchildren. Family is important."

"It surely is." Lacey nodded soberly. No one knew that better than she.

As Grace stepped away, Del approached. "The newspaper is selling like hot cakes. And the books aren't doing too bad, either." He gestured to the rest of the display, which included books and pamphlets from the museum's bookstore. "I sure appreciate your being here today."

"I'm glad the project is a success," Lacey

said, as she nodded to a couple that stopped by the table.

"No doubt about that. We sold at least a dozen special editions with the last tour. And the mannequins you dressed got a lot of compliments. You're talented, Lacey."

Del's compliment rang with sincerity, and Lacey took in a deep, satisfied breath. "Why, thank you, Del."

The front door opened, and a group entered. "What time's the next tour?" a man asked.

Del checked his wristwatch. "In about five minutes. Come on in and sign our guest book while you wait." He motioned for them to approach the counter.

Lacey straightened the stack of newspapers and the display of books. When she looked up, Rory stood at the table. Her heart skipped a beat.

"Hey, looking good."

"Me, or the newspaper?"

He swept his gaze over her. "Both."

"You're not bad yourself," she said, admiring the way his Silver River Days T-shirt stretched across his broad chest.

Rory turned to Del. "Okay if I take your

star away for a while? It's time for the car rally."

"Why, sure." Del's eyes twinkled. "Y'all go on now, and have a good time."

Outside, the celebration was off to a good start. People strolled the sidewalks, popping in and out of the stores to see their special displays. In the park, a band entertained with country music. People sat on benches or on the grass to listen while they enjoyed food purchased from nearby vendors.

While she and Rory stood on a corner waiting for the traffic light to change, Jorgen Miller stepped to her side. Lacey stiffened. She hadn't spoken to the restaurant owner since their unpleasant interview.

His "hey, you two" was cheerful enough, though, and so she added a smile to her "hello."

Rory leaned around her to ask, "How's your special menu doing?"

"Real well. We've had a lot of compliments from the lunch crowd." Jorgen shifted from one foot to the other and cleared his throat. "Ah, Lacey, I read what you wrote about The Owl in the newspaper's special edition…"

Expecting to hear a complaint, she held her breath.

"Good job," he said.

"Glad you approve, Jorgen."

After she and Rory crossed the street and Jorgen was out of earshot, Rory said, "I'm guessing that was also an apology for giving you a hard time when you interviewed him."

"You may be right," Lacey said. "If that is the case, I accept."

They reached Main Street, where the classic cars were lined at the curb, all polished and gleaming in the sunlight, many with their hoods open and engines running.

"There's Tom Jackson's Model A." Rory pointed to the car at the end of the line. "It was his grandfather's."

They stopped to talk to Tom for a few minutes, admiring the car and its restored leather interior. Then they worked their way down the line of cars, chatting with the owners and others who'd come to see the show.

The car at the head of the line was Rory's '57 Chevrolet.

"She looks beautiful." Lacey ran her fingers over the smooth, shiny green fender.

"I worked hard to get her ready for the show." Rory opened the passenger door and motioned Lacey inside. He took his place behind the wheel and flashed her a smile as he started the engine. "Here we go!"

They started off, the other cars falling into line behind them. They cruised Main Street, waving at the crowd lining the sidewalk, and then followed the highway out of town.

Rory turned on the radio, and music filled the air. Lacey focused on the passing scenery, her emotions tumbling one over the other.

After a while, Rory said, "You're so quiet. Aren't you enjoying the ride?"

"Yes, I am. But I'm still reeling from that bombshell you dropped on Gram the other day. Restoring the house."

"Are you doubting my sincerity?"

"No, but I can't quite get used to the idea. I'm so accustomed to seeing the house as it is now."

"Do you think your grandmother will go for my idea?"

"I don't know, but even before your visit, she mentioned it might be time to move on. Still, I can't see her letting go of the house."

At the Suttons' ranch, they parked with the other rally participants in front of the freshly mowed field where picnic tables were set up under a bank of trees. Herb and his wife, Molly, had the tables loaded with fried chicken, baked ham and a variety of salads and desserts. Not surprisingly, the talk centered on the cars. Rory had had a hand in restoring several of them. Judging from the comments Lacey witnessed, he'd gained quite a reputation.

Lacey chatted with people she knew, and some she didn't. She felt more at ease than she had at the Youngs' party. More...at home.

But was that possible? Could she really be at home in Silver River again?

The caravan returned to town under the glow of the setting sun. But instead of going all the way back with everyone else, Rory pulled off to the side of the road and let the Model A behind him take the lead. Everyone honked their horns and waved as they passed by.

"What are you doing?" Lacey asked.

"We're taking a little detour." He grinned.

"Rory..."

"Come on, you know you're safe in my hands."

When the last car in the rally had disappeared over a rise in the highway, Rory continued on. But not far. He soon turned off on Linton Road, and then she knew exactly where he was going.

"Oh, Rory, are you sure you want—"

"Yes, I do. I'm not taking you back just yet."

They wound up on the familiar road to the maple tree, and Rory pulled to a stop under the canopy of branches, just as he had a few weeks ago and before that years ago, so many times.

He cut the engine, and they sat there, both staring out of their sides of the windshield.

"Rory—"

"Lacey—"

They both laughed. "You first," Lacey said.

Rory cleared his throat. "I don't have a prepared speech, but okay, here goes. As you know, I left A.J. to go off on my own."

"That was a big step," she said, thinking of how she, too, had left her job in Boise.

"But I need something else to make my world complete."

"What's that?" she asked in a cautious tone.

"You. We belong together, Lacey. We always have. Ever since we met back in Mr. Callahan's class. What happened with our parents tore us apart for ten long years. But something else happened when you came back to town this time. Maybe the universe said, 'Enough, already. It's time for these two to be together again.' And so, here we are."

"This time has been different."

He shifted in the seat to face her. "I love you, Lacey. I always have and I always will."

"Oh, Rory."

"And I believe you still love me, too."

"Yes, yes, I do. I've been fighting my feelings because I didn't believe we could ever be together again. But even now I don't see how—"

"I know there's much to be settled yet. We don't know the outcome of Chief Barnett's investigation, and we don't know what your grandmother will decide about the house. But as long as we love each other and vow to be together no matter what, I believe everything will work out." He put his arm around her and pulled her close. "So, what do you say, are we a couple again?"

"Yes. Oh, Rory. I love you so much!"

"I love you, too, my darling Lacey." He tipped up her chin and kissed her. And, with all her heart and soul, Lacey returned his kiss, happier than she'd been in a long, long time.

The moon had reached its zenith by the

time Rory pulled into the driveway at Sophie's.

"I don't want to let you go," Rory said, "But I'll see you tomorrow night for the street dance."

"I'll look forward to that."

"It won't be as fancy as the prom we missed, but there might be a surprise or two." His eyes glittered in the light from the streetlamps.

"What? Rory, I know that look. What are you up to now?"

"You'll see."

CHAPTER NINETEEN

"YOU LOOK LOVELY, DEAR," Gram said. "Is that a new dress?"

Lacey smoothed the skirt of her blue cotton dress. "No. I brought it along for church, but it'll do for the dance. More dressy than my usual tights and tees, anyway. Now, what are you going to wear?"

"Something pink."

Lacey laughed as she wheeled Gram into her bedroom. "You have a lot of choices. Your closet is full of pink."

"Pull out that silk blouse and pleated skirt, and the white cardigan with the pink rosebuds embroidered on it. The one Hal gave me for my birthday."

"He likes you," Lacey teased as she rummaged through the closet.

"Maybe he just wants me to be his Scrabble partner 'cause I win a lot."

"Nooo, he likes you because you're cute

and charming." Lacey brought out the requested clothing and laid the items on the bed.

Gram laughed. "Charming? Okay. But cute? Maybe fifty years ago."

Lacey freed the blouse from the hanger. "I'm glad you'll be at the dance, though. You and Granddad used to dance a lot, didn't you?"

"We did." Gram pressed her lips together in a sad smile. "And I will again."

"I know you will," Lacey said as she helped Gram change her clothes. "Especially now that you have a new partner."

"GREAT CELEBRATION THIS YEAR," Sam commented to Lacey while they shared a dance later that evening.

"It is," Lacey agreed. "There's certainly a good turnout for this occasion." The street was full of couples dancing to the tunes of a lively Western band. Spectators sat on benches or on blankets on the grass. Overhead, a sprinkling of stars and a three-quarter moon added a silvery glow to the scene.

When she and Rory had first arrived, they'd joined some other couples, including Sam and Kris, at one of the picnic tables. Lacey didn't think Sam and Kris were actually a couple, though. They'd arrived separately, each with other friends.

The song ended, and Rory and Kris, who'd been dancing together, made their way through the crowd toward them.

"She step on your toes?" Sam joked to Rory.

Before Rory could answer, Kris poked Sam in the shoulder. "Careful, or I'll do more than step on *your* toes."

Sam raised his hands to ward off another poke. "Is that a promise or a threat?"

"You'll find out." Kris grinned.

The band struck up another tune.

"C'mere, lady." Sam pulled Kris into his arms. "See you guys later," he said over his shoulder as they danced off.

"They seem to be getting along well." Lacey watched the two disappear into the crowd. "Do you think they'll get back together?"

"I don't know. They're good at kidding around, but when the serious issues come up, they freak. But come on, our turn now." He put his arm around her waist and pulled her close.

Lacey pushed away her worries and gave herself up to the pleasure of being in Rory's

arms. The years since they'd last danced together faded away, and they fell into step
as though it were only yesterday. He held
her hand close to his chest, the way he used
to, and she wound her arm around his neck.
The warmth of his body both comforted and
thrilled her. How wonderful to be in his arms
again.

They danced to several more tunes, and
then the bandleader, his guitar slung over
his shoulder, stepped to the microphone. He
tipped back his cowboy hat and, shading
his eyes with his hand, peered at the crowd.
"Rory Dalton, you out there?"

Lacey jolted. Why was he looking for
Rory? Was there an emergency?

"I'm here." Rory waved.

"Come on up, Rory." The bandleader beck-
oned.

"C'mon, honey." Rory grabbed Lacey's
hand and pulled her toward the bandstand.

"What's going on?" Lacey skipped along
to keep up with him.

"You'll see."

"Rory…"

The band struck up a tune. The crowd
parted, and Rory led her across the grass to
the bandstand. She glimpsed Gram in her

wheelchair and Hal on a bench by her side. Gram's eyes were wide. Lacey managed to shrug as she and Rory hurried by.

He kept a tight grip on her hand, tugging her up the steps and onto the platform. The bandleader sliced the air with his hand, and his band stopped playing.

Rory stepped to the microphone. "Good evening, everyone. I'm Rory Dalton. If you're from Silver River, most of you know me, and I know most of you. And this is Lacey Morgan." He gestured to Lacey. "Although she hasn't lived in town for a while, she's been visiting and this year has joined our celebration."

Lacey's heart beat wildly, but she managed a smile and a nod. The bright lights on the bandstand kept the people beyond in shadow. She could only imagine who all was out there witnessing this…this whatever. What *was* Rory up to?

Rory continued, "I have an important question to ask Lacey tonight, and I wanted you all to be witnesses." He reached into his pocket and pulled out a small square box. He flipped open the lid. A diamond ring sparkled under the lights.

Lacey gasped and pressed a hand to her chest. "Oh, Rory..."

Rory took the microphone. Dropping to one knee, he gazed up at her. "Lacey Morgan, I fell in love with you back in high school, and I've never stopped loving you. We have been apart way too long. Will you marry me so that we can spend the rest of our lives together?"

Lacey could hardly believe this was happening. Only yesterday, they'd come together again as a couple. Now, he was proposing marriage. Was she ready to be his wife? Silence hung in the air as everyone waited for her answer.

"Lacey?" Rory prompted.

Lacey took the microphone and looked directly into his eyes. "I love you, too, Rory Dalton. And you're right—we've been apart too long. Nothing will keep us apart ever again. I'd be proud to be your wife, so, yes, I'll marry you."

The crowd cheered. Rory rose to his feet. He took the ring from the box and slipped it on Lacey's finger. The square-cut diamond, with three smaller stones on either side, sparkled in the moonlight.

"It's beautiful," she whispered.

Rory pulled her into his arms and kissed her. Lacey returned his warm and tender kiss with all her heart and soul. The crowd went wild.

The bandleader stepped forward and took the mic from Lacey. "Congratulations, Rory and Lacey," he said. "Come on, everybody, join them in their first dance as an engaged couple."

"DO YOU UNDERSTAND why I wanted to propose to you in front of an audience?" Rory said later to Lacey.

They were sitting in the '57 Chevy in the parking lot at Sophie's. It was past midnight, the luminous moon, now low in the sky, casting pale shadows over the foothills. The dance was long over, but the group they'd been with had insisted on buying them a celebratory drink afterward.

"I think so." She looked down at her ring glittering in the moonlight. The ring still felt strange on her finger.

"I wanted to make up for not standing by you ten years ago. And I wanted to give you a chance to stand up in front of everyone and say, 'Here I am, folks, and I'm going to stay.'"

"I think you achieved your purpose," she said dryly.

"You're not mad at me?"

"No. Mad *about* you, maybe, but not *at* you."

He grinned. "That kind of mad I can live with." He drew her into his arms and kissed her.

They sat there for a long time afterward, talking for a while, and then kissing some more, until the moon disappeared behind the mountains, spreading a soft, warm glow over the land.

EPILOGUE

Two weeks later

"I'VE CALLED THIS town meeting tonight," Mayor Palmer said from his position at the podium, "because new evidence has been brought to light concerning a crime committed in our town." He cleared his throat and smoothed his gray hair with the palm of his hand. "I'll give you some background, and then Chief Barnett will fill you in on the details." He gestured to Police Chief Barnett, a head shorter than his own six-foot-two inches, who stood at his side.

From where she sat with Rory in the front row, Lacey surveyed the packed room, with the overflow standing at the back. Elton Watts was there, of course, representing the *Sentinel*, as well as a crew from KCVM. Jorgen Miller from The Owl, and Bonnie and Tom Rosen, Sophie and Hugh Bennett, and Claire and Clint Roche, Kristal and Sam, and many others from their high school days. Hal had brought Gram, who looked tense and worried.

Mayor Palmer shuffled some papers on the lectern. "Many of you were here ten years ago when we lost one of our prominent citizens in a terrible crime. Alfred James Dalton Jr., better known as Al Jr., was gunned down, shot in cold blood, in the back—"

Lacey felt Rory stiffen. She reached over and grasped his hand.

"—on the Whitfields' property," Mayor Palmer went on. "Another one of our citizens, Richard—or Rick, as he was better known—Morgan, was tried and convicted of this crime. Mr. Morgan died in prison. We're sorry he isn't here today to see justice served. And now I'll turn the meeting over to Chief Barnett, who will give you the details."

He moved aside, and the chief of police took his place at the lectern.

Chief Barnett took a moment to shuffle papers again and then looked out at the audience. "Several weeks ago, my office was presented with a document purportedly written by the person who committed the crime against Al Dalton, Jr. This document was a confession and was authenticated by several handwriting experts employed by the Idaho State Police Forensic Services. The document was written by another one of our citizens, Calvin Trenton."

A collective gasp came from the audience.

Chief Barnett waited until the commotion died down, and then he continued. "Even though all the participants in this crime are now deceased, their relatives reside here." He focused his attention on Lacey and Rory. "And we felt obligated to set the record straight."

Lacey nodded in response to the chief's attention.

"We'll take questions now," Chief Barnett said.

A man in the front row raised his hand.

Barnett pointed at him. "Yes, Bert?"

"Is this so-called confession something anyone can see?"

"The court has jurisdiction over evidence. I suppose if you got a court order, you could examine it."

A woman raised her hand and received a nod from the chief. "What about the buildings named after the Trentons? Will the names be changed?"

"That's a question for the town council to consider," the chief said.

Several others asked questions that the chief answered. Then the audience fell silent. Barnett stepped aside, and Mayor Palmer took over again.

"If there are no more questions, this concludes our meeting. Thank you all for coming."

Lacey and Rory stood, and a crowd formed around them. The urge to run gripped Lacey, but instead she stood tall.

A woman she didn't know spoke up. "I never liked your father, Lacey. But if he's innocent, I'm all for justice."

"Thank you," Lacey murmured.

"Good to see you two together again," another woman said, looking from Lacey to Rory. "Congratulations on your engagement."

"Thanks, Martha," Rory said. "We appreciate your support."

Several others spoke to them, all with positive comments; but, finally, only Lacey, Rory, Mayor Palmer and Chief Barnett remained.

"How is Cora doing?" Lacey asked the mayor.

"She's been holed up in Wildwood since

Chief Barnett told her the news. She's still in shock."

"And denial, I bet," Rory said.

"Did she ever confess to being behind the slashing of my tires?" Lacey asked.

"No, but we think we've got the guy who hired Alfie. He's in jail right now on another charge, and he may agree to a plea bargain."

"Did Cora know Cal was the killer?" Rory asked.

"She either knew or at least suspected he was," Chief Barnett said. "She might've seen him with the necklace before he pawned it. She sure didn't know it was in his cuff-link box, though, or the confession, either."

Rory shook his head. "Hard to believe that after all the good she did, she could be so… so evil."

"It is hard to believe," the chief agreed.

Mayor Palmer nodded. "Adjusting to this will take time—for all of us."

LATER THAT EVENING, Lacey and Rory stopped by Gram's apartment. Gram gave them each a hug. "I'm so happy for you both," she said. "Lacey, you know I never thought your father was good enough for our Norella, but I need to tell you I'm glad he's not a murderer. I'm glad you found out the truth."

"Thanks, Gram. Although I always believed in his innocence, I'm still getting used to it being a fact."

"Adjustment will take time, honey." Gram turned to Rory. "And your father, bless his soul. I hope he rests in peace now that the truth is known."

"Thank you, Remy."

They all were silent a moment, and then Gram said, "But now you two can move on with your lives."

Rory grinned. "Yes, we can. But speaking of moving on, have you made a decision about the house?"

Gram's expression turned sober. "Yes, I think I have."

"Good. I have some plans to show you, as well. How about taking a ride out to the farm tomorrow and discussing everything then?"

"I'll be ready," Gram said.

"HERE THEY ARE." Rory nodded to the car coming down the road.

Standing beside Rory in front of the Whitfield farmhouse, Lacey shaded her eyes against the sun. "Yes, that looks like Hal's car."

"Hmm, a new Buick," Rory commented. "Nice set of wheels."

Lacey laughed. "I think you'll find he's a nice guy, too."

The car pulled to a stop. While Lacey and Rory went to meet them, Hal popped from the driver's side and hurried around to open the passenger door. He extended his hand, and Gram stepped out. Then he pulled out a cane and handed it to her. With one hand on Hal's arm and the other on her cane, Gram came toward them.

Lacey stared. "You're walking!"

A big grin lit Gram's face. "Uh-huh. Told you I would. I've been practicing for a couple weeks now with my therapist, and today he gave me the okay to be on my own."

Lacey and Rory gave her a hug, and then Rory and Hal shook hands. "Good you could come," Rory said.

Hal nodded. "I've heard a lot about this place, but not being from around here, I hadn't seen it." He looked up at the house. "It's due for a makeover, all right."

"You said you had some other ideas, Rory," Gram said.

"I do. I had an architect friend draw them up. Come take a look." He waved them over to the '57 Chevy where a large sheet of paper was spread across the trunk.

When they were gathered around, Rory said, "First of all, Lacey and I want to buy the property. Then it will stay in the family."

"I was thinking to make it a wedding present," Gram said.

"Oh, no, Gram…" Lacey put her arm around Gram's shoulders.

Gram waved a hand. "We'll argue that out later. I want to see what Rory's got."

"Okay," Rory said. "This building here—" he pointed to a spot on the drawing "—will be the Dalton Classic Car Museum." He paused and looked at Gram.

"What a great idea," she said. "I remember you talked about having a museum for collectible cars when you were back in high school."

Rory nodded. "It's long been a dream of mine." He turned back to the drawing. "And all this area would be a park."

"A park?" Hal said. "Open to the public?"

"Yes, the Whitfield-Morgan Memorial Park. It'll include a picnic area and a playground for kids and gardens and whatever else a park should have."

"What do you think of that, Gram?" Lacey asked. Rory had of course shared the plans with her earlier, and she loved the idea of a park named after both her grandfather and her father.

Gram pressed a hand to her cheek. "Why, I—I'm speechless."

"Oh, oh, I've never seen you speechless before," Hal teased.

"I don't think I ever have been," Gram said. "But the museum and the park would be a wonderful tribute to all our families."

"That's what I thought," Rory said, looking pleased.

Hal surveyed the drawing. "That still leaves quite a bit of land."

Rory nodded. "Right. Not sure what we'll do with the remaining acreage. I may want to move my shop here. Depends on what happens to the house."

They all turned to look at Gram.

"Tell us what you've decided," Lacey said.

Gram gazed up at the house, took a deep breath, and said, "I want you to tear it down."

"Tear it down?" Lacey echoed. "Oh, Gram, are you sure?"

Gram nodded. "It's time. You and Rory are moving on. I need to move on, too." She and Hal exchanged a meaningful look.

Lacey struggled with a mixture of emotions. She gazed up at the house she'd lived in until the tragedy that had changed her life forever. Run-down and dilapidated and no longer fit for habitation, and yet, at the thought of the house being destroyed, her chest tightened and tears filled her eyes.

Rory put his arm around her. "Will you be okay with your grandmother's decision?"

"Yes, eventually. In my heart, I know you made the right choice, Gram, but saying goodbye after all these years is hard."

"I know, I know…" Gram bit her lip and looked away.

"Do you want to go inside one last time?" Lacey asked.

"Oh, no. I'd rather remember it the way it was when we all lived there than be reminded of how it looks inside now."

No one said anything. The wind rustled the leaves of the willow trees and stirred the grass in the meadow. In the distance, two blackbirds swooped low over the river.

The sound of an approaching car captured Lacey's attention. She looked around to see a silver BMW rounding the bend in the road. "Who's that?"

"It's A.J." Rory propped his hands on his hips. "What's *he* want? I don't have anything to say to him."

"Now, Rory," Gram warned. "He is your grandfather, after all."

The BMW pulled to a stop, and A.J. climbed out. "I was driving by and saw your car, Rory," he said as he approached them. "Decided to stop. Hello, Lacey, Remy." He nodded to the women and then studied Hal. "Don't believe we've met."

Gram introduced the two men, and A.J. stepped forward to shake hands. Then he gestured toward the house. "What's going on here?"

"Remy's selling the property to Lacey and me," Rory said.

A.J. raised his eyebrows. "Is that so? And what do you plan to do with it?"

"My classic car museum will be built here. And a park."

"A park?"

"Yes, with a playfield and gardens."

"What about the house?" A.J. gestured to the house.

Gram spoke up. "It'll be torn down."

"Well, I'll be." He shook his head. "Are those the plans?" He pointed to the architect's drawing.

"They are," Rory said.

"Mind if I take a look?"

"Okay…sure, if you're interested."

"I am."

Rory stepped aside to make room for his grandfather, and they bent their heads over the plans. When they finished, A.J. said, "Looks like you're making good use of the land."

"We think so," Rory said.

A.J. turned to Lacey. "I didn't get a chance to tell you at the city hall meeting the other day that I'm glad justice was served."

"Thank you," Lacey said. "We are, too."

"We are," Gram echoed.

An awkward silence followed. Then A.J. looked at Rory. "When you get set up here, how about restoring the Dodge?"

Rory grinned. "Are you serious?"

"I am. It's been sitting in my garage long enough. I wouldn't mind taking a drive in it now and then."

"Well, sure, I'll fix it up for you. I've been wanting to get my hands on that car for years."

"I know," A.J. said in a dry tone. "Give me a call when you're ready to take it on. And the door's always open if you want to come back to work, too."

Rory sobered and shook his head. "Oh, no. Not a possibility."

A.J. spread his hands. "No pressure. I'm just saying."

Another awkward silence, and then A.J. said, "I'll be on my way, then. Nice to see you walking, Remy. Nice meeting you, Hal. Good to see you, Lacey. And you, too…son." His gaze lingered on Rory before he turned away and walked toward his car.

Rory took a step after him and then stopped. He looked at the others.

"Go." Gram flapped a hand.

Rory grinned and then took off after A.J. When he caught up, he slung his arm around the older man's shoulders. "Thanks for stopping by…Granddad."

"You know me and property around this town," A.J. said. "I gotta know what's going on."

Soon after A.J. left, Gram and Hal said they must leave, too. "We have a Scrabble game this afternoon," Gram said.

"Can't miss that," Hal said. "We're on the way to winning the tournament. And when we do, we'll all go out on the town and celebrate."

"That's something to look forward to." Lacey kissed her grandmother's cheek and gave Hal a hug.

Rory and Hal shook hands. "Thanks for coming today," Rory said.

After they were gone, Rory rolled up the architectural plans and put them in the car's trunk. "How about a walk down by the river?"

"I'd like that."

Rory took her hand, and they walked along the driveway, past the barn and across the field to the river. A warm breeze swept down from the mountains, and the sun beamed over the valley. At the river, they stood on the bank watching the silver water flow peacefully, rippling here and there over rocks and fallen branches.

"I love the river," Lacey said. "Living here again will be wonderful."

"It will be for me, too, now that we're together again. And to celebrate, I have something for you." He pulled a small box from his jacket pocket and held it out.

"What's this?"

"You'll see. Go ahead, open it."

Lacey took the box and lifted the lid. Inside was a gold bracelet with amethyst stones. "Oh, Rory, it's beautiful." She ran her fingers over the shiny stones and the delicate filigree. "This matches Mother's necklace. Where did you—"

"I had a jeweler in Milton make it. Here, put it on." He lifted the bracelet from the box.

Lacey held out her arm. Rory wound the bracelet around her wrist and fastened the clasp. The gold felt cool against her skin.

"We're starting a new tradition," he said, "Or, rather, adding to an already existing one. Now, you'll have both the necklace and the bracelet to pass down to our daughter—or daughter-in-law, as the case may be."

The thought of having children together, to love and cherish, gave Lacey a warm feeling.

"Thank you, dear Rory. I love your precious gift. And, I love you."

"I love you, too. More than you'll ever know, and for all time." He tipped up her chin and kissed her.

Lacey wrapped her arms around Rory and returned his kiss. Happiness and contentment filled her. The journey back home had been long and sometimes painful, but she was here at last, and here she would stay.

* * * * *

LARGER-PRINT BOOKS!

**GET 2 FREE
LARGER-PRINT NOVELS
PLUS 2 FREE
MYSTERY GIFTS**

Love Inspired®

SUSPENSE
RIVETING INSPIRATIONAL ROMANCE

Larger-print novels are now available...

WESTERN WP PROMISES

YES! Please send me **The Western Promises Collection** in Larger Print. This collection begins with 3 FREE books and 2 FREE gifts (gifts valued at approx. $14.00 retail) in the first shipment, along with the other first 4 books from the collection! If I do not cancel, I will receive 8 monthly shipments until I have the entire 51-book Western Promises collection. I will receive 2 or 3 FREE books in each shipment and I will pay just $4.99 US/ $5.89 CDN for each of the other four books in each shipment, plus $2.99 for shipping and handling per shipment. *If I decide to keep the entire collection, I'll have paid for only 32 books, because 19 books are FREE! I understand that accepting the 3 free books and gifts places me under no obligation to buy anything. I can always return a shipment and cancel at any time. My free books and gifts are mine to keep no matter what I decide.

272 HCN 3070 472 HCN 3070

Name	(PLEASE PRINT)

Address	Apt. #

City	State/Prov.	Zip/Postal Code

Signature (if under 18, a parent or guardian must sign)

Mail to the **Reader Service:**
IN U.S.A.: P.O. Box 1867, Buffalo, NY 14240-1867
IN CANADA: P.O. Box 609, Fort Erie, Ontario L2A 5X3

* Terms and prices subject to change without notice. Prices do not include applicable taxes. Sales tax applicable in N.Y. Canadian residents will be charged applicable taxes. This offer is limited to one order per household. All orders subject to approval. Credit or debit balances in a customer's account(s) may be offset by any other outstanding balance owed by or to the customer. Please allow 4 to 6 weeks for delivery. Offer available while quantities last. Offer not available to Quebec residents.

Your Privacy—The Reader Service is committed to protecting your privacy. Our Privacy Policy is available online at www.ReaderService.com or upon request from the Reader Service.

We make a portion of our mailing list available to reputable third parties that offer products we believe may interest you. If you prefer that we not exchange your name with third parties, or if you wish to clarify or modify your communication preferences, please visit us at www.ReaderService.com/consumerschoice or write to us at Reader Service Preference Service, P.O. Box 9062, Buffalo, NY 14240-9062. Include your complete name and address.

LARGER-PRINT BOOKS!
GET 2 FREE LARGER-PRINT NOVELS PLUS
2 FREE GIFTS!

HARLEQUIN *super romance*®

More Story...More Romance

YES! Please send me 2 FREE LARGER-PRINT Harlequin® Superromance® novels and my 2 FREE gifts (gifts are worth about $10). After receiving them, if I don't wish to receive any more books, I can return the shipping statement marked "cancel." If I don't cancel, I will receive 4 brand-new novels every month and be billed just $5.94 per book in the U.S. or $6.24 per book in Canada. That's a savings of at least 12% off the cover price! It's quite a bargain! Shipping and handling is just 50¢ per book in the U.S. or 75¢ per book in Canada.* I understand that accepting the 2 free books and gifts places me under no obligation to buy anything. I can always return a shipment and cancel at any time. Even if I never buy another book, the two free books and gifts are mine to keep forever.

132/332 HDN GHVC

Name	(PLEASE PRINT)	
Address		Apt. #
City	State/Prov.	Zip/Postal Code

Signature (if under 18, a parent or guardian must sign)

Mail to the **Reader Service:**
IN U.S.A.: P.O. Box 1867, Buffalo, NY 14240-1867
IN CANADA: P.O. Box 609, Fort Erie, Ontario L2A 5X3

Want to try two free books from another line?
Call 1-800-873-8635 today or visit www.ReaderService.com.

* Terms and prices subject to change without notice. Prices do not include applicable taxes. Sales tax applicable in N.Y. Canadian residents will be charged applicable taxes. Offer not valid in Quebec. This offer is limited to one order per household. Not valid for current subscribers to Harlequin Superromance Larger-Print books. All orders subject to credit approval. Credit or debit balances in a customer's account(s) may be offset by any other outstanding balance owed by or to the customer. Please allow 4 to 6 weeks for delivery. Offer available while quantities last.

Your Privacy—The Reader Service is committed to protecting your privacy. Our Privacy Policy is available online at www.ReaderService.com or upon request from the Reader Service.

We make a portion of our mailing list available to reputable third parties that offer products we believe may interest you. If you prefer that we not exchange your name with third parties, or if you wish to clarify or modify your communication preferences, please visit us at www.ReaderService.com/consumerschoice or write to us at Reader Service Preference Service, P.O. Box 9062, Buffalo, NY 14240-9062. Include your complete name and address.

HSRLP15